Italian Stallions

Italian Stallions

KARIN TABKE
JAMI ALDEN

APHRODISIA

KENSINGTON BOOKS

http://www.kensingtonbooks.com

APHRODISIA BOOKS are published by

Kensington Publishing Corp.
850 Third Avenue
New York, NY 10022

All Kensington Titles, Imprints, and Distributed Lines are available at special quantity discounts for bulk purchases for sales promotions, premiums, fund-raising, and educational or institutional use.

Special book excerpts or customized printings can also be created to fit specific needs. For details, write or phone the office of the Kensington special sales manager: Kensington Publishing Corp., 850 Third Avenue, New York, NY 10022, attn: Special Sales Department, Phone: 1-800-221-2647.

Aphrodisia and the A logo Reg. U.S. Pat. & TM Off.

ISBN-13: 978-0-7582-2559-7
ISBN-10: 0-7582-2559-8

First Trade Paperback Printing: July 2008

10 9 8 7 6 5 4 3 2 1

Printed in the United States of America

Contents

In His Bed

Karin Tabke

1

"Now, that's a rack!"

"Shut the hell up, Gordo. You're going to have the whole family breathing down our necks," Gabe hoarsely whispered. He didn't bother looking at his hormone-infused partner. Instead he glanced around them, ascertaining that no one had bothered to look over at the cluster of oleander bushes they were hiding in, focused his binoculars, and zeroed in on the object of Gordo's comment. Gianna Michaela Cipriani. Grieving daughter of the recently departed Alberto "Cappy" Cipriani.

A soft breeze stirred her long dark hair. With her head bent, her hands clasped tightly in prayer as the good padre's deep melodic voice droned last rites, he could only catch a glimpse of her flushed cheeks and full lips. Gathered tightly around Gianna was her extended family and half of San Francisco's Italian population. If Gabe was a betting man, he'd lay odds his Southern California Italian family shared some of the same gene pool.

From Gabe's vantage point, all he could see was a body shrouded in a shapeless dark dress his nona wouldn't be caught dead in.

"How the hell can you tell she has a rack in that bag-lady dress?"

Gordo chuckled. "I have X-ray vision."

"Well shut it down. We're not here to sniff out your next lay."

"Yeah, yeah, yeah. You watch Tucci; I'll watch the girl."

Reluctantly, Gabe dragged his binoculars from the demure Gianna Cipriani to every God-fearing Italian's nemesis, Don Fabio "the Blade" to those who knew the true nature of the man. Tucci however preferred the Don "Juan" moniker. The prick fancied himself a lover and connoisseur of all things female. Gabe scowled hard. The mob boss, was, in Gabe's highly trained estimation, looking a bit too long and too predatorily at the bereaved daughter. The smarmy bastard! "I bet that prick tries to swindle that restaurant right out from under her," Gabe mused out loud.

"Yeah, and if his lover-boy approach doesn't work, you think he'll take her out like he did her old man?"

Gabe swung his binocs back to look at Gianna. Her pale face was practically hidden behind huge dark sunglasses. Not that she needed them. The low clouds were dark and ominous in the sky hovering over Holy Cross Cemetery, typical October weather for the Bay Area. The wind picked up, lifting Gianna's long black skirt. He caught a glimpse of a shapely ankle and calf before she hastily pushed it back into place.

"Nice legs too!" Gordo exalted.

Gabe looked at his partner's grinning face and shook his head. Gordo's flushed fleshy jowls and wet lips reminded him of a slobbering St. Bernard. He turned back to his job. Surveilling Tucci. "Next time, jerk off before we go into the field."

"Nah, jerking off ain't half as fun as the real thing. I think maybe tonight I'll go over to Ciao Bella and have me a bite or two." Gordo wagged his eyebrows, and Gabe just shook his head again.

"You do that, but don't blow your cover. I don't feel like breaking in a new asshole."

Gordo harrumphed at the insult but continued to watch the Cipriani girl. Gabe watched Tucci watch Gia. His blood warmed. Tucci had a nasty way with women. Hence "the Blade" moniker. Gabe had seen firsthand the aftermath of the hookers he liked to tenderize after he sliced and diced them. The man lived at his strip joint impersonating a steak house, Roberto's, where he had his pick of the crème de la crème. Fear, drug addiction, and the promise of starring in one of Tucci's notorious X-rated film noirs was a strong aphrodisiac for many women. It always amazed Gabe how low one would sink for a buck or the promise of fame and fortune.

Gabe hadn't much minded hanging out at a high-class strip joint and keeping a watchful eye on the lothario who presided in his upstairs office overlooking the main dance floor like Julius Caesar lording over a harem. It was part of his undercover. The eye candy was primo, and the info he racked up while the flavor of the night ground away on him in a lap dance was as good as reading it in the *Chronicle*. And the food? Roberto's did have one hell of a steak. So, yeah, as strip joints went, Roberto's was top-notch.

Gabe shook his head. But the girls. They might look as good as any Victoria's Secret model when they stepped on the dance floor for the first time, but it didn't take long for that vacant look to appear in their eyes. He'd seen more than a few girls show up to work with bruises covered with makeup. Some never came back. They dummied up the minute one of his task force partners popped in for a chat. Gabe knew he could get more out of them than could a female agent, but if he did that, his cover was in serious jeopardy of being blown. And no way was he going to see almost two years of hard work go down the drain. So, he did what he always did. Kept his head down, his ears open, and the cash flowing from his wallet into the strippers' G-strings, courtesy of the U.S. government. Gabe cringed. He'd been catching a lot of heat for his flamboyant expense requisitions. But in his mind it was worth every penny and then some to nail Tucci's ass to the concrete walls of Leavenworth.

His brows furrowed. Tucci was a slippery scumbag of the highest order, and if his task force didn't nail him this time around, Gabe was tempted just to relieve the taxpayers of another trial that would cost them a fortune only to see the slippery Don waltz out of the courtroom for the third time.

Gabe's hands tightened around the thick black plastic. It wasn't that they didn't have the evidence. It was the star witnesses. Even with them in deep witness protection, the bastard had managed to get to them every single time. Fucking mistrial after mistrial. He was sick of it. And he was positive that the Don had made sure Alberto had *accidentally* fallen down the stairway into his basement wine cellar, and then intentionally made sure his neck was broken in three places.

"Hey? Who's that?" Gordo asked.

Gabe shifted his binocs back to Gianna and the woman who had maneuvered through the voluminous crowd to take the girl's hand. "Theresa Bellesi, cousin on the mother's side. She arrived from New York last night."

Gordo put his glasses down and looked at Gabe. "Don't you sleep, man?"

Gabe shook his head and continued to look at the cousins. "Nope. I want Tucci."

Gordo looked back through his glasses at the voluptuous Theresa, smacked his lips, and said, "I want the cousin."

"Miss Cipriani, my sincerest condolences on your loss."

Gianna looked from the perfectly manicured hand extended to her, up his arm, to his neck, then to the face attached to it. Olive skin pulled tight over severe features that reminded her of a hawk, complete with dark predatory eyes that regarded her with what her gut told her was false concern. A hard shiver sprinted down her spine. Intuitively she knew this man was not someone her father would approve of. She sniffed back a sob. Papa. Gone. Just like that. One minute they were laughing about Zia Cece sneaking cannoli when she thought no one was looking, then Gianna returned from the bank thirty minutes later to find her father dead at the bottom of the wine cellar stairway.

She swiped a tear away and looked harder at the man. She supposed many women would find his classic, albeit sharp, Italian features handsome. She did not. Malice lurked behind the dark eyes. This was not a man to say no to. Even though her experience with men was nil, Gianna intuitively knew that even under the most urgent, desperate duress, she would never succumb to this man's manufactured charm.

But she was not stupid either. Slowly she took the extended hand. Long, thin, cold fingers wrapped around her hand and pulled her ever closer to his overcologned body. "My name is Fabio Tucci. Your father was a distant business associate of mine. I will miss his good humor."

Gianna flinched under the unrelenting grip and the cloying scent of his cologne. "Thank you, Mr. Tucci." She pulled her hand from his grasp; he tightened it.

"Miss Cipriani, I understand you are grieving right now, and I will certainly respect that with a day or two of time to yourself, but I need for you to understand." His voice lowered to a threatening pitch. "Alberto and I had some unfinished business."

Gianna's heart thumped harder against her chest. As far as she knew, her father's only business interests lay with the restaurant, and as his sole heir, she was aware of every dime coming and going.

She yanked her hand from his grasp and shoved it into her jacket pocket. "I'm sure I don't understand."

Tucci grinned, showing straight white teeth, the canines

elongated, reminding her of a hungry dog. "Come to my restaurant, Roberto's, tomorrow night. I have an excellent chef who will prepare whatever dish you desire. We'll have a glass of wine and discuss your options."

"I'm afraid that isn't possible. I'm needed at my own restaurant. Perhaps you could stop by Ciao Bella and we can discuss this 'business' you speak of."

Tucci shook his head and moved in closer. "No, bella." He lowered his voice and continued. "You strike me as a smart girl. So understand right now—*my word is law*. Do not turn me down again."

He strode past her then. Slack-jawed, Gianna turned and watched the smarmy man, along with the goombahs who circled around him protectively, stride to a waiting black stretch limo.

"Who was that?" Theresa asked.

Gianna turned to her cousin. While she wanted to shrug the answer off nonchalantly, the icy fingers of doom scratched at her arms. "Some guy named Fabio Tucci."

Theresa's eyes widened. "Don *Juan* Tucci."

A sudden creepy feeling encompassed Gianna's body. Of course! Don Juan! The man was notorious for his womanizing. What the hell did he want with her? *She* hadn't earned the moniker "Madonna" for nothing.

"What did he say?"

Emotion sprang up in Gianna's chest. Fresh warm tears welled in her eyes. "He said Papa and he had some type of unfinished business."

Theresa's perfectly arched brows furrowed. "Doesn't sound good to me, Gia."

"He wants me to go to his restaurant tomorrow night to discuss my 'options.'"

"You aren't going, are you?"

Gianna swiped at the nagging tears and shook her head.

"No. I invited him to Ciao Bella, and he told me he calls the shots." She pulled a damp hanky from inside her long-sleeved shirt and blew her nose. "I don't like him."

Theresa looked past Gianna's shoulder to the big black stretch pulling away from the curb. "Me either."

Before Gianna could comment further, she was swarmed with genuine friends and family who offered their condolences. She held back her tears and stood stalwart as she always had. For the sake of her father and the rest of the mourners, Gianna would once again put her own feelings aside for the greater good of the family.

Several hours later, after the last mourner left the restaurant, Gianna climbed the back staircase to the spacious apartment she shared with her father. It was the only home she'd ever known. After her gypsy mother told her and her father she was going out to the store and never returned, it had been Gianna and Alberto against the world.

As she kicked off her sensible heels, Gianna groaned. Her feet were killing her. She plopped down on the sofa and rubbed them, thinking how terrified she was when her mother didn't return home that night. They called the cops, along with the entire family.

Never suspecting Tina would have deserted them, Alberto nearly died on the spot when the cops pointed out his wife's empty closet and dresser. Alberto later discovered that the secret cash stash only he and his wife knew about had disappeared with her.

It was crystal clear to everyone what had happened.

To a seven-year-old girl, it was the harshest of betrayals. Her father had sunk to his knees and cried inconsolably for weeks. Gianna knew a new terror. What if Papa left her too?

When he finally came back to reality, he begged Gianna never to leave him. And she had given her word, begging the same promise from him. Twenty years later, she now felt completely alone. No siblings. No living grandparents. Just cousins, aunts, and uncles, but mainly her father's sister Cece, who had failed filling in as a mother figure, though she had tried valiantly. Cece was lovable, but she was more interested in letting the world know what a horrible woman Tina Cipriani was. For that, Gianna could not forgive her. Tina had abandoned her, true, but at the end of the day, she was the woman who had given birth to her, and that counted for something in Gianna's book.

Tears welled again, and Gianna moved over to her father's recliner, took the afghan her nona had made years ago, and wrapped it around her shoulders. She curled up into a ball, closed her eyes, inhaling the warm spicy scent of the only man who had been in her life, and cried.

Gabe sat across the street from Ciao Bella, hunkered down in a battered black van. From behind a half-empty cup of coffee, he watched the upstairs apartment light go on, then a slender shadow pass in front of the window. He knew it was Gianna, and he knew she was alone. He also knew she was in for a whole lot more hurt.

Gabe's eyes moved from the window down the street to his left to the blacked-out Escalade hugging the curb on the same side of the street as he. Tucci had his own men keeping an eye on the little Italian girl. He wondered how far the Blade would go to get what he wanted from her. Which broached the question: What *did* Tucci want with the girl?

Gabe took a big swig of his coffee and contemplated the answer. One of two things. He wanted to extort the money from Gianna that Alberto owed him, or he wanted the quiet demure virgin. It was an open secret on the streets that "Madonna" Cipriani was as cloistered as any nun in a convent. Now that her overprotective father was out of the way, the ocean was teeming with circling predators. At the gravesite, he'd watched the way the men, including his partner, had salivated over the prospect of popping such a sweet cherry.

A twinge of heat speared Gabe's dick. He pushed against the rise in his slacks. "Down boy," he muttered. He finished off his coffee and tossed the empty cup into the black hole of the back of the van. His dick reared its head again. Gabe groaned but didn't bother pushing it down. It had been months since he'd come inside of a woman. And that was no easy feat considering where he spent most of his evenings. He looked up at the now-darkened window.

He had a yearning all right, but he realized it wasn't for those sleek, high-end, world-class bodies. No, he was in the mood for a good old-fashioned home-cooked girl. The kind of woman who had some meat on her bones and, more than that, a genuine smile and a zest for the same pleasures he craved. Good food, good wine, and some lusty, twisting-the-sheets-till-they-were-ringing-wet sex.

Blood surged to his dick. And this time Gabe fought back. With the heel of his hand, he pushed down firmly against his hard-on. He closed his eyes and groaned. *Not helping.* "Son of a bitch!" he growled. He fought the urge to take the matter into his own hands but somehow couldn't justify it on company time. Instead, he rearranged himself and willed his hard-on to go away.

2

Gianna lay in bed for several long moments. She squinted as the glare of the morning sun blinded her. It was supposed to rain. Instead sunshine greeted her. She rolled over and stuck her head under the pillow, not wanting to open the restaurant. She let out a long relieved sigh when she remembered she told the employees she was going to close today. She needed time before she could pretend to the world her heart was not broken. What surprised her most about her decision was the fact that she was, for the first time, doing something for herself and not thinking of others first.

Gianna flung the covers from her body and sat up in bed. She looked down at the thin beige flannel nightgown she'd worn for the last two years with sudden contempt. Such was her life. Colorless, but safe and warm. Her shoulders slumped forward. It wasn't so bad.

She lay still for a long time and realization dawned. She was taking the time off because it wasn't what *she* wanted, she was being forced to by her family! She sprang up straight in the bed as a shot of rebellion surged inside. Was she destined to do what was deemed best for her by others? Her entire life she'd gone with the flow. If Papa said it were to be, it was to be. Zia Cece was an indomitable force, and well, Gianna had always done the right thing. It never occured to her to rebel. Why should she?

She slumped back into the pillows and reasoned, in the end it was good for her. So be it.

With no one needing her at the moment, and nothing better to do, Gianna snuggled deep beneath the covers and slept.

A distant thud woke her from a fitful slumber. She'd dreamt her mother came for her with Papa, and together the three of them welcomed family and friends to Ciao Bella, like they used to in the old times. Gianna could still remember sitting on the stool while her nona flicked gnocchi with her thumb from the potato dough she'd rolled out. As hard as Gianna tried, she could never perfect her grandmother's technique. It died with her several years ago.

The thudding increased in velocity and repetition. Gianna popped up in bed, her long hair covering her face. She swiped the heavy mass from her eyes to more clearly see the shadowed room.

More pounding. Like a hammer. From downstairs. She glanced at the clock and gasped. One o'clock it the afternoon! Gianna grabbed her robe and tied it securely around her waist, then hurried from the apartment down the back stairway to the back of the restaurant, then to the kitchen door where the incessant pounding came from.

She flung open the door and nearly screamed.

Two men, the same two who had walked with Mr. Tucci back to his limo at the cemetery, stood big, mean, and foreboding in her doorway. They pushed her back inside and shut the door behind them. Gianna shivered in her bare feet, her toes curling against the chill of the tile floor. "Wha-what do you want?" she meekly asked.

The bigger of the two, the one who looked like his face had single-handedly stopped a truck, grinned. His toothy smile reminded her of a jack-o'-lantern. "Don Tucci wanted us to give you a little reminder about tonight. He expects you at eight o'clock sharp. He'll send a car. Be ready by seven-thirty."

Gianna forced her shaking limbs to still. She raised her chin and pursed her lips. Setting her hands on her hips, and grateful for the long robe and long nightgown, she said, "I told Mr. Tucci yesterday I was unable to do that. He is welcome here to discuss business."

The smaller guy—not that his three-hundred-pound frame would ever constitute small, but in comparison to his three-hundred-fifty-pound, six-foot-six friend, he was smaller—stepped forward. His nose had obviously had a few run-ins with doors but was not nearly as damaged as his friend's, and he said, "Don Tucci don't make social calls."

Gianna's sudden burst of defiance evaporated when the big one stepped closer and reached out a ham-sized fist to her. She flinched and stepped back. He grabbed her by the front of her robe and lifted her clear off the floor. "If we gotta take you kicking and screaming, we will." He let go of her, and Gianna sprawled onto the floor. Her robe and nightgown hiked up to her thighs. Hastily she pushed the fabric down, then looked up at the two thugs. Their black eyes brightened. Gianna moved back. The smaller one moved toward her. The big guy grabbed his arm. "Mario, you gonna pay for that piece with your dick on the block?"

Mario stopped and snorted. "I'm patient. I'll take the Don's sloppy seconds any day."

Both men turned from Gianna as she scrambled to her feet, pushing past Theresa who was just coming through the door, but not before each of them gave her an appreciative leer.

Theresa gave them the international sign of peace minus one finger, then hurried to her cousin. "What the hell, Gia?"

Gianna smoothed her robe with shaky hands. "I'm okay. Those guys came by to remind me that Mr. Tucci was expecting me tonight and that they'd be by with a ride."

Theresa steered Gianna to a nearby chair and pushed her down into it. Hands on hips, she announced, "I'm going with you."

Vehemently, Gia shook her head. "I'm not going!"

"What are you going to do when they come looking for you? Do you think Tucci gives a flying fuck that you don't want to meet him? He wants something from you, Gianna, and the sooner you know what he wants, the sooner we can take action."

Gianna smiled. She'd always loved Tressie's moxie. As girls, her cousin, although a few years younger, was always the adventurous one. Gianna had taken the heat more than a few times for Tressie's ill-fated antics.

"He scares me," Gianna muttered.

"He should. That guy thinks he's Casanova twice over. He gives me the creeps." Tressie looked down at her cousin. "But that aside, take the Italian slime ball by the horns and let's see what he wants."

Gianna nodded, wondering what hole she could hide in until Tucci forgot about her.

"I'm glad I came by to check on you and the restaurant. Who knows what those goombahs would have done."

Gianna stood and tightened her belt. Then smiled at her perky cousin. She was so jealous of Tressie. She was gorgeous and dressed like she had stepped out of *Vogue*, but what Gianna admired most was her cousin's adventurous spirit. Never in a million years would Gianna have picked up and taken off for New York City like her cousin had a few years ago. It had caused a huge rift between Tressie and her father.

No, Gianna didn't have a wild bone in her body. Always the good girl, she did what was expected of her. And never thinking of the grass being greener on the other side, she was content. But now? She thought about how she felt. She wasn't sure what it was, but she knew something had ignited last night as she sat curled up in her father's chair. Anger, resentment, and a deep yearning to explore the world. "I'm looking forward to you working here with me," Gianna said.

Theresa smiled and hugged Gianna, then said, "I appreciate the offer. I need to keep busy and my mind off other things." She looked around the spotless kitchen. "So show me around. I didn't have much of a chance last night with the entire city here!"

Later that afternoon, after Tressie had left, Gianna took a long hot bath, then a nap she didn't really need. When she awoke, an odd restlessness she couldn't put her finger on engulfed her. She dressed and puttered around the apartment, still feeling at odds with herself. Once again her solitude was interrupted by a loud knock on the door. But this came from the apartment door. Whoever it was had a key to the restaurant.

Gianna opened the door and blinked. "Tressie? What are you doing here?"

"I'm here to stage an intervention," Tressie said, moving past her and into the living room where she plopped what looked like an oversized tackle box and a duffel bag onto the coffee table.

Gianna closed the door, confused. "Intervention? I'm not hooked on drugs."

Tressie whirled around and stared down her cousin. "I'm talking a beauty intervention, Gia. If you're going to meet up with Tucci, we need to do some . . . polishing."

"Polishing? That man is a letch. If you polish me, he'll . . . he'll, well, he'll want something else!"

Tressie didn't seem to care about *that* minor detail. "Look, Gia, I know how sad you are about Uncle Berto, and I know how much you miss him. But if you want to find out what the hell that creep Tucci has up his sleeve, you have to drop the Madonna-in-tears thing and show Tucci you have your act together."

Gianna threw her shoulders back and stepped toward her cousin. "I *have* my act together. I'm an accomplished business-woman. Who do you think has been running Ciao Bella for the last ten years? Dressing up like Zia Lola will only get me laughed at."

Theresa didn't back down. Nope, Gianna watched her four-inch heels dig into the carpet.

"The way you look now, Don Juan thinks he can walk all over you."

Gianna headed toward her bedroom, Tressie hot on her heels. "I'm not doing it, Tress," she said over her shoulder. "*If* I go, I go as I am. I can't act like . . . well, I just can't be someone I'm not."

"I'm not talking about you walking in there with the girls hanging out Gia, you know I love you, but the way you dress . . ."

Abruptly, Gianna turned around, narrowed her eyes, and asked, "What girls?" Then looked down at her black ankle-length wool skirt. "And for your information, I bought this at Macy's! It's respectable. Like me."

"You know? The girls," Theresa said, cupping her own full breasts for emphasis; then she cocked a brow and gave a walleyed look at the skirt. "As for that skirt, it's straight out of Nona's wardrobe, is what it is. I don't care where you bought it." Tressie held up the tackle box and duffel bag. "I promise not to dress you like a slut. I just want to make you a little less Nona and a little more Zia Lola."

Gianna sighed heavily and plopped on the edge of her bed. She stared at the ceiling, knowing her cousin was not a patient woman and, more frustrating, knowing Tressie was right. If she presented herself to Tucci as a woman in control, not one hiding behind wool and flannel, maybe she could maneuver him. She chewed her bottom lip. But maneuver him from what? What did he want?

"Fine!" Gianna said unbuttoning the pearl buttons at her throat and wrists. Pulling the lace and linen shirt off, she handed it to Tressie. "*This* was Nona's."

"I told you! *Santa madre di dio*, Gia. You dress like you're headed for the convent."

"I might as well be."

Theresa cocked a brow. "What do you mean by that?"

Gianna's face tightened as she caught her cousin's eyes in the mirror. "Tress, I've never . . ." Heat flushed her cheeks. She couldn't quite say it.

"Never what?"

"Never, *anything*," she whispered. And it was true.

Tressie's big eyes widened.

"C'mon, Gia, you've never had sex?"

Gianna shook her head, suddenly feeling like a freak.

"Really? Not even when you were dating Tommy Verrastro after you graduated from high school?"

Gianna snorted. "Dating? You call going to Friday night Mass dating? Papa made sure the boys sniffed elsewhere." A sudden flash of anger erupted. "In fact, Papa made darn sure the only thing the boys left with was a cannoli." Gianna turned and faced Tressie. "What's it like?"

She watched her cousin's eyes darken, then look away.

"I'm not exactly rolling in experience here, Gia. Remember, your father and mine came from very similar schools of thought when it came to raising their daughters. Keep them cloistered and virginal until they walk down the aisle."

"No kidding. Alberto Cipriani wrote the book on that topic." And with that, Gianna made a decision. She moved over to her dressing table and sat down. She smiled into the mirror, catching Tressie's deep dark eyes, which were so much like her own. "I'm really glad you came."

Tressie smiled back. "Me too."

Gianna looked away, her original question still burning hard. Her cheeks flushed hotter. "Papa told me boys were nothing better than rutting pigs, and once they got what they wanted from me, they would move on to the next girl. But that never squashed my curiosity. I always wanted to know what it *feels* like."

Theresa looked away and shrugged. "Sad thing is, Uncle Berto was probably right. As far as how it feels? My only experience was with Mark, and judging from that, you aren't missing much."

Sensing Mark was probably one of the reasons Tressie jumped at the offer to come help out, Gianna didn't push. But she still wanted to *know*.

"I'm sorry it didn't work out, Tress. But Mark's loss is my gain!" Gianna turned back to the mirror and took a deep breath. "Okay, from this moment on, Madonna is dead, and the real Gianna Cipriani is coming out!" She grinned, looking up at Tressie. "Do your worst, cousin. When I'm done with Tucci, he won't know what hit him." Gianna swallowed thickly and wondered who the heck she was kidding.

The shadow across Theresa's face vanished as she rubbed her hands together in anticipation. She cupped Gianna's jaw, tilting her face this way and that, frowning and making little "hmms" to herself.

"Am I salvageable?"

Tressie nodded. "You've got the Cipriani cheekbones, sculpted, exotic, very Sophia Loren."

"Am I too fat? Guys like those stick girls. I am *so* not a stick. More like a log."

"I prefer to use the word *lush* to describe the Saccamano

ass." Theresa grinned and swung her own curvy rear seductively. "You're the exact same size as me. You just have to learn how to work it." She ran her hands through Gianna's hair, stretching it out to its full length. "And your hair is amazing, but we're vertically challenged, so this much hair can be overwhelming. How about I give you a trim?"

Gianna nodded.

Theresa went to her tackle box of stuff and rustled around for a moment, emerging with a pair of shears. She sliced the air in pretend menace. "Come here, my pretty."

Gianna nodded again, knowing she was safe in her worldly cousin's hands. "I'm in your hands, Tress. I'm going to close my eyes, and when I open them, I want to be the Italian version of Cinderella." Gianna closed her eyes, then opened one. "And that includes the glass slippers and Prince Charming."

"In that case, I'm going to need a lot more light. Let's go into the bathroom." She steered Gianna down the hall to the bathroom and draped a towel around her shoulders. For the next forty-five minutes, Gianna heard nothing but the slice of the scissors. Occasionally, Theresa would pause and make another one of those "hmm" sounds as she contemplated her next move. After what seemed an eternity, Theresa finally said, "Perfect, but don't look yet." She made another disapproving clucking sound. "We have *got* to do something about these," she said, touching between Gianna's eyebrows.

"My eyebrows are fine!"

"No offense, cousin, but do people ever call you Bert and ask you to do the pigeon?"

Gianna giggled and swatted Tressie's butt. "I thought I was your favorite cousin." When Tressie stood staring down at her, unmoving, Gianna sat back and closed her eyes. "Fine, pluck away."

"I need to get out the heavy artillery for this." She pulled a jar and what looked like a tongue depressor out of the box. "Where's your microwave?"

Gianna groaned and pointed toward the kitchen.

Once she was convinced Gianna's face was completely devoid of hair, Tressie explained to her as she expertly applied makeup, "You need to walk into that restaurant like it's yours. Keep your eyes focused ahead of you. Your chin level with the floor or, better yet, a notch higher, and for God's sake, don't look down!"

"What if he puts his hands on me?"

"Then scream bloody murder and kick him in the balls. And if that doesn't work, act like you're giving in, then grab his balls and twist them until they break off."

Gianna cringed. "Jesus!"

Theresa stepped back and set the container of eye shadow down on the sink. "Look, these guys understand one thing. *Power.* If they think they own you, they will act like it. Remember: You are cool; you are confident. You eat sleaze balls like Tucci for breakfast. Think it, act it, be it."

Gianna nodded. "I eat sleaze balls like Tucci for breakfast. I have the power."

Theresa nodded, picked the eye shadow back up, and in a few minutes she was done. "Now, get dressed in the outfit I brought, then come back out here."

Gianna hurried to do just that. Despite where she was going, excitement skittered through her. She felt alive. Excited. Womanly. Not the demure little house mouse everyone smiled at one minute then forgot about the next.

Reverently, Gianna slid her fingers across the smooth black leather of the midthigh skirt. As she zipped up the back zipper, the sound of it jolted her. Warmth filled her. She'd never worn anything higher than calf length before. Next she slipped on a modestly cut button-down V-neck sapphire-colored cashmere sweater that seductively hinted at the curves that lay beneath. The smooth soft feel of the fabric felt as good as the luxurious bubbles in her bath earlier. Black patent leather stiletto peekaboo pumps completed the ensemble. Gianna didn't dare look at herself. She was terrified the warm sexy feeling encompassing her would not be reflected in the mirror.

Carefully she negotiated her way back into the bedroom where Theresa stood. She watched her cousin's eyes widen; then a radiant smile spread across her face.

"Now you're ready to go head-to-head with Tucci." Theresa came to her and turned her to face the full-length mirror. Gianna gasped at her reflection. That was not her! The woman who stared back in shock *was* beautiful. She looked . . . sophisticated. She had a shape! Her father would roll over in his grave if he saw her like this.

"You look amazing, Gianna. Sexy and classy at the same time. Tucci thinks he's dealing with a frumpy little church mouse. You go in looking like this and he'll be so distracted trying to get into your pants, you'll have him eating out of the palm of your hand, and he won't care what he thinks he wants from you so long as you act like he has a chance."

3

"I eat slime balls like Tucci for breakfast. I eat slime balls like Tucci for breakfast. I eat—"

The limousine came to an abrupt halt, cutting off Gianna's mantra. Her knees shook and her hands were damp. "I eat slime balls like Tucci for breakfast." Why didn't she let Tressie come with her? Because if there was going to be any trouble, Gianna didn't want her cousin in the mix.

The door opened and Mario looked in. "C'mon, the boss is waiting."

Gianna took a deep breath and scooted out of the backseat. It occurred to her that they were in the Tenderloin. And while there were lots of restaurants and shops in the area, the Tenderloin had long been known for one thing and one thing only—the strip joints and peep shows. But the building she stood in front of with a half dozen suited doormen looked innocuous enough. Maybe Tucci had a legit place? Perhaps it *was* just a steak house. Somehow she doubted it, despite appearances. Roberto's profited from meat of a different kind.

No sooner had Gianna been escorted into the building than

she was greeted by a beautiful woman in a skintight hot-pink vinyl miniskirt and halter top. "I eat slime balls like Tucci for breakfast," Gianna muttered to herself.

"Miss Cipriani?" the tart asked.

"Yes."

The woman smiled, her overblown lips as pink as her plastic outfit. Gianna didn't contemplate where the huge chest came from.

"I'm Taffy. I'll take you to Mr. Tucci. He's expecting you."

Gianna continued to repeat the mantra in her head as Taffy led her through a large room with a stage at the end. Hanging from the poles like upside-down worms were women in various stages of undress. "I eat slime balls like Tucci for breakfast," Gianna said out loud.

"Did you say something?" Taffy asked.

"Nothing you'd be interested in hearing," Gianna said. They wound around a wide stairway that circled the stage. As they came to the next level, a long chrome bar complete with topless women shaking and blending drinks for the rapt men leaning into the bar stopped Gianna dead in her stilettos. Open-mouthed, she gazed at the bulbous breasts pounding up and down as the women shook metal shakers.

Gianna started to cross herself but stopped, and swallowed hard. Turning from the women, embarrassed for them, she was met with an even more disturbing scene. In a pitlike lounge, several men sat back on overstuffed red velvet-backed seats, as naked women ground and gyrated on tented trousers. Her cheeks flushed hot and her fingers went cold.

She turned to back out, but Mario and his buddy blocked her way.

Gabe choked on his scotch and pushed the pair of triple Ds out of his face. Who the hell was that? The sexy voluptuous brunette seemed hauntingly familiar to him. The brand-new pair of tits smacked his cheeks. "C'mon on, honey, I got more than that little girl," the dancer said, smashing her slick mounds in his face. A nipple dragged across his nose. Gabe pushed her off his lap. She squealed as her ass hit the carpeted floor.

He watched Tucci's two goons, Mario and Eddy, push the girl who stood rooted to the floor toward Tucci's office. The lightbulb went on in Gabe's head. Gianna Cipriani! Here? And where the hell did she get that body?

Gabe's natural male instinct was to grab her by the arm and drag her out of the club, but his cop instinct kept him in position. Tucci wanted her for something, and while Gianna looked as if she might be having second thoughts about being there, he knew it was crucial to his case that she see it through.

"C'mon, Gianna, go with the big ugly apes," Gabe muttered.

He couldn't help an appreciative sweep of her curvy figure. The leather skirt and sweater hugged her curves, accentuating every lush peak and valley. Gabe's dick twinged. Her long hair was thick and dark with subtle golden highlights, the wispy strands accentuating the high cheekbones and full sensuous lips. The image of them locked around his swelling cock sent a hot jolt of blood south.

Damn it! By the time he had his cock under control, Gianna disappeared up the hidden stairway to what he knew was Tucci's office. Gabe moved up to the long bar, where he nursed his watered-down scotch and waited.

Gianna entered Tucci's office muttering her mantra over and over. By the time she came face-to-face with the slime ball, she prepared herself for the worst. Instead of a frothing mad dog with a raging erection, she found Tucci sitting comfortably in a chair with a glass of wine in his hand. He stood when she entered the room, his cologne reaching her before he did.

"Gianna, welcome. I'm so glad you came."

Gianna smiled. Like she had a choice.

"I'm glad I did too, Mr. Tucci. I've had quite an adventure getting here."

"Please, my name is Fabio, like the model. I would be honored if you'd call me by my given name."

"Of course—Fabio."

He took her hand and pulled her to a chair that matched the one he'd just sat in. "I have a wonderful Chianti from my family's estate in Tuscan. Would you like a glass?"

Gianna shook her head. "No, thank you."

Tucci ignored her answer and poured her a glass. "Please, sit."

As she did, she caught his appreciative leer on her legs.

"You look beautiful, Gianna. I had no idea."

"I only dress like this for . . . special people."

Tucci pressed the glass of wine in her hand. "Please, join me in a toast." Gianna nodded and raised her glass. "To our future, may it be profitable for us both."

Gianna clicked her glass against his and took a sip. She smiled and settled back into her chair. It was comfortable. "So, Mr., ah, Fabio, tell me about your business with my father."

The don took a long drink from his glass and refilled it. "I can think of far more fascinating things to discuss, Gianna, like how luscious your lips look. Are they all yours?"

Gianna frowned. "Mine?"

"Do you have them injected?"

Gianna winced. "Lord no! I detest needles!"

Tucci's eyes drifted down to her ample cleavage. "Is everything natural?"

Gianna adjusted herself in her seat, subtly jutting her breasts out. This was easier than she thought. Tucci was like a sixteen-year-old aching for his first blow job. Gianna's eyes widened. Had she actually thought that? Holy mother, what was happening to her? Whatever it was, she kind of liked it. All of the sudden she didn't feel so self-conscious in this new skin of hers.

Quite the contrary. She lowered her long lashes and tested the water a little bit more.

"I am as natural as wood-pressed *extra* virgin olive oil."

Tucci caught his breath and moved closer to her. "Speaking of virgins . . ."

Gianna leaned forward, touching her right knee to his left. This was too easy. "Fabio, I didn't come here to discuss virgins. I came here to discuss business."

Fabio smiled. The gesture lit up his sharp features and Gianna felt as if for the first time he was genuinely enjoying himself. "Of course, bella, business first."

Gianna took another sip of her wine, enjoying the warm mellowness of it and her power.

"I met your father a few years ago at Golden Gate Fields."

Gianna scrunched her brows, her newfound sexual sway over this man forgotten. Golden Gate Fields? "The racetrack?"

"Yes, I run several horses there, and, well, Alberto was quite the fan."

"But—"

Tucci waved her off. "One thing led to another, and before Cappy realized it, he was deeply in debt."

"I'm afraid you must be mistaken. My father was not a gambler."

Tucci stood up and went to his desk. He opened a drawer and pulled out several sheets of paper. He handed them to Gianna. She set her glass down on the table, and as she read each page, with her father's signature at the bottom, her stomach became tighter and tighter. The wine soured in her belly. She was going to be sick. She looked up at Tucci. "I don't believe this."

"It's his signature, bella. Your father owes me one hundred forty thousand dollars."

Her hand shaking, Gianna handed Tucci the papers. "I'm sorry, but I don't believe my father would do such a thing! He would never jeopardize our future."

"It is unfortunate that he had this addiction."

Gianna's eyes narrowed. "An addiction you encouraged!"

Tucci smiled. This time it was not so genuine. "I race my horses for the love of the sport. Those who wager? Not my concern."

"But you do nothing to stop it!"

"That is not my responsibility."

Gianna stood. "Neither is my father's debt."

Tucci remained sitting. "I'm afraid that isn't acceptable to me, bella. I expect you as his daughter and heir to see to his debts. I will take a percentage of Ciao Bella as a down payment." Tucci grinned and sipped his wine, then stood and walked closer to her. He reached out a hand and swept her hair from her shoulder. He closed his eyes and inhaled. "You smell fresh. Wholesome. I want you, Gianna, and I am willing to pay any price you name to be your first man."

Gianna slapped his hand away. "I'm not for sale!"

Tucci laughed. "Everyone has their price. Name yours."

"I want nothing from you, except for you to leave me alone." How dare him?

"There, you see? You do have a price. For what you ask, I want something in return. Your cherry. Willingly given."

Gianna moved to the door and turned the knob. When she jerked it back and it didn't open, a hard shard of fear tore through her. She turned to face the grinning don. "Would you rape me?"

"No," he said, smiling. "I want you willing."

"That will never happen."

"Not even to save your restaurant?"

Gianna was adamant. "No."

"How about your sweet little cousin Theresa?"

"You wouldn't dare!"

"You will soon find out, Gianna, that I am a man who ultimately gets what he wants."

"*You* will soon find out, Fabio, that *I am* a woman who ultimately gets what she wants." Gianna pointed to the door. "Please open that. Our business is concluded."

Tucci moved to her and placed his hand on the knob. He lowered his voice, the sound of it menacing. "I'll give you two weeks to either come up with the money owed me, or I will come for the deed to the property Ciao Bella sits on."

"That lot is worth six times what my father owed you!"

"Then I suggest you take out a loan."

"Mr. Tucci, I have no intention of paying you one red cent."

"You'll change your mind." He moved into Gianna, his hands spanning her waist, his lips hovered over hers. The stench of garlic hung heavy between them. Gianna gagged. Tucci moved in to kiss her, but she turned her head. His hands gabbed at her breasts, and his lips trailed along her neck. "Gianna, I'm always up for option two."

Gianna shoved him away from her. "There are no options."

He chuckled and opened the door. Gianna moved as quickly as her stiletto heels would allow.

4

Gabe moved stealthy in behind Gianna as she hurried down the last stairway, then into the open vestibule of Roberto's. She pushed the doors open and darted outside before one of the doormen could get to it. Gabe followed, ducking behind a concrete pillar as she quickly turned, looking wide-eyed and panicked over her shoulder to see if she were being followed. He caught sight of her a minute later as she ducked into the Kat's Meow, a seedy topless lounge.

"Jesus Christ," he muttered as he hurried in behind her. For a Wednesday night, the place was quiet. But he had no doubt that in a few hours, the shrouded cubicles where patrons could have "privacy" would be full to busting. Long before his Fed days, he'd worked the streets of San Francisco, vice to be exact. He was all too familiar with the goings-on in the Tenderloin.

As he pushed open the black furry doors to the club, he heard a familiar voice behind him. "Mario, she went his way!"

Gabe kept his back to the street and stiffened at the other man's words. "I swear to God, Eddy, if I don't get my hands on that girl tonight, I might have to break a few heads."

"You might, coz I'm gonna beat you to her."

Gabe knew who the two thugs were, and he knew who they were talking about. If there wasn't so much at stake, he'd turn around and use those bastards' heads as bowling balls. Gabe pushed into the darkened vestibule of the Kat's Meow. Sleazy music infiltrated the equally sleazy lounge area. He didn't have to look far to find Gianna. She sat at the far end of the chrome and black leather bar. She looked like a rare gem in a dime-store jewelry case. Gabe sauntered to the opposite side where he would have an unobstructed view of her profile and contemplated his next move.

Gianna tried to smile at the weasel-looking bartender. Instead she winced. She'd run from Tucci like a ninny! She'd acted like a ninny! She *was* a ninny! Her cheeks flushed warm in shame. She didn't eat guys like Tucci for breakfast—they ate her!

Tressie would be so disappointed. Lord knows she was with herself. Was this to be her life? Talk the talk but when it came time to walk the walk turn tail and run as fast as she could to the next safe hole and jump in and hope she wasn't followed?

She let out a long exasperated sigh. Well, she started out okay, the seduction part came a little too natural, but she didn't fight it. She liked it, in spite of the lech she practiced on. From the moment she saw herself in the mirror after the transformation, she not only acted different, she *felt* different. She would have hung in there if the news of her father's gambling hadn't blindsided her. Or the fact that he owed a bundle to the dirty don. But what rattled her most was the man's sexual persistence. Her sudden sex-kitten act had been played out too well. Tucci's ardent response at the door terrified her. His proposition disgusted her.

She would decide on who got her cherry—not some dirty don!

Gianna rolled eyes. Who was she kidding? She was doomed

to live the life of a spinster. She'd look like Lily Tomlin, with the hair net, long dress coat, and super thick brown knee-highs.

"What'll it be, toots?" the bartender asked. Gianna looked up, so lost in her thoughts she didn't remember where she was. She looked around the room and swallowed hard. Another one of *those* places. The topless cocktail waitresses pranced in and out of the lounge into what was the stage area, as if showing their breasts was as common as wearing a hat. Her gaze continued around the dark leopard-spotted room and abruptly stopped when they clashed with dark eyes at the other end of the bar. A slow warmth filled her, and her belly did a slow roll. The guy staring back at her with the intensity of tiger on a deer caused her mouth to go dry. He was big, dark, and intense. He raised his glass in a subtle salute, then drained it.

"Toots?" the bartender prodded.

Gianna dragged her eyes from the man at the end of the bar and said, "A glass of Chianti, please."

"Chianti? This ain't Scoma's."

"Ummm." Gianna looked down the bar to the dark-haired man and nodded. "I'd like one of those."

"You want him on the rocks?"

Gianna smiled, suddenly feeling very bold. "No, I'd prefer him straight up."

As the bartender moved down to the end of the bar, Gianna suddenly felt foolish. A man like that would never be interested in a girl like her. Suddenly she found her lap more interesting than her surroundings.

"I prefer my drinks straight up as well."

Warm breath assaulted the back of her neck, and Gianna could swear every hair on her body raised in awareness. Long thick arms, one on each side of her, circled her.

Swallowing hard and feeling extremely daring, Gianna turned on the barstool and came face-to-face with the man from the end of the bar. His dark intensity startled her; his toxic sensuality enveloped her, and for the first time in her life, she squirmed in her seat over a man. He smiled and she nearly swooned. He slipped a big arm around her waist and pulled her against his chest. Her nipples puckered, her breasts thickened, and she had the unadulterated urge to rub against him.

"Hello, gorgeous," he softly said. His dark chocolate-colored eyes scanned her face. From her eyebrows to her eyes to her nose and then her lips. Slowly he lifted his eyes back to hers. "You have amazing lips." Gianna licked said lips. The man groaned. "Baby, you have no idea how sexy that looked."

Every cell in her body warmed. She closed her eyes and inhaled. He smelled good. Clean. Like soap and lemons and spice.

"You smell really good," she whispered, opening her eyes to his hot gaze. Not sure what to say or do next, she knew what she wanted to do, and the thought shocked her. Just ten minutes ago, Gianna had been sickened by Tucci's advances, and here she was in a two-bit strip joint with a stranger who had her so hot and bothered that if he let go of her, she'd puddle onto the floor.

"Let's get a booth over here," he cajoled. Taking her hand into his big warm one, he pulled her along to the booth farthest from everyone and slid her along the smooth vinyl. His body slipped in beside her.

He leaned into her and softly asked, "What's a nice girl like you doing in a place like this?"

"What's a bad boy like you doing in a place like this?" He grinned like a wolf, and Gianna suddenly had an urge to be bitten. Hard.

Nervousness skittered through Gianna's body, warming her in a tingly way that was anything but unpleasant. The big man sitting so close to her made her feel things she wasn't aware she was capable of feeling. His big dark eyes were hooded and framed by thick black lashes. When he smiled, as he did now, a dimple in his right cheek deepened. He reminded her of a very Italian Magnum PI.

"My name is Gabriel. What's yours?"

His thick husky voice made her squirm in her seat. "Um . . . I . . . my name is Gianna."

He grinned deeper, revealing big straight white teeth. The vision of them laving her nipple shocked her. She gasped and sat back, wide-eyed. He moved in closer. In a slow unhurried motion he traced a big finger across her collarbone. "Don't be afraid of me, Gianna. I only bite if you want me to."

Her heart hammered against her chest, and to her utter shock and amazement, his hand slid down to rest just above the swell of her breasts, his little finger resting on the plump rise. "Your heart is beating like a drum."

She opened her mouth to tell him that she was shocked by his boldness and more so by her reaction to him. Never had a man touched her as he did, and, well, she liked it. The words failed her when he touched his fingertip to her bottom lip. "Your lips are soft."

Were his? He moved in closer, his warm breath caressing her skin. Her breasts trembled, and she felt herself begin to melt. "Can I kiss them?" he softly asked. Completely under his spell, she nodded.

His lips touched hers, and a hot shot of heat speared right between her legs. Like an electric fizz, her body jolted. Gianna closed her eyes and leaned into him. He tasted like hot sex and aged scotch. Gabe groaned and slipped his arms around her waist and pulled her hard against his chest. His lips parted, his tongue swirled along her mouth, and his kiss deepened. Gianna didn't know what to do. Quickly she decided she'd let his experience guide her. And Gianna was not disappointed. Gabe swirled his tongue along her lips, his teeth nibbled her bottom lip. His warmth, his scent, his masculinity combined into a heady cocktail. She sighed, loosening against his hard warmth, wanting him to teach her more.

Ever the willing student, tentatively, she touched his tongue with hers and angled her head to get more of him. She grabbed his shoulders, and in a sudden swell of desire, Gianna pushed him back against the padded back of the booth seat, and nearly climbed in his lap.

She felt Gabe grin beneath her lips and he tightened his arms around her. Gianna had a fleeting feeling of embarrassment, but her desire to learn more, to feel more, to do more, overrode it. Gabriel turned her on, and for one living in the dark for so long, she was desirous with the need for light.

Gabe's hand slid around her waist to her breasts, his big hands softly caressing her. Her nipples were so hard and tight, she had the unexpected urge to pull down her bra and shove them in his face, demanding he kiss them like he kissed her lips.

Reading her mind, Gabe trailed his lips to her chin, then to her throat. Gianna cried out when he pressed his mouth to her nipple, only fabric separating them. Slick warmth infused her thighs. She wanted more. Her hands moved across the hard planes of his chest. Gabe pressed back warm and hard.

"Touch me harder," Gianna begged.

He'd awoken Sleeping Beauty and Gabe obliged. He wanted to lose himself deep between her thighs. To feel the warmth of her bare skin against his. He wanted to take a nipple into his mouth and lick and suck it to the roof of his mouth until she screamed for him to stop. He slid his hands up to the top button of her sweater and deftly unbuttoned several. Her full luscious breasts heaved beneath his hands and he squeezed. She moaned and thrust harder into his hands. He slid a finger beneath one bra strap and slipped it down her shoulder. Then the other one. The only thing holding the bra in place was the hardened tips of her nipples. Her skin was creamy smooth and flushed in excitement. He looked into her deep hazel eyes and smiled. She was like a child in a candy store for the first time in her life. A quick stab of guilt raced across his consciousness. It was quickly replaced with two things—his libido and his sense of getting the job done. And while he would never do Gianna in a place like this, or any place for that matter, he wasn't above some serious petting to find out what Tucci wanted with her. He had no doubt that whatever it was, it was illegal and a means to the dirty don's end.

So, he felt no guilt. Not really. It wasn't like he was going to pop her cherry.

"Gianna, you have beautiful breasts," he breathed as he drew down her bra, exposing the cherry-colored nipples. He traced a fingertip across each of them. The skin pebbled, and he felt Gianna tremble in his hands. He lowered his head to one and licked the tip, and she reared against him. With his hands, he slid her across his lap so she was now straddling him with her knees on the seat. He took her nipple into his mouth and slowly sucked while his other hand palmed and caressed the other. Gianna threw her head back, and her long hair cascaded around her shoulders, her hips gently thrust forward, her soft perfume intensified in the warm confines of the booth. His dick hurt it was so full, and he knew that unless she was numb, she could feel the length of him against her panties.

Gianna held on to his shoulders and moaned, thrusting her breasts into his face. "Gabe," she breathed hard, "I've never felt like this before."

Her innocent confession stopped him cold. Guilt washed across him, as effective as a bucket of cold water. He stiffened. And stopped his assault.

"No, don't stop," she begged.

"Gianna," he softly said.

"No! Don't say no to me. Not tonight!"

Gabe looked at her moist eyes. He brushed a strand of hair

from her cheek and pressed a kiss to her lips. "Gianna, this isn't the place—"

"I don't care!" She pushed his head into her breasts, and Gabe, being a man, could not resist. He gave in to her demands but controlled the situation.

He licked and kissed her breasts, his hands molding to her ass, his fingers digging into her luscious skin. His dick swelled again, and if she kept moving against him the way she was doing, he was going to make a mess on them both.

"Gianna," he said, caressing her ass and licking a taut nipple. "Why are you here?"

"I was looking for you," she breathlessly said.

"Baby, I've been looking for you all my life."

Gianna unbuttoned his shirt and shoved it wide open, her hot hands caressing his equally hot skin. "I like the way you feel," she said, then kissed him and rose up. With her legs spread on either side of him, her skirt was hiked up her thighs, and her warm musky scent drifted to his nostrils. Gabe groaned and pulled her harder against him. If he wasn't careful, he was going to take her right there. When her hand reached down to his crotch and pressed his raging erection, Gabe about came on the spot. For one who supposedly was inexperienced, Gianna Cipriani was one aggressive girl. She grabbed his hand and put it on her thigh. Then proceeded to thrust her hips against him. She had yet to sit back down in his lap. Instead, she spread her thighs wider. He couldn't resist her invitation. His hand slid up her thigh, her skin warm and smooth like velvet. When the tip of his finger touched her damp pantie Gianna flinched. Her thighs tightened, and he felt her body go rigid. He didn't move. He pulled his head back and looked into her hooded eyes. He saw fear, excitement, and trepidation.

"It's your call, Gianna," Gabe said. She closed her eyes and threw her head back.

Her tits were in his face, her ass in his hands, and her pussy wept for him to touch. When she failed to give him the green light or even the red light, Gabe pressed his lips to a nipple. "You have the breasts of a goddess, Gianna."

She moaned.

His lips suckled, his teeth nibbled, his hips rocked. "Your skin is like warm velvet."

Gianna closed her eyes and sighed. His hand on her thigh moved closer to her core, and when he traced a finger along the satin of the panties shielding her pussy lips, she trembled. But still she gave him no indication of how far he could go. And he wanted to go all the way. If she unzipped him, all he had to do was slide the thong she wore aside and fill her to the hilt. The image of that action caused Gabe to surge against her. He pulled her down to him and ground against her dampness. It was the last straw for Gianna.

She pressed her hand to his and cried out. Her hips undulated, and moistness filled his hand. Gianna's eyes flew open in shock and she gasped. "Take me here, Gabe."

"Jesus, Gianna," he whispered. Gabe's hard-on battled with his shaky sense of propriety. He couldn't have sex with her. No penetration. He would *not* cross that line. But he could do the next best thing.

Gabe slid a big finger between her panties and her slick wet folds. Gianna nearly died of sheer sensory overload. Her entire body stiffened. Never had she thought another human could make her body feel like it did at this moment. She pressed harder against his hand. She wanted penetration. But his finger only moved along her outer lips. When he slid a fingertip over her hardened clitoris, Gianna cried out. Her wetness lubricated his finger, and in a slow swirling cadence, Gabe moved his finger around her stiff clitoris. His lips latched on to a nipple, and his teeth laved her. His other hand pressed against her right butt cheek, pressing her hard against him. Gianna's hand locked onto his shoulders. She squeezed her eyes closed and bit her bottom lip, pressing into him harder, spreading herself wider, hoping, praying he would slip a long thick finger into her.

The fact that she was engaging in a sexual act with a complete stranger didn't faze her in the least. What shocked her more was how good it felt. She was done playing the virgin act. She wanted to live and feel alive, and Gabe was the man to take her there.

Even though he didn't enter her, Gabe's hand wreaked havoc with her body. He quickened his motions around her clit. On her knees, she stiffened as he moved back and forth, the slick sound of her juices on his hand heating her more. She arched her back, as a deep hard swell of sensation coiled tightly inside of her. She knew when it unleashed, the sheer force of it would make her want more. And more after that.

5

Two facts slammed hard into Gianna's conscious. One, she had never felt so lit up in her life, and second, she was allowing a complete stranger, albeit a very handsome, yummy-smelling one, to touch her in places only she had touched herself. And with that realization, she added a third fact: She wasn't ashamed! Not really.

Her breasts ached, her womb ached. Like a fever, her body ached. She could not sit still. But realization filtered into the fog of her sexual haze. He was a stranger. A stranger with his hands in her pants.

"Gabe, please," she whispered against his hot lips.

"Tell me what you want," Gabe said, his lips trailing to her chin, then her neck, then her collarbone. "Anything," he breathed just as he latched on to a very hard, very excited nipple.

Gianna moaned and rolled her head back, pressing hard against him. Just another minute. It couldn't hurt. . . .

"I want to see you after tonight," Gabe said against her breath.

If it were possible, more excitement tore through her body.

She'd never been asked out by a man like this before. She melted into him. How ironic, she thought. It took her father's death for her to come alive. A sudden rush of guilt infused her and reality began to seriously infiltrate the sexual haze. "I . . . I can't. I don't know you."

Gabe chuckled and pulled back enough to look at her. He slid his fingers from between her legs. She felt her cheeks warm. "I think we're a bit beyond the acquaintance stage." His left hand squeezed her thigh, but he did not demonstrate to her just how acquainted they were. She liked that. He was sexy as all get out, but he didn't force himself on her. Indeed, she had practically jumped him. Gianna pushed off of his lap and suddenly felt very naïve and very foolish. She was not the sexy siren she pretended to be. *If* she saw him again, he'd see past the expertly applied makeup and borrowed clothes and see her for the fake she was. Panic rose, as well as sudden humiliation. Who was she trying to kid? She was Gianna "Madonna" Cipriani. She was too set in her ways to change now. And if she chose to later on? It would be on her terms and at a much slower pace. Gianna looked hard at Gabe. He was the kind of guy who had trophy girlfriends. Not good Catholic girls.

"I . . . um . . . I made a mistake. I need to go." Gianna literally climbed over his lap to get away. As she did, her wrist snagged on his shirt. Her bracelet! She tugged it, freeing herself, then moved as quickly as she could away from him.

A shiver of panic tore through her as realization settled in. Not only had she nearly had sex with a stranger, but she had also been given an ultimatum by Tucci. An ultimatum she could not deliver even if she wanted to.

Gianna almost cried as a cab pulled up in front of her like a magic coach sweeping her away from a Prince Charming who would find out Cinderella was really an imposter. And one with a price on her head to boot.

Gianna looked over her shoulder to see Gabe running from the club, looking both ways for her. She ducked and said, "Lombard and Columbus."

Gabe stood at the curb and watched the yellow cab hurl itself into the brisk traffic. He brought his right hand up and looked at the dangling gold charm bracelet. A soft whiff of musky scent swirled around his nose. Gianna's sexy applied scent mingled with her natural scent. He closed his eyes and inhaled deeply. His blood quickened and he smiled. She had turned out to be a very nice unexpected perk. He opened his eyes again just in time to see a black town car take off in the same direction as the cab.

"Fuck!" he muttered. On the run to his car, he pulled his cell phone out and called Gordo. "If you're anywhere near Ciao Bella, hightail your ass over there and look like a drunk hanging out at the back entrance. Our girl is being hunted. I'll be there in ten."

"I'm around the corner at Lucia's."

Gabe hopped into his cover car, a sweet little Carerra. Compliments of Search and Seizure. Not his natural style, but for a hot-shot real estate developer, it worked.

Gabe downshifted, taking the corner of O'Farrell and Mission at forty-five miles per hour. His urgency to get to Gianna disturbed him. Not that he wouldn't break his ass to save any victim, but he realized there was more to it with his Cinderella. In the time between seeing her at the cemetery and her bold moves on him at the Kat's Meow, she had made an emotional impression on him. She was that fresh breath of air in a stale bar. A clean slate. Normal, natural, and uncomplicated.

His life was a quagmire of complications. From his parents' acrimonious divorce when he was twelve to his own less-than-civil divorce five years ago, topped by the undercover work these last few years. He'd lost count of how many IAs he'd managed to back out of. At thirty-five, he was tired of all the bullshit of constantly being on, of the lies and the sleight of hand.

He banked the next corner at fifty-five and downshifted. He couldn't help the grin that broke out across his face. The power of the sports car vibrating beneath him coupled with the sensitive handling and the remnant of the hard-on induced by Gianna Cipriani warmed his entire being. He loved the rush, the feeling of excitement, the not knowing what was hiding around the next corner. He didn't fool himself; as much as he disliked some things about undercover work, there was more of it he loved.

Gabe pulled up on the opposite side of Lombard, across the street from Ciao Bella just as Gianna inserted the key into the gate leading along the side of the restaurant and back to the door leading to the kitchen and what he knew was a stairway up to her apartment. Two big shadows followed her and Gordo was nowhere in sight.

Gabe slammed the car door shut and rushed across the street to grab the wrought-iron gate as it swung closed. The lock clicked. Damn it! Adrenaline shot through him. When he heard Gianna scream, he was over the spike-tipped gate like a billy goat over a boulder.

The harsh glare of the porch light clearly illuminated Dumb and Dumber, and a terrified Gianna Cipriani plastered against her front door holding her key in front of her like a dagger. Gabe rushed up behind the two gorillas, butted their heads together, and shoved the six hundred pounds of pasta-fed flesh into the door.

He let go and the Roman columns toppled.

Without a word, he grabbed the key from Gianna and inserted it into the door. He pushed her through as it opened, then shut and locked it. He heard the gate rattle and a loud *whoosh* as a body tumbled over it. Gordo, no doubt. He'd figure out soon enough that Gabe had beat him to the punch again.

Gabe turned to a shaking Gianna. Wide-eyed, she stared up at him. He pulled her into the circle of his arms and smoothed her hair. "You're okay, Gianna. Those guys won't bother you anymore tonight."

She pulled slightly away shaking her head and looked up at him. "How did you—?"

He smiled and pulled her tighter against him, feeling more for this girl than just a cop protecting a victim of what would have been a really ugly crime. Gianna's innocence was refreshing, and in his tainted world, he had the overwhelming urge to nurture it.

"You left so fast, I wanted to get your number. I saw those two guys go after you and, well"—he looked down at her and smiled again, then said in a goombah voice—"a guy's gotta do what a guy's gotta do." He shrugged his shoulders and rolled his head. "You know what I mean?"

Gianna laughed and pulled away. "I should be really mad at you for following me. I . . . I didn't want you to know where I live."

Gabe continued to smile down at her. Her warm scent encompassed him, keeping his senses on high alert. "Yeah, well, sorry about that, but now that I know, whatcha gonna do about it?"

Gianna's body heated up in his presence. The adrenaline already in her system continued to spike. She felt safe in this big man's arms. She leaned into him and decided she could just this once show him her gratitude. On tiptoes, she moved up against him. Slipping her hands around his neck, she brought his lips down to hers. "This is what I'm gonna do about it."

What began as a simple kiss quickly turned into a firestorm of passion.

His lips were warm, they were firm and they fit hers perfectly. For the second time that night Gianna found herself responding with years of pent up passion to this virtual stranger. Gabe pulled her into him and maneuvered her up against the nearest wall. Gianna lit up like a Roman candle. Her previous terror had long since evaporated, to be replaced with white-hot desire. She felt more than grateful to this stranger for saving her from what would have surely been a brutal sexual attack. Instead, she had an entirely different sexual attack on her mind.

Gabe's hands and lips were everywhere—her breasts, her waist, beneath her skirt on the hot flesh of her thigh. He moved his knee between her knees and parted them. In the club, he had only pressed against her; now his fingers gently probed the moist fabric of her panties, the tip of one pressing slightly into her. Gianna arched and hissed in a deep breath. Her thighs parted more; her hips moved in a slow sensual undulation against him, pushing her hot wetness down and around his finger. His thick erection pushed hard and insistant between them. Gabe's big hand slid around to her buttocks and squeezed, lifting her from the floor. Gianna wrapped her right leg around his thigh and pressed harder into him. When he slid a finger into her, she caught her breath and closed her eyes. "Oh, God, Gabe, that feels so good," she moaned.

Gabe froze. Her hot sweet muscles clamped desperately around his finger. His dick flinched. God she felt so damn good. So innocent and this situation was getting away from him. He didn't mean for it to go this far. Her hand slid boldly over his erection. He closed his eyes and grit his teeth. Jesus Christ. "Gianna, don't. I'm going to come all over us both."

"I have a towel," she offered.

He wrangled his libido into a semblance of order and, he pulled back from her, looking hard into her eyes. His belly did a slow roll. Raw innocent desire radiated from her dark eyes. He wanted to take her upstairs to her bedroom and make love to her all night long. But he couldn't. He'd managed to get himself in hot water once. It nearly cost him his job. "Gianna, I—"

Her face clouded with sudden embarrassment. He felt her ardor cool and her body tensed. As much as he wanted things to cool off, he was disappointed. She pushed his hand from her and slipped out of his arms, rearranging her mussed clothes and hair. "I'm sorry. That's twice I forced myself on you tonight." She walked to the door and peeked out the window, then unlocked the dead bolt. Head down, she pulled open the door. "Thank you for helping me tonight."

Gabe stood beside her, resting his hand on hers. "Gianna, if you hadn't been so bold, you would have been fighting me off."

She looked up at him and smiled. "That's nice of you to say." She pulled her hand from the knob and stepped back. "Good night."

He stepped through the threshold, his heart not in it. He reached out to touch her, but she stepped away. In the glow of the porch light, he was sure he saw the twinkle of a tear. He felt like a pile of shit. "Gianna—"

He was answered with the door closed firmly in his face.

Shit! Not only had he managed to make her think he wasn't into her, but he'd also managed to make it so she wanted nothing to do with him. How the hell was he going to stick close if she was water to his oil?

Gianna felt like a fool. A complete and utter fool! What guy turned down what she was offering? Either a gay one or one who was not into her at all. Heat infused her cheeks, shame infused her heart and sexual frustration trumped them both. Was she destined to be a virgin? "Madonna?"

She ran up the narrow stairway to her apartment, double locked the doors, and strode directly into her father's bedroom and pushed up the mattress. His handgun. She hadn't a clue how to use it, but if one of those thugs came back, hopefully she'd learn real quick or she'd scare them away. Or maybe, she'd use it on Gabe!

For a long moment Gianna concentrated on calming herself down and tamping her rabid libido.

There was more at stake then losing her cherry. She laughed harshly. Her cherry! It's what Tucci wanted and was willing to pay for it. Never! After what Gabe had made her feel, there was no way that even if she had considered Tucci's proposition, which she had not, she would allow him to touch her. Not after she knew how it was supposed to be. Her body, still warm from Gabe's touch, warmed hotter. He wasn't so easy to shake.

She strode into the bathroom and looked at herself in the mirror. Despite the lack of lipstick, thanks to Gabe, and her subtle makeup, she looked the same. Yes, her hair was cut more stylishly, and her eyebrows had the perfect arch of a *Vogue* model and she'd acted like a sex-starved loser. No wonder Gabe bolted twice. Maybe if she kept up the makeup and bought some new clothes, she could gradually work her way into the butterfly Tressie had created. Maybe a guy like Gabe would come around.

Gianna washed her face and crawled into bed, the gun within reach on her nightstand. For long minutes different emotions swirled in her head. She stared at the shadows on the ceiling, listening to the distant rumble of traffic. She closed her eyes and inhaled, and could not help smelling Gabe's lingering scent on her. It smelled good. Potent. Her skin warmed, her nipples tingled, and heat speared between her thighs moistening her. Biting her bottom lip, Gianna moved her hand down her belly and over the flannel fabric of her nightgown. Slowly she hiked up the fabric.

When she touched the moist spot between her thighs, she gasped. And moved her legs farther apart. She pushed the covers off and lay exposed from the waist down. She pressed her fingertips to her mound and caught her breath again. Sharp spears of desire pierced her skin, heating her hotter. She pressed her other hand to her right breast and squeezed. Her back arched and her hips rose against her hand.

Closing her eyes tighter, Gianna pressed a finger between her slick folds. She was so wet, so warm, so aroused. A soft cry escaped. She wanted Gabe's hand there, not hers. She wanted more of him than his finger. She wanted to feel him inside of her. She wanted wild, wanton, sweaty sex with him. She pressed her finger deeper into herself and moved against the pressure. Her tiny nub jutted out from its hood, demanding satisfaction.

Slowly she rubbed her fingertips across it. Sweet wisps of ecstasy swept through her. Her hand moved faster. Her hips pressed into the air, her legs rigid and her back arched. She wanted more than what she could give herself, and for the first time, she felt no guilt, no shame in touching herself.

She had visions of Gabe raised above her, his big body naked, covered in slick perspiration as he slammed into her. Gianna's breathing turned harsh and labored as her hand swept back and forth across her clitoris; her body rigid, feeling just out of reach of that place she so desperately wanted to go.

Just as she climbed the peak, the heat of her body almost too much to bear, the phone rang.

"Argh!" Gianna cried out. She rolled over, shoving her nightgown down, and grabbed the phone. "Hello," she grumbled.

"Gia, are you all right?"

She sank back into the pillows. "I'm fine, Tress."

"You sound . . . busy."

"Nope, just lying here in my boring bed."

"What happened with the Dirty Don?"

"Oh, he told me I had two weeks to cough up the hundred forty K my father owed him and that he'd knock some off for the pleasure of popping my cherry."

"Oh, my God! What a pig!"

"I told him no on both accounts."

"My God, then what happened?"

"I left." Gianna didn't tell her she was afraid he would hurt her family if she didn't comply. She figured she had two weeks before she'd have to alert them. Maybe then she'd go to the cops. As a last resort. She didn't trust them. Her father taught her that.

"I'm coming over!"

"No, Tress. I'm in bed, and I have to sleep. I'm opening to-morrow; then I decided I'm going to do some damage in Union Square."

"Oh, yippy skippy! I don't have to be in until five. I'll pick you up at noon!"

6

"What the fuck happened to you being just around the corner at Lucia's?" Gabe demanded, getting real close to Gordo. His partner opened and closed his mouth like a floundering catfish gasping for breath.

"I got there, but those goons were just getting up from whatever the hell you did to them!"

"No shit, 'cause you weren't there!"

Gordo pulled his shirt from Gabe's grasp and looked around the darkness of the street. "Hey, I had to, uh, you know, use the can. I got a bug going through me."

Gabe moved backward and shook his head. "Next time, when I call for backup, Gordo, you can shit your pants on the way. That girl was almost raped!"

Gordo perked up. "She want to press charges?"

"If it were so easy. She's afraid of them. I don't blame her."

"Why didn't you tell her you were a Fed?"

"And have her slam the door in my face permanently?" Gabe shook his head. He needed a drink. "No way. I'm playing this one close, real close. That slime bag Tucci wants her, and so do his gorillas."

Gordo grinned. "Just how close you gonna play it?" He leaned toward Gabe and sniffed loudly. "Smells like you've already made some headway."

Gabe shoved him away and started for his car. "Gordo, did it ever occur to you that the reason you don't get laid more often is because the ladies smell the dog in you long before they see you?"

Gordo laughed. "Yeah, but when they find out this dog can hump like a lion, they come back until they can't stand."

Gabe hit the key fob and his car lights blinked on and his dick sprang up. "In your dreams, old man, in your dreams."

Once settled in his car, Gabe called in to SFPD dispatch and asked for a detail to keep a sharp eye on Gianna's addy. He doubted the gorillas would be back but didn't want to take anything with Tucci for granted.

Gabe sped past his partner, who stood in the middle of the street giving him the finger.

Gabe raised his right hand to his nose. Essence of Gianna swirled about his senses. His dick swelled, and he wanted to turn around, climb up the fire escape, creep into Gianna's apartment, and slip between her sheets. The urge to turn around was so powerful, he found himself braking, then signaling to turn right. He shook the urge off, and though it was fifty degrees outside, he turned the AC on full blast and cursed all the way to the Marina district, where he had an appropriate flat for his cover.

Once inside, Gabe poured himself a stiff bourbon, tossed it down, then poured another one. He paced the floor of his living room. What he knew was that Cappy Cipriani was into Tucci for a hundred forty large. He'd bet the meeting tonight was to discuss repayment options. Tucci would force Gianna to pay off her father's debt. How the hell was she supposed to do that? The only thing of value she possessed was the restaurant.

Gabe snapped his fingers. "That's it!" Quickly he put a call into the task force secretary's voice mail.

"Hi, Jan, I need you to run a title search on Ciao Bella. It's on Lombard, but start with Alberto Cipriani, then Gianna Cipriani, and find out the balance on the mortgage. I need that info like last night." He hung up the phone.

If Tucci wanted the restaurant, that would explain why he let Cappy run up his pony bill so high. Most bookies would have cut him off at ten grand. He'd bet his hazard pay that the dirty don told Cheeks the bookie to let him ride. After all, when he dug himself in too deep, there would be only one re-course: hand over the restaurant and the property it sat on.

Gabe poured another bourbon. He moved to his panoramic window and gazed out over the bay and the lights of the Golden Gate Bridge.

A question niggled at his brain. Why Ciao Bella? He sipped his drink, this time savoring the smooth bite of it. The answer wasn't what was important. Because in the end, it wouldn't matter. His time to leave this city by the bay was near. Gianna was his ticket to Tucci, and once he was arrested, his work here would be done.

He tossed back the rest of his drink, which suddenly bit too hard. Another reason he couldn't let things with Gianna go too far. He'd love her then have to leave her, and for a man who didn't do morning coffee with aplomb and was more comfortable slip-ping out before there was any uncomfortable morning-after conversation, he didn't want to hurt the innocent Gianna. She was a pawn, the key to the prize. And as such he owed it to her to leave her alone.

Gabe looked at the nearly empty bottle of JD. Enough was enough. He began to unbutton his shirt and head for the bath-room. He needed a shower. A really cold one.

* * *

Gianna spent a fitful night dreaming of Gabe coming to her, waking her with kisses, and roaming his hands over her body—only to be interrupted by Mario and Eddy bursting into her bedroom, their eyes wild, their teeth gnashing like rabid dogs and their hands, long furry claws like a monkey's, reaching for her. Several times she woke wanting to call Gabe. But she had no way to reach him. Even if she did, she would not call him. He'd made it clear he wasn't interested in her.

The next morning, Gianna jumped into the shower, then started to replicate what Tressie had done to her the night before. And though she tried, she could not make her hair look anything close to the miracle Tressie managed. Instead she settled for it hanging straight, letting the wispy edges frame her face and decided it didn't look too bad. After she applied the few cosmetics she possessed, Gianna looked at herself in the mirror. Not bad. Better than before Tressie had her intervention but not the sultry siren who walked out of here last night.

Gianna found herself immersed in the daily operation of the restaurant. The cozy red and white checkered tablecloths beckoned her with friendly warmth. The bottles of Chianti that lined the wall behind the bar promised a smooth companion to the pasta dishes Marlene and Dante could whip up in their sleep. Gianna had taken more interest in the kitchen these last few years. She enjoyed the solitude of creating, but more than that, she enjoyed the sharing of her efforts. Several of her own recipes were featured on the menu, and every once in a while, when one of her chefs could not make it in, Gianna gladly put on the apron and spent the evening running between the kitchen and the hostess stand. One of her dreams was to go to Italy and spend a year working in various restaurants. In her entire life, she had never left the Bay Area. Maybe, just maybe, it was time to spread her wings. She smiled. Maybe. Someday.

The fresh scent of basil, thyme, and oregano wafted from the kitchen, mingling with the pungent scent of fresh garlic. It was perfume to her. She would never tire of the scents. As long as she lived, those herbs would give her comfort and joy. Like a teddy bear.

The restaurant was immaculate. Her family and guests who had cleaned up after the reception two nights before did a stellar job.

It was still early, not even seven-thirty. Paulie, her prep boy, would be arriving soon, followed by Marlene, who would make her fresh pastas from scratch. Soon the kitchen would be bustling with activity and scrumptious aromas.

And so the day went. At noon Tressie showed up, ready to melt Gianna's credit card and leaving the hostess stand in Zia Cece's capable hands. Gianna spent a whirlwind afternoon with her cousin trying on clothes, hats, and shoes and getting a full makeover at the MAC counter at Nordie's. Gianna didn't think of her dead father, Tucci, or his two goons, instead she thought of spreading her wings a little at a time, and, a certain dark-haired man who made her feel things she now craved more than any dish on the menu.

As the dinner hour rolled around, Gianna was dressed in a shirt and skirt, and not one that stopped at her ankles. While black, this skirt fell midthigh. She loved the shirt. The minute she'd spied the deep emerald-colored button-down cashmere form-fitting sweater in Nordstrom's, she knew she had to have it. The color brought out the green in her hazel eyes. While it was form-fitting, it did not reveal too much of her ample cleavage but showed it off in simple classic tailored lines. She wore dark hose and three-inch Kate Spade peekaboo pumps Tressie insisted she buy.

Despite the smiles from her regulars, Gianna still felt like somehow she was an imposter. Not worthy of the smiles and looks she garnered. Even when old man Amato came in for his weekly penne all'Arrabbiata and Chianti fix, removed his glasses, cleaned them, then smiled and said, "I'm not seeing things. You are more beautiful than an angel, Gianna. Fie on Berto for keeping you hidden away all these years." He took her freshly manicured hands into his gnarled ones and kissed them. "Don't be afraid to go find a nice Italian boy. You deserve to live a little." He patted her hand, then said almost to himself, "We all do."

Gianna smiled. The door to the restaurant opened, and the regular courier stepped through. His eyes widened when he realized who he was looking at. "Dayum, Gianna, you look hot!"

Gianna laughed, the sound foreign to her. She was not feeling so light. "Thanks, Mark."

He hurried and crossed himself. "Oh, sorry, I forgot. My condolences." He dropped his shaggy blond head and handed her the box in his hand.

There was no label on the finely wrapped package. Smooth gold-toned vellum wrapped with creamy silk ribbon covered the heavy box. "You don't have to sign for it, but I was told I had to give it directly to you."

Gianna frowned. "Who sent it?"

Mark looked down at his clipboard and shrugged. "Dunno." He turned from her and said over his shoulder, "Sorry I can't chat. I have two more deliveries; then I get to go home. Ciao!"

"Ciao, Mark," Gianna said as she turned with the box in her hand. She hurried over to the hostess stand. Excitement skittered through her. Was it from Gabe? Did he want to see her again?

A minute later, Gianna stood horrified, holding a crystal bowl full of big ripe blood colored cherries. "Oh, they look delicious, Gianna," Zia Cece said as she ambled closer. Plucking a cherry from the crystal bowl, her aunt chewed and smiled. "So juicy. Who sent them?"

Gianna shoved the bowl into her aunt's hands. "I have no idea, but you are welcome to them."

Anger clouded her vision. How dare Tucci? *How dare he?* She didn't have time to seethe, as several regulars came in. Quickly Gianna morphed into the hostess with the mostest. Until fifteen minutes later when Mario and Eddy walked in; but, she smirked, she was happy to see them sporting lumps on the sides of their heads.

Feeling safe on her home turf, Gianna strode up to the two thugs. "Get out of here before I call the cops."

Mario smirked. "Better yet, call your boyfriend from last night. We got a score to settle with him."

"He's not my boyfriend." The minute the words left her mouth, Gianna wished she hadn't said them. Let the two dumbasses think she had a boyfriend who wasn't afraid of them. Quickly she tried to retake the statement. "Not yet anyway."

Eddy shrugged. "Don Tucci wanted to know how you liked the cherries."

"Tell him I threw them in the trash."

Mario shook his head, his great jowls slinging back and forth. "He's not going to be very happy with you."

Gianna watched the door open again and caught her breath when Gabe strode through like he owned the place. He was more handsome than she remembered. Her cheeks flushed hot. She turned to Tucci's men. "You tell your boss, I'm not interested in any gifts from him or doing any business with him. Tell him if he continues to harass me, I'll call the cops."

Eddy stepped closer, so close she could see the dull beige flecks in his dung-colored eyes. "You go ahead and call the cops, girlie, but take a look around here before you do, 'cause every single person in this joint will be sleeping with your father if you do."

Blood drained from her cheeks. The two men moved past

her and settled into a round table for four in the center of the intimate dining room.

Gianna turned to Gabe, who stood behind her. "I can take out the trash if you'd like." His warm breath caressed her ear. Gianna's knees wobbled. Gabe took her elbow and turned her around to face him. "Jesus, Gianna, you're as white as a ghost." He steered her toward the back of the restaurant, out of the way of the goombahs' prying eyes. Zia Cece bustled out of the kitchen with bread baskets in each hand.

Her brown eyes scoped out Gabe before they landed on Gianna. They quickly morphed from teasing to concern. She set the baskets down on a nearby table. "Gia, *stai bene?*"

"*Si*, Zia, I'm okay. Just felt a little light-headed for a moment."

Cece clucked several times like a hen. "I told you it was too early for you to come back to work." She raised her hands to Gabe. "Does she listen to me? She is like a daughter to me, but she is as stubborn as a goat."

Gabe smiled. "I agree on the stubborn part."

Cece narrowed her eyes and took a closer look at Gabe. "Calabrasi?"

"Siciliano."

"Ah!" Cece cried, crossing herself. "No more Sicilians. Tina was Sicilian. She left a daughter and a husband. Shoo. Go away."

"Hey," Tressie said from the kitchen as she wrapped an apron around her tiny waist. "I'm Sicilian, too, don't forget. I'm not going anywhere."

Cece threw her hands up in the air, grabbed the baskets, and hurried out to the waiting diners.

An awkward silence fell between the three. Tressie stuck her hand out to Gabe. "My country cousin forgets that in the big city, it's customary to introduce strangers. I'm Theresa Bellesi, fellow Sicilian, and damn proud of it."

Gabe smiled and shook her hand. "Gabe LaMotta." Then he handed her his card and grinned at Gianna when he said to Theresa, "Hold on to this for Gianna, she might need it."

Gianna felt the heat rise in her cheeks again. "I'm sorry, I just—forgive my bad manners. Tress, Gabe, Gabe, Tress. Now, Gabe?" She turned a smile to him. "Did you come to eat dinner or annoy me?"

Gabe's eyes twinkled, and Tressie crossed her arms over her ample breasts, not taking a step away. Gianna gave her cousin a look that said, Scram. Tressie smiled and slowly shook her head no. "Fine, you two can stand here and play games. I have a restaurant to run."

The next hour went by in an uncomfortable blur. Gianna was extremely aware of Gabe sitting in the back circular booth. Tressie informed Gianna he had insisted on sitting there. Of course, he could watch Gianna run around like the proverbial chicken with her head cut off, *and* Tressie informed Gianna, Gabe insisted on waiting for Gianna to eat dinner.

Gianna strode up to his table after an hour. "Mr. LaMotta?"

Gabe held up a hand. Warmth spread across her skin as she looked at the big thick fingers and neatly manicured nails. Just one touch of those big hands made her feel things she'd never felt. Gianna licked her lips and looked at him. He grinned wide, his white teeth shining in the low candlelight of the table. "I think, Gianna, we have gone past the formalities of mister and miss."

Heat scorched her cheeks and zipped southward to her thighs. Her nipples tingled. Gianna shifted her feet. "Gabe, I have a long night ahead of me. Please, go ahead and eat."

He sipped his wine and shook his head. "I had a late lunch. I'll wait."

Gianna spun around on her heels and was glad to see Tucci's men gone. But she knew they were now aware of Gabe. He'd made no effort to hide his disdain from them. Several times she found the three of them doing the old stare-down.

Gianna steered clear of Gabe for the better part of the evening. Tressie however, had a sparkle in her eye that made Gianna very nervous. Several times her cousin walked past her with a shit-eating grin plastered across her face and acted like she had a big secret. Try as she may, Gianna could not extract information from her.

Finally feeling as if the joke was on her, Gianna marched up to Gabe's table. "Mr. LaMotta, we're going to be closing in thirty minutes. I'd like to close out your tab now."

Gabe poured another glass of wine from the half-empty bottle. His dark eyes glowed seductively in the candlelight of the table. Gianna groaned. Her skin flushed, and she wanted to slide in next to him in the spacey booth.

"I've been waiting for you."

She raised a brow. "Really? Twice last night you couldn't wait to get rid of me."

Gabe reached out and touched her hand. Her skin warmed. "I'm here to beg your forgiveness."

Gianna slapped his hand away. "Save your sweet talk for someone who'll appreciate it."

She turned and hurried away from him, nearly laying flat Treesie and the laden tray she held out. When she turned the CLOSED sign over for the evening and saw the last diner out from the restaurant, Gianna turned to the back of the dining room.

"Mr. LaMotta, it's time for you to go."

"Oh, no, Gia, his dinner is finally ready," Tressie said as she sashayed past her with a tray containing enough to feed a dozen people. The fresh-cooked aromas of garlic and butter tempted her more than it should have. It occurred to Gianna she had not eaten. From the moment she had opened the box of cherries, to the arrival of the goombahs, and then Gabe's arrival, she had not been able to contemplate food. Suddenly she was ravenous.

Gabe smiled at her and raised his glass. "Come have a glass of wine with me, Gianna, and some dinner. I don't want to eat alone."

She moved toward him. Her gaze did a quick scan of the plates. Shrimp scampi, veal piccata, and rosemary rack of lamb? "You ordered lamb?" It was one of her favorites and not on the menu.

"Tress told me how much you enjoyed it."

"But it's your dinner."

"*Our* dinner." He scooted over and patted the burgundy leather seat. "C'mon. Sit down."

"I have a restaurant to close."

"I'm on it, Gianna," Tressie said, her voice bubbly. Gianna wanted to shove a breadstick in her mouth.

Gianna turned to her cousin and narrowed her eyes. "Are you, now?"

Tressie nodded and put a large plate of spaghetti and meatballs on the table. Gianna gave her a look that said, "What the hell are you doing?"

Tress smiled, "*Mange.*"

Then she proceeded to stalk off to the kitchen. Gianna

looked around the restaurant. The bussers had cleared and reset all of the tables, save Gabe's. Jimmy came in with the vacuum cleaner and did a quick thorough job of vacuuming the tile and carpeted floor.

Gianna turned back to face Gabe. He watched her quietly. "I'll leave, Gianna, if I make you uncomfortable."

She collapsed next to him and pushed him over with her hip. "You don't make me uncomfortable," she lied.

"I'm glad to hear that."

He poured her a glass of Chianti. She noted the vintage of the bottle and smiled. It was one of their best and most expensive. He raised his glass to hers and said, "To second chances."

Gianna raised a dubious brow. "You had a second chance."

He clinked his glass to hers. "Then to the third time being the charm."

A wave of warmth rippled through Gianna's body. Gabe's dark eyes twinkled in the candlelight. His big fingers held the wineglass, almost covering it. He had big hands and big thick fingers, square fingernails with blunt fingertips. She looked up at him. "What exactly do you do for a living, Mr. . . . . Gabe?"

"Real estate."

"What kind of real estate?"

"Commercial, industrial. I specialize in cross acquisitions."

She wrinkled her brow. "Cross acquisitions?"

He nodded and set his glass down and proceeded to place several fat juicy shrimp on her plate. "When someone needs money and has a piece of real estate they want to hang on to but don't want to sell outright, I locate either a temporary buyer or a suitable partner to regenerate a cash-flow problem for the property owner. Or, sometimes for legal reasons, a person needs to look as if they don't own property. I find a legitimate tenet to hold the property in trust, so to speak, until such time the owner requests full ownership and deed returned."

"Isn't that illegal?"

"Nope."

Gabe smiled and plucked one of the shrimp from her plate. He held it out to her lips. "If this tastes half as good as it smells, I might take your chef home with me tonight."

Gianna laughed and leaned into his hand. "I don't think Dante will like that."

He moved closer and traced her lips with the shrimp. She opened her mouth, and he placed it on her tongue. When he didn't pull his finger away, she closed her lips around his finger and softly sucked it before moving back. Gabe's eyes darkened, and she heard a small intake of breath. Slowly Gianna chewed. After she swallowed, she licked her lips. Gabe moved in close to her. He smiled and lowered his head, and licked at the corner of her mouth.

"You missed a spot."

The contact sent her senses reeling and her world tilted. Quick intense jolts of desire pricked her senses. Gianna looked over her shoulder to see if anyone witnessed his touch. She closed her eyes and breathed a sigh of relief. Most everyone was busy shutting down for the night.

Gabe speared another shrimp and plopped it into his mouth. He chewed with gusto. Mesmerized, Gianna watched the full curve of his lips move in sync with the strong line of his jaw. His eyes locked with hers.

"Gianna?" Tressie called as she made her way to the back of the dining room. Gianna tore her eyes away from Gabe's mouth and turned to see her cousin saunter their way. A smirk hovered on her lips. Gianna flushed and smirked back. "I'm heading out for the night. Everything is cleaned and locked up except your plates."

Gabe stood and extended his hand to Tressie. When she gave him her hand, instead of shaking it, he brought it to his lips and kissed it. "Theresa, *grazi*, for everything."

Tressie grinned and withdrew her hand, looking down at Gianna. Her smirk turned into a knowing secret smile. "Anytime. *Ciao!*" She said over her shoulder as she strode from the room. Before Tressie exited the room, Dino's "That's Amore" piped softly through the sound system.

"You're fired," Gianna called to her retreating cousin. An answering laugh was followed by the slam of the front door, then the lock turning.

"I like your cousin," Gabe said, scooting closer to Gianna. She scooted away. "I used to like her."

"Why are you afraid of me?"

"I'm not afraid of you!"

"What happened to the firebrand who jumped me last night?" Gianna frowned. "She got a grip."

Gabe plucked another shrimp from the plate and wagged it in front of her mouth. Gianna reached up and tried to take it from his hand, but he shook his head. "Open."

She kept her lips shut. He slid the shrimp along the crease of her lips. "C'mon, Gianna, you know you want it."

"No—" He plopped the shrimp in. She pulled away from his fingers. He grabbed a tender piece of lamb and took a bite of it right off the bone. He chewed slowly. "Mmm, that is delicious."

"That's my recipe."

He took another bite and slowly chewed, savoring the taste. "Perfectly grilled. It's so pink and juicy. Like you."

He took another rib and held it for her to bite into. Gianna snatched the bone from his hand and sunk her teeth into the rare meat. She twisted her head and ripped it off the bone. As she chewed and swallowed, Gabe grabbed another rib and wagged it under her nose. "C'mon, Gia," he softly said, "take another bite."

When she moved forward and opened her mouth, Gabe's

lips swooped down on hers. He set the rib aside and plundered her mouth. His body swelled when he felt Gianna's breasts press against his chest in response. Slowly he tasted her, his lips nibbling her tongue, and he tasted the lamb and the essence of Gianna.

He moved back and, only a few inches from her face, brought the rib bone up to her lips. She took a bite. He took one as well. They both chewed, their eyes watching, their nostrils flaring, each very aware of the other. Gabe swallowed and grabbed his glass of wine. He pressed it to Gianna's lips. She took a sip; Gabe took a sip. Her lips glistened a deep burgundy color. Gabe kissed her again, softly this time, a savoring exploration.

He felt her muscles loosen. Gabe smiled against her lips. "You taste better than anything on this table."

He smiled down at her then and looked over at the plate of spaghetti and meatballs. He took his fork and twirled a gob of pasta. "Open," he said. Gianna complied. He put the fork full of pasta in her mouth. A long strand hung out. Gabe nibbled at it while Gianna chewed. "Mmm," Gabe murmured. He sipped his wine again and gave some to Gianna. He went back to the shrimp and by design dropped it. The succulent meat plopped onto the high swell of her breasts, then landed between her ample cleavage. Gabe smiled. "Oh, I'm so sorry, Gianna," he said. "Let me get that."

He licked the trail of butter and garlic sauce on her right breast and then dipped his mouth down into her cleavage and sunk his teeth into the shrimp. Gianna arched against him. Her breath hissed as she inhaled.

Gabe chewed the shrimp and moved slightly away. His dark eyes glowed molten in the low candlelight. He was having one hell of a time sticking to his keep-your-dick-in-your-pants policy. "Gianna, I want to touch you more."

He touched her thigh near her knee.

Heat flared in every inch of Gianna's body. Her hands trembled; her lips twitched. Her gaze traveled across Gabe's rugged face. She wanted him to touch her more too. A lot more. "I . . . I . . ." She couldn't tell him she wasn't given the name Madonna for nothing. And despite last night with him, he'd probably run to the front door and crash through it if he knew she was a virgin. Guys like Gabe liked slick, sophisticated, experienced women. Not little Italian church mice.

Suddenly she felt like a freak again.

Gabe's eyes twinkled as he regarded her. Did he suspect?

He took her face between his hands. His eyes glowed; when he spoke, his voice dropped several octaves. "Just a few more tastes, Gia."

He brought her lips to his but dropped his right hand to her thigh. In a slow slide, he pushed the skirt back, then slid his big hand between it and her skin. Her leg trembled. His thumb swirled in slow light circles on the tender skin of her inner thigh. Her skin reacted, skittering against his fingers. Gianna gulped in a deep breath. Her defenses were easily foiled. She'd tried really hard to ignore the man's sensuality. But when she felt her pulse lurch in her throat, and he looked at her with that deep soulful look that said she was the only woman in his world, she couldn't resist. She was weak. She was vulnerable, and she didn't care.

"Why me?" she managed to squeak out.

Gabe smiled slowly and pressed his forehead to hers. "Because, if I don't, I won't be able to concentrate on another thing until I do." His thumb brushed the fullness of her bottom lip. "Please, Gianna . . ." A violent tremor passed through her.

Her tongue darted out and touched the tip of his finger. A hot rush passed through her womb at the simple sensuous gesture. She liked the alternately smooth and rough texture of his skin. His sharp intake of breath set the rest of her body into a spiral plunge. Gianna surged against him. Gabe dug his fingers deep into her hair and pulled her lips to his. The contact was violent, fast and explosive. It knocked Gianna for a hard loop she was not prepared for. Terrified by the tide of desire she experienced, she pushed Gabe away. Her body trembled. She looked at him and read the same shocked expression in his eyes.

Gianna backed away. Gabe pulled her toward him. "What's wrong?"

She hung her head, unable to explain her feelings. Heck, even she didn't know what to make of them. She really wanted to go all the way. *Really*, she did. And she wanted to with Gabe, but she felt stupid. Fake. Like a freak. "I can't do this with you."

His dark brows crashed together. His big warm hands slid up her arms to her shoulders. "I won't push you, Gianna. But if it's me, tell me. I can take it like a man."

Gianna almost choked. Her eyes scanned his face; she wanted to tell him it wasn't him. No, he was what schoolgirl wet dreams were made of. It was her, pure and simple. As usual, when it came time to do something for herself on a purely selfish level, she balked. She'd been the insignificant Madonna for so long, she didn't know how to accept attention. She wasn't comfortable with it. When her breasts emerged one day, Papa explained she was cursed with the body of Sophia Loren, but God showed her mercy when he gave her a plain face. It would keep the boys from panting at her doorstep, and in so doing save herself from a world of hurt. Because, he told her repeatedly, the boys only wanted the goodies. And they would promise the world to get them. Gianna hunched back into the padded leather booth but continued to contemplate the man next to her.

He was exquisitely constructed in a rugged manly way. Every hard sensuous line of his face flowed effortlessly into the other. His black hair held the unruliness of a boy, yet the fire that burned in his eyes was that of a full-grown man. A man who made passion a way of life. A man used to having the crème de la crème between his sheets.

Not her.

What could he possibly see in her? As she traced his face with her gaze, she wished she were braver. Exciting. Lusty.

"I'm not cut out for this kind of stuff. I'm a frigid ice queen. And I'm okay with it." The minute she said the words, she felt like a complete idiot.

Gabe slowly moved toward her. A flirty smiled tugged at his lips. New heat rushed her cheeks. He knew she was looking for an out. And he wasn't going to give it to her. He reached out a finger and traced the subtle curve of her jaw. She couldn't help the warm flush that flashed in its wake.

"Does an ice queen respond like that?" He drew her closer to his chest. Warmth emanated from him. She just wanted to melt against him and let him make love to her until she couldn't move. He pressed his lip against the shell of her ear. "Does a frigid woman's skin warm like yours is now?" His fingers swept her collarbone. The warmth of his lips followed.

Gianna moaned against the pressure of his lips.

"Gianna, there is nothing cold about you. You'll have to come up with a better excuse to keep me away."

How about that she was embarrassed as hell by the fact that she was a twenty-seven-year-old virgin? Maybe she should hire a pro to pop her; then she could enter a sexual relationship with confidence.

"I'm a virgin." There, she said it! Gabe's body stiffened. She caught the look of pity in his eyes.

He tried to cover it up by smiling at her. She pushed away and exited on the other side of the booth. Humiliation encompassed her. God she felt foolish!

"Gianna—"

She put her hand up. "No! Don't. I knew if I told you, you'd think I was a freak of nature. And, well, I guess I am. So, you are majorly off the hook. I'd like you to leave now." He made to move toward her. "No!" she screamed. Hot tears stung her eyes. "Don't you see?" She ran her hands over her clothes, then flung her hair over her shoulders. "I'm a fake. The girl you met last night? Pretend. I'm Gianna Cipriani, a twenty-seven-year-old virgin who has never been outside of the Bay Area. I go to church three times a week and live in flannel nightgowns. I'm not sexy. So don't pretend that I am! Now please go!"

She turned and ran through the dining room into the kitchen, then up the back stairway to her apartment. She slammed the door shut and leaned against it, feeling like the biggest schmuck in the world. Oh, God, what did she just do? What *was* wrong with her? She wanted him! He wanted her. At least he seemed like he did; then she went and killed it.

She squeezed her eyes shut. Humiliation rode her hard. She'd never be able to face Gabe again. She could just see Tressie now, tsk-tsking her, shaking her head. Gianna pushed off the door and strode into her bedroom. Angrily she stopped as she caught her reflection in the full-length mirror near the bathroom.

Pulling back her long hair, she fastened it with a tie from her dresser and gave herself a long thorough contemplation. She supposed she *was* plain. Though her features were bold. But they weren't, she thought as she looked closer, so plain after all. She had dark arched brows. Big hazel-brown eyes with long black lashes. High cheekbones and full lips. She licked them, then pressed two fingers to them. Gabe seemed to like them. Her hand dropped to her ample breasts. He liked those better. Was it true? Guys turned into stupid piles of mush when they saw boobs?

Gianna took a deep breath and stepped closer to her reflection. Was there something wrong with her, or was she just a coward at heart? She opened her hands and ran them up along her waist to her breasts. The full heaviness overflowed her hands. Her aroused nipples strained against the silk of her bra and the thin fabric of her shirt. Gianna closed her eyes and tilted her head back. Her fingers applied more pressure, and as a man would, she rubbed the turgid peaks between her thumb and forefinger. An erotic jolt of heat leapt from her nipples to her womb, and in its wake, slickness followed. One hand slid down her belly to the soft mound between her thighs. Warmth emanated. No, she was not frigid. Frigid women didn't respond to stimuli. Frigid women didn't get wet when a man touched her between the legs. And frigid women did not touch themselves like she did now and enjoy it.

Gianna moaned softly as her skin warmed to her own hand. Frigid women did not suck face in a titty bar with a complete stranger and almost rape him.

The vision of her in Gabe's lap at the Kat's Meow sprang into her mind's eye. He felt so good. He was so warm, and so big, and he knew just where to touch.

Gianna caught her breath as sparks of desire pulsed from her clitoris to her womb. No, she was not frigid—far from it. She was a vibrant, feeling, breathing sexual human being. She lifted her skirt and pressed her hand to her damp panties. The imaginary feel of hot breath on her cheek and a strong hand on her thigh spurned her to slowly rub back and forth across her clitoris. Her body flinched at the erotic charge. The ragged breath was her own as was the cry of pleasure. As the tension surged through her body, Gianna's eyes flashed open. She didn't recognize the torrid beauty of the woman who stared back with deep dark eyes. Nor the shadowed man in the corner of her room.

She whirled around and a scream congealed in her throat.

"It's me, Gianna," Gabe said, stepping from the window where he'd obviously climbed up the fire escape.

Humiliation rode her hard again; this time it was more than she could bear. "How dare you!"

With the smooth arrogance of a big jungle cat, he sauntered toward her. Despite her shock, anger, and embarrassment, the hungry look in Gabe's eyes focused on her riveted her to the spot. She could not have moved away had her life depended on it. Her knees weakened and her heart rate accelerated so quickly she thought for a minute she might have a heart attack.

"How long have you been here?" Oh, God had he . . . ? Mortified, she knew the answer.

He stopped only inches from her. "Long enough to know you didn't finish."

Her breath came quick, fast and warm. She could feel it ricochet off the broad width of his chest. "I . . ." She was speechless. She knew she should tell him to leave. Or even call the cops. But she couldn't.

"Gianna, don't be ashamed. You were meant for passion." He reached out and touched her waist. She didn't stop him. "You need to relax and learn to enjoy your sensuality." His fingers slipped through the belt loop at the waist of her skirt. Ever so gently, he pulled her an inch closer. "Show me again," he whispered.

Gianna's jaw dropped. But she could not deny the hot course of excitement that zipped through her at his words. "I . . . I, no." Her skin was so hot; she had the irrepressible urge to rip her clothes free and allow the coolness of the air to bring down her temperature.

"Are you afraid?"

Muted, she shook her head no.

"Shy?"

She hesitated for a heartbeat and then nodded.

"Do you think your body is ugly?"

When she hesitated, she detected a change in his energy. "Who told you that, Gianna?"

"M-my father told me it was a curse."

He chuckled low. "A curse for all fathers. But"—he traced a fingertip across a hard nipple—"a cure for every red-blooded man who lays eyes on you." Gabe pulled her hard against his chest. His breath was warm against her cheek. Sliding his hands up from her waist to her rib cage, he turned her around to face the mirror. "Let me show you how beautiful you really are."

In a dreamlike trance, Gianna allowed him to maneuver her in front of the mirror. His big body surrounded her. She didn't resist. Indeed, she didn't fight the overwhelming urge to lean back against his hard warmth.

"Shall I compare thee to a summer's day?" he whispered against her ear. Gianna stiffened in shock. Was he quoting Shakespeare? She caught his gaze in the mirror. His eyes burned dark and hot. Full of passion. And something else. Sincerity.

Mutely she nodded.

A strong finger touched the full poutiness of her bottom lip. "Thou art *more* lovely and more temperate." He brushed a feather-soft kiss across the throbbing artery in her throat. "Rough winds do shake the darling buds of May, and summer's lease hath all too short a date."

The raw huskiness in his so eloquently spoken sonnet caused something deep to move inside of her. For the first time in her life, Gianna began to see herself as she truly was.

His hand reached out, and with the outside of his palm, he brushed down the curve of her cheek. "Look at this." His fingers traced along the bow of her upper lip. "You have the most luscious lips I've ever seen." Long thick fingers delved into the sleek softness of her hair. As his fingers combed through it, the tie slid off and to the floor. He spread the long strands gently, reverently across her shoulders. "And this?" She felt him inhale her scent. "So soft and smooth." As his fingers treated, one traced the curve of her ear. His lips bent to it.

Gianna watched, mesmerized by his movements in the mirror. When his fingers traced along her arched brows, he whispered into her ear, "Perfect." His lips nibbled her ear and then licked the inner shell.

He moved his other hand from her waist up to her rib cage. She didn't realize he had undone the few bottom buttons of her shirt until his hand slid up the warmth of her flesh. She gasped and stood up straight. Deftly Gabe's other hand came around to the front of her and nimbly undid the remaining buttons. His lips nuzzled against her neck. "Bella, Gianna, you have the most perfect breasts. A work of art." He pulled back the shirt. As his hand swept up the steep curve of her breasts, he unclasped her bra. His sharp intake of breath sent a shattering bolt of desire through her entire being.

Gianna's head reeled. Her breasts heaved as she sought to control her excitement.

A deep moan escaped her chest. And she didn't care. When his fingers rubbed her nipples, Gianna arched against him, leaning into his muscular length. She closed her eyes and bit her bottom lip to keep from crying out.

"Let it go, Gianna. Let your inhibitions go."

"I . . . I can't."

He nipped at the spot where her neck met her shoulder. His teeth grazed the tendon there. "Yes, you can. It's a beautiful thing. Do it. For me."

Gianna shook her head slowly, melting deeper into the heat of his mouth. But she didn't have the nerve to open her eyes and face him in the mirror.

"You want it, Gia. You want to break out and scream. Do it now."

Her nipples strained at his whispered words and in response to his fingertips brushing lightly across her taut tips. "Gia, relax against me."

Oh, God, she wanted to. She wanted to just pour into him.

"Open your eyes. See how beautiful you look right now all flushed and sexy."

"I . . . can't."

She couldn't.

The incredible sensation of him surrounding her was enough. She reveled in it. Her urge was to turn around and encourage him to take her nipples into his mouth and wreak havoc that way. She never had the chance to demand it. His hands slid down the curved length of her waist to the top of her skirt, and without a ripple in the pond of desire he'd stirred up, he unzipped it, then slid it down her thighs.

The sensuous slide of his hands as he pushed the fabric down her hips made her feel so damn sexy. She moaned, deep and throaty. He answered with one of his own. It was the switch Gianna needed. It wasn't herself she wanted to see in the mirror. No, she wanted to look into Gabe's dark hooded eyes and know they had only her in their sight.

Her eyes fluttered open. She gasped at the sight before her as more heat shimmered across her sultry skin.

Her rose-tipped breasts jutted out into the air, impudent and demanding satisfaction; her head rested back against the wide width of Gabe's chest. She licked her full pouty lips and smiled. Her hair hung wildly around her shoulders, with the heated tips of each breast peeking out from the dark strands. The rounded curve of her hips stood out, softly illuminated against the low light. The soft V at the juncture of her thighs hinted at the hot and wanting pussy hiding there.

When she looked directly into Gabe's eyes and their gazes locked and held in the glass, waves of newfound desire rippled through her. She'd never wanted the attention of another person as she wanted Gabe's at that moment. More than that, she wanted to know he wanted her as badly.

"Look at yourself, Gianna. Look at what only God could create, and only on his best day."

She trembled at his words. He made her feel like Venus. His fingertips slipped beneath the elastic of her panties. Gianna watched, mesmerized, as he strummed her skin in slow erotic motions. Her skin plumpened. Her heart rate kicked up to a higher pace, and her mouth was suddenly dry. She licked her lips and arched against him.

"No!" she cried out when his hand slowed to a stop. She grabbed his hand and pressed it hard against her. He laughed low in her ear. "What do you want?"

Embarrassment swept through her, and she ducked her eyes from his. His free hand swept up to her left breast and touched the place over her heart. She felt it leap against his hand. He pressed his lips to her ear and nibbled the lobe. His hand squeezed in a slow discovering cadence over he breasts. "Tell me, Gianna."

She closed her eyes and opened her mouth to tell him, but she couldn't.

Gabe's body stiffened. He flung her hand from his. He grabbed her right thigh and kneaded the skin there, his long fingers working up toward her clitoris. When he brushed bold fingertips across her, it was her turn to stiffen. She stood on her tiptoes to better meet him. "Gabe," she softly cried.

He pressed his palm against the inflamed mound between her thighs. "Open your eyes."

Gianna jerked against his hand, shards of fire sparking from the tension in her body. Her breathing came so hot and forced now that she wondered if she would hyperventilate. Slowly she opened her eyes.

He smiled dark and dangerous from behind her. "Good girl. Now watch."

His fingers slid down into her slickness. The sublime feel of him inside of her was too much.

Gianna screamed.

Using his body to stabilize her, Gabe pushed her skirt down just past her knees with his free hand. With the freedom it gave her, Gianna wantonly opened up to him and pushed against the sinful feel of his fingers. As the thickness of his finger moved in and out of her, her liquid muscles constricted torridly around him. Her inclination was to pump hard against his palm. He denied her, holding her hips at bay. She watched herself in the mirror beg with her body for relief.

"Slower, Gianna, slower," he whispered.

The episode was surreal. There was no way the flushed beauty in the mirror writhing against the handsome Gabe LaMotta's hand could be her. But it was. Gianna watched her tongue lick full lips, then bite at the bottom one as her hand pushed against the one between her legs. She couldn't believe her eyes when she watched her free hand snake backward, wrapping around Gabe's neck, pulling them harder together.

He continued to control the slow rocking rhythm. She continued to increase the momentum. The tip of his long finger tapped on a spot she never knew existed. She bit back a cry of pure ecstasy. His hot breath against her ear encouraged her. Gabe increased the rhythm, pumping, pressing, caressing, repeatedly torturing her with his knowledge of her body. "Let it go, Gianna. Push against my hand; ride it out."

The cradle of Gabe's undulating hips against her bottom and the feel of his full erection digging into her back urged her on more heatedly than any words ever could. Her hips bucked wildly against him as she took the ride of her life. A thin sheen of perspiration erupted, slicking her flesh.

Gabe licked her neck and nipped at her jugular. Gianna went rigid. His hand pumped harder into her. A wave of desire crested, and had he not been supporting her, the velocity of the orgasm that hit her would have knocked her off her feet.

A scream tore from her lips as her whole body crashed against a wall of sublime pleasure. Her hips jerked as she continued to spasm hard against his fingers; they slowed, allowing her to ride out the orgasm. She could feel the warm stickiness of herself against her thighs. Spasms continued to grip her, and Gianna felt overcome with the urge to cry. It felt so damn good.

Gabe turned her in his arms and lowered his lips to hers. In a long, fluid, wild kiss, he took what little control she had left. Gianna melted into him, enjoying the way her body still trembled from the orgasm, the way her sensitive breasts rubbed against the hard planes of his chest, and the way he made her feel as if she were the only woman in the world.

When he drew away, she held him tighter. He took her hands from his and stood back, smiling down at her. "Never question your sensuality again, Gianna. You are sexier than a thousand women combined. Don't ever forget it."

Gianna nodded, afraid her voice would crack if she spoke. Her gaze dipped to his waist, then lower. His trousers rose high with no hint of going down. She smiled, then and moved around to his back. Gently she turned him to face the mirror.

He moved as if to get away from her, but Gianna was determined. "No, Gabe. Stand still, please."

He caught her gaze in the mirror. She smiled up at him and wrapped her arms around his waist. Gianna didn't have the length of arm he did, so she was at a bit of a disadvantage, but she would manage.

Gabe knew he should leave. But damn if he could. The evening had gotten out of hand. Way out of hand. But at least he hadn't fucked her. He'd come damn close to just picking her hot-and-bothered body up and tossing her onto the bed and blowing off some steam. But he didn't. He wasn't a damn cad. He couldn't knowingly take a virgin when he wasn't willing or able to make at least a minimal commitment to her. His back stiffened when those lovely little hands of hers rubbed his dick through his slacks. He hissed in a breath. "Jesus, Gianna."

"Jesus has nothing to do with what I'm going to do to you, Gabe."

She unfastened his belt buckle, then unzipped his slacks. "Look at yourself, Gabe. Let me see how big and beautiful you are," she said from behind him.

Gabe grinned. He pushed down his pants. Gianna beat him to his boxers. In a slow unhurried slide, she pushed them down to his thighs. When he sprang free, he felt her body stiffen beside him.

"Oh, my, Gabe, that is beautiful." He looked down at his cock. He knew he was hung. It wasn't that he was cocky; he just knew he had a dick the ladies loved. Gianna raised her eyes to me his. He grinned and flexed.

"Touch me."

She reached out a warm hand and slowly wrapped it around him. Gabe hissed in another breath. Her touch sent him to his toes. "Gianna, I swear to God, woman, I'm going to come right now."

She rubbed her finger over the tip of his cock, smearing the soft warm precome around the head. She came around to stand beside him, and with both hands she began a slow, methodical pump. He threw his head back and caught her watching him in the mirror. He set his jaw and moved hotly against her hand.

"Gabe," she whispered, "I've never touched a man like this before."

He groaned and she tightened her hands around him. Jesus, he wanted her lips to lock around him and suck every ounce of fluid from his body.

When she pressed her lips to his belly, he groaned, and before he could even try to regulate his body, Gabe felt the tight coil in his balls unwind with a velocity that nearly knocked him off his feet. The hard hot rush of his seed erupted as Gianna pumped him. Her fingers tightened around his pulsing cock but she slowed her momentum, and in a slow slick pump, she milked every drop of come from his body.

He shuddered hard against her and caught her eyes in the mirrow. A slow satisfied smile twisted his lips. "You are a very naughty girl, Gianna Cipriani."

She grinned and released him but quickly grabbed a handful of tissue from the box on the dresser and handed them to him. "I had a good teacher."

In quick fashion, he had himself cleaned up and his drawers zipped and belted. He moved away from her. Cool air swirled between them. "I have to go," he simply said. He pressed a fatherly kiss on her forehead, then slipped out the window and was gone.

Gianna stood breathless, ravaged, and alone in front of the all-knowing mirror. She didn't know if she should be angry, relieved, or exuberant. She decided all three were in order.

She was angry Gabe had left her wanting . . . more. She was relieved that she didn't feel like a freak anymore. And she was exuberant she had had her first bona fide orgasm and had returned the favor to Gabe.

He'd felt so big and powerful in her hands. She'd wanted to do more to him, but she'd chickened out.

Gianna raised her eyes, not recognizing the woman who stared back. Her eyes were heavily hooded, her lips full, and her breasts rosy and full. She looked exactly as she felt. Wanton. Her skin heated up again, and she smiled at the mirror.

She was tired of being a virgin. And if Gabe was stuck on playing coy that was fine with her. He wanted her, that was good enough for her. For now.

Gianna hugged herself and smiled. Gabe's scent mingled with hers in the air around her and lingered on her skin and hair.

Her smile widened and she looked at the mischievous smile reflected in the mirror.

Tomorrow, she suddenly decided, would be the day. She had a little surprise for Mr. LaMotta, and it was going to be her pleasure to deliver it personaly.

8

Gabe whistled as he made his way into the elevator to his undercover office. He had Gianna Cipriani on the mind, and even after jerking off twice since last night, he had a hard-on the size of the Golden Gate Bridge. As the doors closed, a ham-sized gloved hand forced them open. The smile faded as Dumb and Dumber walked in. They looked like poster boys for the thugs they were. Dark hair slicked back. Dark glasses, long black trench coats. Gabe was a big guy, but between them, the duo had over four hundred pounds on him. Mario sported a nice shiner. Gabe smiled. "Nice shiner you got there, buddy."

Mario took a swing at Gabe, who ducked and jammed his shoulder into the big man's gut, sending him into his buddy. He pushed the OPEN button and before the two could regain their balance and launch a new attack, Gabe spun out of the elevator and hoofed to the stairway, running up the four flights of steps to his office. As he went down the hall, he grinned. Standing outside of the elevator were the two thugs.

"I didn't give you two enough credit."

Mario casually held a nine mil at his hip, pointed Gabe's way.

"Too bad for you," the other one said.

Gabe stopped and raised his hands. "What do you two want?"

The elevator the two guys had come up on opened and several people walked out. Mario lowered the gun. Gabe lowered his hands. Mario nodded toward Gabe's office. "Inside so we can talk."

Gabe pulled out his keys and unlocked the door. Donna wouldn't be in for another half hour. He had a semi in his desk, and there was one in Donna's desk. His secretary was as skilled in arms as he was. Gabe smiled. She was also tactically sound. They'd spent a couple of months a few years ago practicing more than defensive tactics on each other.

As Gabe moved for the desk, Mario grabbed him and spun him around. Eddy nailed him in the chest with a solid jab. Gabe shook off the hit and dove into his desk and grabbed his gun. He turned on the two douche bags. "Get the hell out of my office and don't come back unless you want to leave in a body bag."

The two thugs grinned but held off. "Stay away from Ciao Bella and stay away from the girl," Mario warned.

"Or?"

"Or we'll fix it so you got no girlie to sniff around."

"Touch her and you can look for your balls in your mouth," Gabe said.

Mario narrowed his eyes. "Let me tell you this, Superman. She belongs to Mr. Tucci. I know you know who he is 'cause I've seen you hang around all that pussy at Roberto's."

Gabe grinned. "The ladies like it when I spread the love."

"Yeah, well, Mr. Tucci likes virgins, and he plans on seeing the girl that way. Pop her and we pop you. Permanently."

They turned to leave, and Gabe made a calculated risk by

throwing a taunt at them. If he could force Tucci to make a move sooner than later, and an emotional one at that, he might just have him. "I already popped her."

The two thugs' eyes opened to the size of saucers. "Oh, you better be shittin' us, 'cause Mr. Tucci, he's not gonna like that."

"Believe it. Last night on the table in the restaurant. And tell your boss she's what wet dreams are made of. Tight, hot, and me first."

Gabe felt like a sick bastard saying that, but dammit, when Tucci found out, he'd come after Gabe. The guy would be so pissed, he'd react in anger and in so doing, Gabe was betting he'd show his hand—and it would be enough to arrest him. It was a long shot, but one that if it hit would pay off big.

For a long minute, the thugs looked at each other. "I'm not going to be the one to tell him that," Mario said, shaking his head.

"Maybe we won't," Eddy mused out loud. Mario narrowed his eyes at Gabe. "Did she bleed?"

"A gentleman never tells."

"You ain't no gentleman. That girl deserved better."

Gabe bit back a laugh and said, "Like Tucci? Or you morons?"

Eddy turned to Mario. "I'm not telling him. He'll kill us."

Mario shook his head and moved toward the door. "Well, I'm not telling him! You think I want his foot up my ass?"

Eddy shoved Mario through the doorway. "Well, we better come up with something, 'cause he's excepting a virgin."

As they exited through the first office door, Gabe let out a long breath. Okay, so Tucci wants a cherry, does he?

Gabe's dick twitched. So did he, dammit. And resisting Gianna had been one of the hardest things he'd ever done. All for noble reasons. But now? Christ, if she walked through that door, he'd clear his desk and have his way with her right then and there.

If she really wasn't a virgin, would that cool Tucci's obsession? Or did he want Gianna regardless? Gabe set up the coffeepot, then headed back into his office and thought about what his next step would be.

Gianna took the card Gabe gave Theresa with his business address on it and called the office number. "LaMotta Investments," a cheerful feminine voice answered.

Gianna held the phone in her hand, her heart wildly pumping blood through her veins. For a minute, she wanted to hang up, wondering who she was trying to kid. Gabe might take her up on her offer, but that would be it. Once, maybe twice, then she'd leave him the box of condoms she was going to pick up along the way.

"Hello?" the woman's voice said, now aggravated.

"Hi, um, is Mr. LaMotta in today?"

"He is. Would you like an appointment?"

"Um, yes. Does he have one this morning? Say around ten?"

"Let me check. He has an eleven thirty, but he likes to break for lunch promptly at noon. If you can conduct your business in that time, I can get you in."

Gianna smiled. Maybe she'd convince him to have her for lunch.

"Eleven-thirty is perfect."

"Your name?"

Gianna froze. She couldn't tell her her real name. "Angela Dickenson."

"And what can I say this is regarding?"

"A prime piece of real estate in the Tenderloin."

"Okay, we'll see you at eleven-thirty."

Gianna slowly hung up the phone and smiled. She had plenty of time to condom shop and, she decided, to talk herself out of going.

* * *

Gianna hadn't talked herself out of going to visit Gabe. At eleven twenty-five, she found herself standing front of his office building. After several long minutes, she pushed open the heavy glass and chrome doors, walked to the elevator, and pushed the button for the fourth floor. She stared straight ahead, her coat wrapped tightly around her. The cool air from the street had followed her in and wisped up to her warm nether parts. She shivered when she thought of Gabe's mouth there. She closed her eyes and moaned, grateful she was alone in the car. She felt deliciously naughty. So much was her anticipation that she felt her body moisten between her legs. Lord, what if she made a mess?

As she pushed open the door to suit 417, Gianna smiled at the pert little blonde behind the desk. Instantly suspicion rose. Not that she had a right, but her natural female possessiveness grabbed her. If Gabe was her boyfriend, she'd worry for sure, but he wasn't. And despite that fact, jealousy gnawed at her belly.

"I'm Miss Dickenson. I have an eleven-thirty with Mr. LaMotta."

The blonde sized Gianna up before she forced a smile. "One moment please."

A minute later, Gianna was escorted into a decent-sized office. She smiled. The office had a more than adequate desktop. It would give her great pleasure to spread herself on it and let Gabe do naughty things to her. He stood facing the big window, talking on the phone, his back to her.

Gianna smiled and wondered what his reaction would be if she pressed herself against him, and ran her nails down his back.

"All right, Gordo, but make sure you're available tonight. And you owe me big time." Gabe pushed the END button of his cell phone. He did not sound amused.

"Gabe. Miss Dickenson is here to see you," the blonde said from beside Gianna.

Gabe turned around. Gianna had to give him credit. Surprise flashed across his eyes so quickly she wondered if she really saw it. He nodded to his secretary. "Thank you, Donna."

When Donna closed the door behind her, Gianna turned and locked it. She turned around, her back against the door, her hands behind her, and smiled at Gabe, who stood too big and too handsome in front of the huge window.

"Good morning, Mr. LaMotta," Gianna softly said.

He grinned. "Good morning, Miss Dickenson."

Gianna smiled and pushed off the door. She moved slowly toward him, her hands still behind her back. "You can call me Angie."

Gabe's grin widened. "Angie Dickenson?"

"Yes." She stopped in front of his desk and perched a stiletto encased foot on the corner. Her long coat fell away, revealing a smooth black silk stocking. "I have a piece of property in the Tenderloin I'm interested in selling." She leaned forward. Looking deep into his eyes, she cocked her right brow and asked, "Do you know anyone who would be interested?"

Gabe kept a straight face and nodded. Then walked around his desk and stopped several feet away from her. "I might. But my client would want a show of good faith."

All business, Gianna nodded and unbuttoned her long coat. She pulled it back, revealing her leg and the hint of the garter belt on her right leg. Gabe hissed in a breath.

"Is that enough good faith?"

He shook his head slowly. "I don't think so, Miss Dickerson. My client has been burned. He'll need more than a peek at the goods offered."

Gianna nodded again and this time let the coat fall from her shoulders to her hips. Her cleavage spilled out of her demi-cup bra. Gabe's eyes darkened. She watched his nostrils flare. She liked what she did to him.

"More," he said, his voice low, almost hoarse.

Gianna obliged and let the coat slip to her wrists, exposing her hips and panties. "Now, Mr. LaMotta, what will your client give me in return as a show of good faith?"

Gabe moved closer. He reached out a hand and brushed the tops of her breasts with his fingertips. It was Gianna's turn to hiss in a breath. Gooseflesh erupted in the wake of his fingers. She closed her eyes and bit her bottom lip. Just that little touch and her body reeled. She opened her eyes.

Gabe slipped an arm around her waist and brought her hard against his chest. The coat dropped to the floor. Feeling bold and beautiful, Gianna leaned back and wrapped her right leg around his thigh, arching into him.

"This." His mouth slammed down to hers, and in that instant, he made her feel like the most desired woman on the planet. He pulled her tighter against him. His free hand rested on her thigh, his fingers caressing the silk stocking.

His erection swelled against her hips. And Gianna trembled in excitement, anticipation, and a little fear of what she was about to do. But not enough to pull out and run.

She tore her lips from Gabe's and moved back against the desk. The hard edge bit into her bottom. The pain excited her.

9

Gabe's gaze raked Gianna's curvy legs all the way down to her fire-engine red lacquered toes then back to her shapely calves to her full thighs. He licked his lips. Her honey-colored skin whet his appetite for more. She slid a finger under the satin crotch of her thong and moved it slightly aside. Glistening pink lips beckoned him closer. His blood quickened, filling his cock to capacity. When he looked into Gianna's eyes she smiled but a deep flush flared across her cheeks. God, she was beautiful.

He moved right into her, sliding his hands into her hair and pulling her up to his lips. His kiss was hard, possessive, and demanding. It left no question about what he wanted from her. Her lips clung to his, kissing him back fervently.

He tore his lips away. Panting, he pressed his forehead to hers. "Gianna, are you sure?"

Her big hazel-brown eyes glistened, and he thought for a minute she was going to cry. She nodded quickly and reached up to his lips. When he kissed her this time, he savored her lips. The honey taste and sweet smell of her, the smooth softness of them. He didn't touch her below the neck, afraid that if he did, he would come in his pants and embarrass them both.

But Gianna wanted more of him.

She turned in his embrace and forced him against the desk. She swept everything off with a quick swipe of her hands.

Gabe grinned. "You're full of surprises, Gia."

She grabbed him by his tie and pulled him up to her, then straddled him on the desk. "You haven't seen anything yet."

Gianna took a deep breath and told herself that what she was doing was good, because it was what she wanted. It was time to drop the stigma of the Madonna. She wanted sex, and she wanted it with Gabe. If he rejected her this time, she would die of shame.

Nervously, she unbuckled his belt. Gabe grabbed her hand and looked deeply into her eyes. "You sure?"

"Yes. I want you, Gabe. Here. Now."

"Why me?"

Without hesitation she said, "I trust you not to hurt me."

Gabe swallowed. *Shit!*

He reached up and rubbed his knuckles across her cheek. Then he grinned. "I won't hurt you, but I'm not a choir boy when it comes to sex."

Gianna leaned down and nipped at his chest. "Yeah, I'm counting on that."

Gabe rolled her over on the desk. He looked down into her big eyes. "Last chance to change your mind."

She shook her head and arched her breasts against him. He growled and buried his face into her high cleavage. His hands cupped her and squeezed; his lips sucked a nipple through her bra. "God, I love your tits."

Gianna ran her hands up the hard planes of his chest. "I love yours too." And if he didn't do something soon she was going to go up in flames she was so hot for him.

Gabe slowly slipped the straps of her black lacy bra down

one shoulder, kissing its wake, then across the high swell of her mounds to the other side. He slid that strap down her shoulder, then reverently undid the front clasp and caught his breath when her breasts spilled warm and velvety into his waiting hands. Gianna arched into him, luxuriating in the feel of his hot mouth and tongue. She wrapped her legs around his thighs, and pulled him harder against her. His erection pressed firmly between her thighs, against her sensitive mound and she moaned, wanting more than pressure. She wanted penetration.

Gabe slid his right hand down her belly, then farther, and looped his finger around the thin strap of her thong. He slid it down, one agonizing inch at a time.

"Gia, you are so soft," he murmured against her nipple. It hardened further. He flicked it with his tongue. His right hand moved lower, tracing light circles on her skin, getting closer to where she so desperately wanted him.

He slid a finger across her hooded clitoris. Gianna gasped. "Gabe, don't wait."

"Oh, no, Gianna, we're going slow." He kissed her belly button. "Slower." He nuzzled the inside of her thigh and nipped her skin. "And slowest." He licked her slit, deep, long, and slow. Gianna came off the desk. She squeezed her eyes closed and let her muscles relax as she allowed her body to be consumed by Gabe's voracious mouth and tongue. She threw her head back and opened her legs wider, giving him full access to her. He made her feel so, so incredibly delicious; she had no words to describe it. She never expected she would lose her virginity this way or to a man she barely knew, but she had no doubts that Gabe was the man she wanted.

Gabe spread her lips with his thumbs, running his tongue in swirls across her straining clitoris. When he gently sucked it into his mouth, Gianna inhaled a deep breath. Her hands grabbed for something to hold on to. The only thing in reach was the edges of the desk. When Gabe slid a thick finger into her slickness, she came off the desktop again. He settled one hand on her thigh to keep her bucking body from moving off the table.

Gianna moved hotly against his mouth and finger, her wantonness shocking her. Gabe moaned against her, his fingers digging into the skin of her thigh. "Jesus, Gianna," he said against her throbbing pussy, "you are so sweet and so tight." He looked up into her eyes. Gianna trembled. Her juice glistened on his lips, and his dark eyes were hooded with passion. His look was so intense, so possessive, he scared her for a moment.

He must have read the fear in her eyes. He climbed over her and pushed up to kiss her nose. Gianna undulated against him. "Why did you stop?"

"Are you afraid?"

She shook her head. "No."

"No second thoughts?"

"None."

He grinned, his face lighting up. The gesture was pure ego, and Gianna thought she may have just fallen a little in love with him at that moment. He was all man, yet he was considerate.

She pulled him down by his tie and whispered, "If you don't get busy, I'm going to find someone who will!"

Gabe grinned again. His hand slid down over her breasts to her belly, then to her hot mound. He slipped a thick finger into her, and she felt like she was going to swoon. "God, Gabe, that feels so good." She moaned. His lips captured hers, and in a slow rhythmic slide, he fucked her with his finger. A deep swell began to build inside of her, and Gianna knew she was on the verge of a tremendous orgasm. Gabe's lips descended on her breasts, his hand increased in momentum, and his hips moved in rhythm against hers. She came then, in a big bright sunburst of an orgasm. Wave after wave of tension ripped through her. She cried out, and he caught her cries in his kiss.

In slow, agonizing bliss she rode the orgasm out against his hand. A thin sheen of perspiration slicked her skin. Her body continued to convulse. As he slowed her with his right hand, Gianna caught her breath and unzipped his fly. The hard thick length of him rubbed against her hand and she shivered. He was big, and she was not. Adrenaline spiked. She wanted all of him.

Having come this far Gianna had no intention of turning back. She wanted to feel Gabe inside of her. Quickly she slid his slacks down, then his boxers. He sprang free, and Gianna gasped at the heat of his skin.

When she wrapped her fingers around his thickness, he shuddered. "Easy, Gianna, easy."

"Gabe, I can't wait," she panted. A wild possession overcame her. She wanted to mate with this man. Feel him lose himself deep inside of her.

Slowly she pumped him, familiarizing herself with his perfect cock. The head was thick and soft. A bead of come oozed from the opening. Gianna smiled. That was for her. With her thumbs she smeared it across him, then resumed her slow rythmic movement. As he thrust in her hands Gianna maneuvered her steaming box closer to him, then pressed the head of him against her slick folds.

"No, Gia."

Her body stiffened. No? Was he rejecting her *now*? Why? Her chest tightened. Gabe took her face into his hands and kissed her on the nose. "It's not that, sweetheart. I need to get a condom." He looked her deep in the eyes, and suddenly she felt foolish. Then it dawned on her that she had left the box of condoms she bought on the kitchen table!

"I don't have one!"

Gabe smiled and moved from her. He hiked up his drawers and opened the door in the corner of his office. He returned a minute later with a square foil wrapper. "I'm always prepared."

Gianna watched him expertly roll on the sheath, and when

he pulled her to the edge of the desk, he looked meaningfully into her eyes. "You deserve better than this desk for your first time, Gianna."

She pulled him toward her. "It's perfect. Now stop talking and pop my cherry."

Gabe grinned and spread her thighs. But before he brought her into the ranks of an experienced woman, he bent one more time to her pussy. He pressed a kiss to her swollen lips and licked and suckled her slit. Gianna rose off the desk and cried out, and Gabe pulled her straight into his erection. The big head of him softly nudged her swollen lips. Gianna squeezed her eyes shut and slowly exhaled. Gently he pushed harder. The feel of him entering her was beyond her expectations. Every nerve ending pulsed, and as if by some hidden engine, her vaginal muscles pulled him further in.

Realizing she had tensed, Gianna relaxed back onto the hard surface of the desk. His big hands steadied her hips as he filled her inch by delicious inch. She'd never been more ready for anything in her life and never so eager to go. She was tight, especially because of his size. She didn't know how he ranked with other men; all she knew was he had more than enough for her. Despite his eagerness, he was gentle with her. She waited for the rip, the tear, the pain of him busting her cherry, but other than a slight pinch that was over before she realized she'd felt it, the so-called pain was over.

"You okay?" he softly asked, gathering her up to his chest. Gianna nodded, rubbing her lips across his bare chest. She kissed his pectoral and nipped at his nipple. His hips surged and he filled her fuller. She leaned back, allowing his arms to cradle her as he slowly began to rock into her. Gianna closed her eyes and bit her bottom lip. Desire swept across her body, straight to her core, and she felt a wild wave build. She was wet, and hot, and so hungry for him. Gabe answered her. His body slicked with sweat, his cock thrust deeply in then out, then in again, each time pushing her closer to the edge. She reveled in his power, his carnal knowledge, his lust for her. Gianna arched her back, and he caught a nipple in his mouth. She surged against him, and he met her thrust for thrust. Her breath became heavier and forced. He laved her neck, then in a crushing kiss sent her shooting off into the stratosphere. The slick slapping sound of their skin meeting turned her on. He felt hot and wet, his hair was damp, and his breath came hard and heavy. She felt like she was coming to the end of a sprint. "Oh, God, Gabe!" She gasped, digging her nails into his back as a tidal wave of pleasure tore through every nerve ending in her body, only to recede and crest and crash again.

Gabe moaned and his body stiffened, and in one more deep thrust, he came. His hips quivered and his muscles tightened. He held her tight against him; his hips flinched as her muscles constricted around his cock, extracting every ounce of come he had in him.

He collapsed against her on the desk.

Gabe fought hard to catch his breath. He smiled and smoothed Gianna's damp hair from her cheeks. He kissed the tip of her nose. She smiled shyly at him, and he fell for her at that very moment. He hugged her to him and asked, "How do you feel now?"

"Like a grown-up."

Gabe laughed. "You're quite a find, Gianna Cipriani."

"What do you mean by that?"

Regretfully, Gabe moved slowly off of her. If he didn't get the damn condom off, he'd leak the boys into her, and then they'd have a big problem. He was not ready on any level for daddy duty. When he came back from the bathroom, he smiled. Gianna lay on top of his desk like a sated cat. She looked damn sexy all flushed and sultry from their lovemaking. She still wore those sexier-than-hell peekaboo pumps and those hot stockings and garter. She hadn't refastened her bra, and her panties hung around her right ankle. He swiped off the few things remaining on the desk, clearing it of everything except the saucy little Italian girl looking at him with dark hazel come-hither eyes. She was smokin' hot, and damn if he didn't feel his dick responding again so quickly. He'd had more than a few marathon sexcapades in his lifetime, but he couldn't remember filling up so quickly after he came since he'd been a randy sixteen-year-old.

Gianna smiled as her gaze swept down his belly to his rising erection.

"Gianna, you make me want to do very naughty things to you."

She rose up on an elbow and looked at him. Her tits, for as big as they were, sat up firm and high. His hands ached to touch them again. "I want to do very naughty things with you too." She sat up on the edge of the desk and slowly refastened her bra.

"What are you doing?" he asked, moving quickly toward her. He was ready to go a second round. Hell. His dick hurt with want. Gianna put her hand out to his chest and shook her head. "I'm sorry, but I have to get back to the restaurant."

"Right now?" He grabbed her hand and pressed it to his full cock. "My boy wants some more of your girl."

Gianna laughed. "Well, tell your boy down." She leaned into him, though, and smiled. She squeezed his cock gently. And rubbed her thumb over the slick head. "I want to see you again."

Gabe slid his arms around her waist. "Damn straight, you do!" No way was he letting her go. And it wasn't just because she was going to be his star witness. No, Gabe wanted her for himself. She was like a fresh breeze in a stale pool hall. He'd been looking for her all his life and hadn't realized it until just now. The thought sobered him as effectively as if she had thrown a pail of ice water in his face. He dropped his hands from her and stepped back. His erection waned, and he grabbed his shorts and slacks and quickly dressed.

Gianna frowned and opened her mouth but didn't say anything.

"I have work to do too," Gabe lamely said. All of a sudden, he couldn't wait for her to leave. But just as much, he wanted to take her to his place and make love to her in his bed. And not the cover apartment he'd grown to hate, but to his home in LA—a bungalow tucked up in the hills with a killer view of the city. There he wanted to shut the door and spend a month with her in his bed.

Panic filled him. No way! He couldn't settle down! He was undercover, for Christ's sake. And who knew where his next assignment would see him? He was part of an elite mobile team. They moved all over the United States. His life was not conducive to relationships.

"I . . . ah, I'll call you?" Gabe offered, the words sounding lame, just like he meant never to call her.

Gianna looked up from tying her coat belt snugly around her waist. "How about if I call you?"

He nodded. "Okay." And he felt like the biggest piece of shit on the planet.

She turned and walked out of his office. He wanted to go after her. But he didn't.

Donna poked her head in a minute later and scowled at his disheveled appearance. "I see you're up to your old tricks."

"All in a day's work," he flippantly said. He was in no mood to defend what had happened between him and Gianna. Let her think it was nothing. Act casual. And Donna wouldn't make a big deal out of it to their SAC.

Gabe opened his mouth to deny her words, but she was right. He moved to the doorway, and his gut somersaulted when he saw Gianna standing there. She'd heard every word. Her big hazel eyes were bright with unshed tears. He reached out to her and opened his mouth to deny it, but dammit, he couldn't. Maybe this was better.

Gianna turned then and left the room.

10

Gianna couldn't move fast enough from the office where she just lost her virginity. Shame filled her. Not because she was no longer a virgin but because she gave it up to a player! She hit the DOWN button and turned to look over her shoulder, back at the door she'd just exited. Gabe stood there, his shirt hanging from his broad shoulders, the planes of his smooth chest peeking out. His dark eyes were heavily hooded like he'd just fucked someone proper. And he had. She turned around and waited impatiently for the elevator doors to open.

So much for being the one playing hard to get. What the hell was she thinking anyway? Hell, she'd been the one throwing herself at the man. Only a freakin' eunuch would pass up what she offered this morning. Gabe was red-blooded—hell, more so than the average guy. So yeah, what did she expect?

The doors opened, and she walked straight in and faced the wall, not daring to turn around and see if he still stood at the threshold to his office.

When the doors closed, she turned around, grateful she was alone in the car.

She pressed her hand to the apex between her thighs and shivered. She still felt him there. Big, warm, and thrusting. Gianna leaned against the wall and closed her eyes. God, he felt so good. Everything he did, everything he said was perfect. Last night in front of her mirror, he had seemed so sincere. Did he mean those things he said to her? Could he have? How could he turn around and treat her like a casual lay? Was she just another number deposited into his fuck account?

By the time the elevator hit the ground floor, a very pissed-off Gianna Cipriani emerged. She strode out, catching the shoulder of man who stood in her way. Her strides ate up the sidewalk. She didn't look to see who was in her way, she just moved forward away from Gabriel "I Fuck and Run" LaMotta.

She would have walked clear across the Bay Bridge to Oakland if it weren't for the fact that her feet felt like they were going to fall off her ankles. The Kate Spade's were not meant for walking. They were tools for seduction. And they worked all right. Gianna came to an abrupt stop at the corner of Montgomery and Columbus. The shadow of the Transamerica building loomed high above her. The sun had not made much of an appearance that day. A cool swirl of foggy air twisted up from the street to her barely clad ass. Jesus. If she wasn't mistaken for a hooker, she would be lucky.

Quickly, Gianna hailed a cab. She was soon upstairs in her bathroom in the shower, taking the water as hot as she could stand it. She scrubbed every inch of the flesh Gabe had touched. As she dug the loofa into her thigh, tears erupted and she sank to the floor. Pulling her knees up to her chest, she let loose and cried. She cried for her father; she cried for the mother she never knew. She cried for the situation with Tucci and those two thugs who seemed bent on scaring the tar out of her. And she cried for herself and what she thought she shared with Gabe. On her own, she had royally screwed up. How had she made such a mistake? Sex with a stranger! And he was. He proved that today.

Gianna let out a long troubled breath and leaned against the cold tile of the shower stall. The water had cooled and she didn't care. She sat in the shower until the water turned her toes blue. Teeth chattering, she grabbed a big fluffy towel from the hook on the wall and wrapped herself in it, then plodded to the bed where she wrapped herself in her down comforter.

The room had darkened by the time she woke to a persistent knocking on her door. Disoriented for a minute, Gianna sat up in bed. The soreness between her thighs immediately reminded her of why she had cocooned herself away from the world.

"Giaaaana?" Zia Cece called.

Gianna hurried to the door, careful not to trip and break her neck. She opened the door to her concerned aunt.

"Gianna!" Zia Cece gasped. "What—?" Concern laced the old woman's face and words. "Oh, *cara*, *cara*, I'm so sorry. Go back to bed. Take all the time you need to mourn your papa. I'll handle the restaurant tonight."

Gianna smiled and let her aunt think she was crying over her father. And while that was part of it, it wasn't exactly everything she was crying over. "It's okay, Zia. I took a nap. I feel better. I'll be down in forty-five minutes."

True to her word, Gianna was. She had hoped the new clothes would make her feel better. But they didn't. She thought if she looked sexy and sophisticated with her designer cosmetics, she would feel better. She didn't. In fact, the new clothes, new hair, and new face made her feel like a fake.

Life was much simpler when she was Gianna "Madonna" Cipriani. Now she just felt . . . empty. And she put the blame squarely on Gabe's shoulders. He blew excitement into her flat nonexistent life, he filled her cells, he brought her to life, and now? She felt as dead as her father. She went through the motions of work. Smiling on demand. She was glad Tressie had taken the night off. Otherwise she'd have to spill the beans to her cousin. Not that that would be a bad idea. She really felt the urge to talk to someone.

Later, as Gianna said good-bye to the last customer and turned the OPEN sign over to CLOSED, she realized the one person she wanted to talk to was Gabe. And she had no idea why.

After everyone had gone, she sat by herself, totaling the night's receipts, and indignation flared. She poured herself a glass of Chianti and poked at the adding machine like it was a pin cushion.

"You just waltz into my life, turn me inside out, take advantage of my vulnerability, and then holster your dick and stalk off to your next conquest?"

She ripped the adding machine tape and slapped it on the stack of credit card slips. "No! It doesn't work that way!"

She stood and began to pace the floor. Why, she'd like to give him a piece of her mind. If she knew where he lived, she'd call him and tell him off. Gianna grabbed the phone and called information. Hell, it was worth a shot.

She hung up the phone thirty seconds later, staring at an address she was given that was no more than a few miles from where she stood.

Nervously, she started to twirl a strand of hair and began to pace in earnest. She should just let the sleeping dog lie where he fell. He was not interested in her. Besides, he probably had some other woman in bed. Her fury mounted. Forgotten just like that. Good Lord, did it not matter to him that he had been her first?

Gianna pulled her hair, then flung it from her. She was going for a walk.

Thirty minutes and a cab ride later she stood in front of a

nondescript building. Despite its brown brick façade, she saw trendy garden patios overflowing with flowering plants.

She pressed the button for his loft. She stood for nearly five minutes before she pressed it again. She didn't know if his loft looked down at the street, but there was a camera behind the dark glass above the building plaque. She knew he was up there, and she knew he was avoiding her. Cowardly bastard! His lack of response only made her dig in deeper.

She stood aside and pulled her cell phone out and pretended to be chatting on it. It didn't take long for a resident to buzz open the door on their way out. Gianna slipped through the door before it closed. She snapped the cell phone shut and walked up to loft 214. Before she knocked, she pressed her ear to the metal door. Barely audible was what sounded like a television. Bastard! He was home! She banged on the door. "Gabe LaMotta! You open this door right now!" she yelled at the top of her lungs. He'd have to let her in now or face the wrath of his neighbors. The door jerked open, and a firm hand yanked her inside. The door shut behind her.

She turned a fierce stare on Gabe. He stood clad in only a pair of worn Levi's. His face closed. His arms crossed over his chest. Gianna swallowed hard.

"I didn't come here to throw myself at you again. I came here to tell you that you're a slimy bastard, and I wish I'd never met you! I hate you!" The eruption caught her off guard. Gianna lunged at him and pummeled his chest. He didn't flinch as she unloaded on him.

"You told me I was beautiful! You told me I was special! You . . . you said you dreamt of me!" She threw her hair back over her shoulder and looked up at him through hot tears. He didn't look at her. He looked over her head at the wall. His jaw was tight, set like granite. "Argh!" She lunged at his face, her nails bared like a hissing feline.

He caught them in his and held her away from him. She was not even close to being done with him. She kicked him and twisted in his hands.

"That's it!" he roared, dragging her backward, deeper into the apartment. Gianna twisted and screeched, flailing in his grip. He tossed her onto a leather sofa. She jumped up like a jack-in-the-box and lunged at him again. "How can you stand there and act like today never happened?"

She took her shoe off and flung it at his head. He deflected it. When he turned those dark brown eyes on her, they sparked in anger. Gianna swallowed hard. What if he attacked her? Oh, God, she didn't know this man at all, and she came into his home and attacked him? She backed up into the sofa, the edge catching her behind the knees. She flopped backward, losing her balance in her one shoe.

She bounced back up. "I—" Damn, what was she supposed to say? She needed a quick out. *Now!* "Um, listen, I didn't take my meds today. You know, for my outbursts." She moved past him toward her shoe, which had landed on the shelf behind him on his dead rhododendron. "I'll just get my shoe and be on my way." She darted past him and grabbed it. As she hopped on her shod foot, jamming her toes into the other shoe, she lost her balance and tumbled onto the floor. Gabe stood staring down at her. Her rancor rose anew. Bastard couldn't even be a gentleman and give her a hand up. It was almost like he couldn't stand to touch her. Hot tears stung her eyes temporarily blinding her. Was she that repulsive?

She shoved the pump on her foot and stood. She turned then and hurried from the apartment. After she slammed the door behind her, she pressed her back against the wall to the right of his place. Her heart pounded like a freight train in her chest. Gulping air, she closed her eyes and steadied herself.

It was okay that she made a fool out of herself. She was just grateful he didn't call the cops on her. Hastily, Gianna crossed herself. "Holy Mother Mary, what was I thinking?" Gianna hurried to the stairwell and hurried down to the lobby. As she was about to push the big glass front door open, she caught her breath and stepped back out of sight. Mario and Eddy? Her heart hammered in her chest. What were they doing here? Had they followed her? She looked back to the stairwell. She could go back to Gabe's. Hell no! She'd knock on a stranger's door first.

She bit her bottom lip. *Think, Gianna.* What should she do? Call Tressie to come for her? No. Her car was in the shop. The cops? And tell them what? Tell them she was scared to death! Gianna dug for the cell phone from her purse.

When her fingertips didn't find it, she dug deeper. Where was it? *Oh, my God!* Had it fallen out in Gabe's apartment when she pounded the crap out of him? Or when she went flying onto the floor?

The front door buzzed. Oh, God! She hurried to the stairwell and ran up past the second floor. Maybe they were there to see Gabe? Maybe they figured out it was him who took them out the other night. Oh, crap! The door to the stairwell opened. Gianna hurried into the hallway with the apartments and ran to the other end. She'd go down the stairwell on the opposite side and then hurry down and exit the building.

As she heaved open the door, she screamed. Eddy was coming straight for her. She turned and ran to the opposite stairwell and down. But as she got to the second-floor landing, Mario was looking up at her from the first-floor landing. Gianna pushed through the door leading to the second-floor lofts. As she ran past Gabe's door, he pulled her inside and locked the door.

Her heart beat so hard and her breath came so fast, Gianna could not get a deep breath.

Gabe pulled her back into his living room, silencing her with a finger to his lips. "Gianna, you're safe. Try to slow your breathing down. You're going to hyperventilate."

Gabe reached out, wanting to cradle her in his arms and tell her it would be all right. As he did, he retracted his arms. No. Stay the course. No more emotions. No more sex. No more nothing! Gordo had followed the goombahs who followed Gianna. He got the call just as he stepped out of his apartment to go find her before the bastards did.

Tucci must want her real bad. Virgin or not. Gabe was going to make sure that didn't happen. He just wasn't sure how he was going to go about that. Blow his cover by telling her what was going on? Ask for her help? No fucking way! He'd be damned if he'd put her right into that creep's hands.

Donna and Gordo thought it was a damn good idea. His SAC encouraged him to call on her and offer protective custody if she'd wear a wire.

He looked down into her terrified hazel eyes, and he melted. "Dammit, Gianna!"

He smiled as she sparked in anger in return. He knew she was a spicy little fireball, but when she had come at him earlier, he'd been shocked. And in a twisted way pleased. If he didn't mean anything to her, she wouldn't have come over and said and did what she did.

He grinned. Her eyes narrowed. Ah, the rub.

11

Gabe's cell phone rang. He flipped it open, and as he did, a loud thud on the front door made Gianna jump. They'd found her! She turned wide-eyed to Gabe, who scowled and spoke quietly but definitively to the caller. He didn't appear to be worried.

The thudding increased in volume. Gabe finally flipped his phone closed, scowled at her, then grabbed her by the arm. "Come with me."

Gianna didn't ask where they were going.

His bedroom. He grabbed a really big gun off the nightstand and slid it down the back of his pants, then pulled on a pair of tennis shoes and slipped on a T-shirt before moving through the room to the window. He hoisted the window up, reached out, and pulled down the fire escape. "C'mon, Gianna."

She didn't question him. Gabe followed her down to the alley at the back of the apartment building, and to her surprise there was a waiting car. She scowled as she recognized one of her customers behind the wheel.

Gabe hustled her into the backseat, slammed the door shut, then hopped in the front passenger seat.

"Go," he said, and the driver took off.

As they zoomed through the streets of San Francisco, Gianna's fear took a backseat to her curiosity. Before she could ask what the hell was going on, Gabe's phone rang again.

"LaMotta."

She heard a voice, but the words were too faint to decipher. "We'll be there in less than ten." He flipped the phone shut and looked to the driver. "We're a go."

Gianna had had enough of the spy routine. "What's a go? Where are we going?"

"You're in no danger." Gabe curtly answered.

"Great, now answer my question."

Gabe half turned toward her. "You'll have all of your answers in less than ten minutes, Gianna." He turned giving her a great shot of the back of his head.

His tone left no room for discussion. Gianna sat back and crossed her arms over her chest, and decided further prodding would only get more non-answers.

Several minutes later, she was ushered into a nondescript building on the other side of town and into what appeared to be an office. There was a keypad on the outside of the metal door, and Gabe quickly punched in a sequence of numbers, and it buzzed. He opened it and stood back for Gianna to walk through ahead of him. She caught his gaze. For a brief moment, his dark eyes softened, and he softly said, "It's okay."

And she believed him. Gianna strode through the door and was surprised to see Donna, Gabe's secretary, and a man she didn't recognize. He smiled, and while she got the feeling he didn't do it often, she smiled back.

"Gianna, I'd like you meet John Moncada, special agent in charge of Operation Cannoli."

Gianna laughed. Operation Cannoli? He was kidding, right? John extended his hand. "A pleasure to meet you, Miss Cipriani."

Gianna took his hand and said, "How did you know my last name?"

"Special Agent Donna Sweeney, Gianna Cipriani." And then Gabe said, "Special Agent Angelo 'Gordo' Torres, Gianna Cipriani."

As introductions were made, it occurred to Gianna that Gabe was not a real-estate mogul.

She turned on him and said, "Let me guess. Special Agent Gabriel LaMotta? Or is that name as fake as you are?"

Gabe frowned but he nodded. Her anger rose. "So, Mr. Special Agent LaMotta, what does seducing a virgin have to do with your Operation Cannoli?"

SAC Moncada coughed and cleared his throat. He stepped between Gianna and Gabe.

"Miss Cipriani, please sit down and I'll be happy to explain why we've brought you here."

Gianna eyed Gabe like he was covered in scabs.

Once she was seated, she looked up expectantly at the SAC, who pulled a chair from the wall and moved it closer to her. He sat down and smiled. "I believe you are familiar with a certain Fabio Tucci."

She nodded.

"This task force has been working diligently for several years to nail the bastard. Twice we've had him on the hook and twice he's slipped off."

"What does that have to do with me?"

"We believe he was responsible for your father's death, and—"

"No! Papa fell!"

"We think he was pushed. A man was seen entering the restaurant and leaving within ten minutes of the accident. We haven't identified him, but we compared the times to your 911 call. It fits. We know your father was heavily in debt to Tucci. We also know he has pressured you. For what? We're hoping you will share that with us and in so doing, help us find a way to nail him and put him away for good."

Gianna turned to look up at Gabe. "You were at the Kat's Meow on purpose."

"I saw you run out of Roberto's, and I heard Mario and Eddy saying they wanted a piece of you."

Gianna stood up. God she was a schmuck! "And so did you! Except you got it, didn't you?"

John stood. "Miss Cipriani, I apologize for my agent's poor decision making. He'll be reprimanded. But I'm asking you to put your emotions aside for a minute and tell us what Tucci wanted from you."

Gianna sat back down, all the while glaring at Gabe. She turned to face the SAC. "He told me my father owed him one hundred forty thousand dollars. He wants part of Ciao Bella as payment. I told him no."

"And how did he feel about that?"

"He wasn't happy. He gave me two weeks to sign it over."

"Did he threaten you?"

"Yes."

John looked at Gabe, then Gordo, then Donna before looking back at her. "Miss Cipriani, would you consider wearing a wire and engaging Tucci in a conversation that may incriminate him?"

Gianna swallowed. But her decision was made the minute she realized Tucci had killed her father. She would do anything to see him behind bars.

"I . . . I . . . yes. But what if he doesn't tell me what you want him to?"

"Then we go to Plan B."

"What is that?"

"I'll let you know when we know."

Gianna took a deep breath. "Tell me what you want me to do."

At her words, the Feds gathered around her and laid it out.

More than two hours later, Gianna's head felt like it was going to explode with information overload. When Gabe made a move like he was going to take her home, she shot him a glare. Instead she turned to Donna. "Would you give me a ride home please?"

Donna and Gabe made eye contact, but the woman nodded. "Of course."

As Gianna walked out the door, she heard John's furious words. "What the fuck were you thinking? Are you looking to get booted out of here? No fucking victims!"

Gianna cringed at the harsh words.

"Ignore them, Gianna. They're nothing but a bunch of pricks," Donna said.

"No kidding."

Once in the car, and after several minutes of silence, Gianna asked, "Do these set-up things go wrong very often?"

Donna glanced at her. A tight smile played on her lips. She was pretty, Gianna decided. One of those take-charge type of women. And she knew instinctively that Gabe and Donna had been intimate at one time.

"They can get pretty dicey. But as we explained, the club will be filled with agents. Our surveillance truck will be in the alley. Worst-case scenario for something like this? You might get a few bumps and bruises out of it."

Gianna nodded, and as much as she didn't care for Tucci, she didn't see him killing her. She swallowed down the huge lump in her throat. Unless he figured out she was wearing a wire.

Several more moments passed in silence. Gianna wrestled with a question she was dying to ask Donna but would feel foolish if she did.

"Did you love him?" Gianna blurted out. So much for looking foolish.

Donna's body stiffened at the question, her hands grasped and ungrasped the steering wheel. By her body language alone, Gianna had her answer. "I'm sorry, that was rude of me."

Donna shook her head but kept her eyes on the road. "It's kind of hard not to fall for Gabe LaMotta."

Gia nodded. "No kidding."

Donna gave her a quick smile before turning back to the road. "Gabe and his wife were having problems. She didn't like his constantly being gone. But she knew the score when she married him. I don't know why she thought it would change. They got into it one night right after a long stint in Phoenix. She kicked him out. He came to my place looking for a couch to crash on." Donna's fingers continued to open and close around the steering wheel. "We got drunk. And, well, I gave him more than a couch to crash on." She laughed bitterly. "I have to hand it to him. He went straight to Debbie the next morning and told her what he did, and then he told her, if he slept with me, he'd sleep with anyone."

Gianna gasped. "How horrible!"

Donna pulled up in front of the restaurant and said, "What he meant was, if he could stray once, he'd stray again, and he didn't want to be in a marriage where he wanted other women."

That surprised her. Not that Gabe had been unfaithful to his wife, but that he had been honest with her about it and realized his weakness. Most guys would have never told their wife and kept tomcatting around. Her eyes narrowed when she thought of how she like Donna and no doubt dozens of others had been caught up in his seductive web.

Donna touched Gianna on the arm. "Try to give him a break. He's been undercover on one assignment or another for the last seven years. I don't think he knows who he is or what he wants anymore."

Gianna nodded, feeing a little less angry with him. But not enough to forgive him.

"We'll have a car out here keeping an eye on you," Donna said. She scribbled a number down on her card and handed it to Gianna. "Call me if you get scared."

Gianna nodded and hurried into the restaurant, then up to her apartment. She triple-checked the dead bolts before she jumped into the shower. She turned out all the lights and went to the window in the living room that looked down at street. A dark van was parked a half block away. As she stepped back, a dark blacked-out sedan pulled up behind it. Her heart leapt in her throat as she watched Gabe get out and talk to the driver of the van. They switched vehicles. Before Gabe climbed into the van, he looked up at her window and stared. Gianna stepped back, allowing the heavy drapery to fall into place.

When she slipped between the sheets in her lonely bed, Gianna thought how easy it would be to call Gabe and invite him up to warm her. Not that he'd come. And seriously, not that she'd have him. Although the sex with him had been beyond her wildest expectations, Gianna realized that while she could change her virgin status, she couldn't change her traditional good-girl status. It was who she was. And while she would give an Oscar-worthy performance for Fabio Tucci tomorrow night, it was just that, an act.

She was Gianna Michaela Cipriani. Good Catholic girl who, while she wanted to explore more of the world around her, did not want to do it with casual relationships littering her wake. The next man she had sex with would be a man who accepted her as she was, not who she could act like. She closed her eyes and snuggled against her pillow. And she was okay with that. A smile tugged at her lips. But she had to admit, another round or two in the sack with Gabe wouldn't be such a bad thing either.

Gianna was up early and called Tucci. She told him she'd made a decision that he might be interested in hearing. She'd like to see him later that evening to discuss it. At his place if that was okay with him.

The don tripped over his words as he hurried to assure her he would count the seconds until eight o'clock.

For self-preservation, and the fact that she was still steamed at him, Gianna refused to allow Gabe near her as she was being wired. She was relieved to see it wasn't a big bulky device like she'd seen on the movies. No, the device she was wearing was worked expertly into a heavy chunky gold belt she would wear. It went perfectly with her skimpy outfit. Since there would be nothing taped to her chest, she felt confident that if Tucci got suspicious, she could persuade him he was being paranoid.

"Gianna, we have another toy for you," John said as he handed her a small black clutch purse with a big onyx button snap. He tapped the stone. "A lens."

Gianna scrunched her eyebrows in confusion.

He explained. "Have you ever heard of a nanny cam? It's like that but more sophisticated and compact. When you get into Tucci's office, set this down and position it so we can get a full view of the room. If we lose you on the wire, we can see what's going on."

Gianna relaxed. She was double covered.

Tucci called an hour before she was ready to leave, insisting Mario and Eddy would pick her up. Gianna said she was hoping for a ride since she didn't know if she'd be returning home and didn't want to leave her car parked in the Tenderloin. She smiled when Tucci was speechless for several seconds. When he spoke, his voice quivered. "Gianna, I cannot tell you how happy I am you are coming to me tonight."

Gianna hung up the phone, giving it a sneer. Men. They only thought with their dicks and didn't care a whit about anything else.

She had been nervous the first time she had slid into the back of the black stretch, but Gianna was calm this time. She understood the power she held over a man. And she understood it had little to do with superficial beauty. It had to do with attitude. It had to do with a natural sensuality you could not practice and perfect. It had to be a natural occurrence. And she discovered that night in front of her mirror that she had it spades. Men looked at her completely different now that she took herself more seriously. It felt good. Empowering. Coupled with the fact that her resolve had galvanized, and in the last few days she had gone from a timid virgin to a woman with a vendetta to serve.

When Eddy and Mario smacked their lips at her like she was a piece of candy, she scowled and said, "Do you kiss you mother with those lips?"

Both men looked at her in surprise. Gianna pushed harder. "How do you think your boss will feel when I tell him you two have been hitting on me?"

"Hey! We—" Eddy started.

Gianna waved him off. "Do you think he'll believe you or me?"

Mario elbowed his partner. "Just shut up, E. We'll get the seconds."

Gianna scoffed. "I'll geld you first. And don't for a minute think I won't."

She slid into the back of the limousine without their help.

Several minutes later, she was escorted into Roberto's. While she kept her eyes forward, she noticed Donna and Gordo act-

ing like a couple. She also saw John hanging out at the bar closest to Tucci's office. Gabe was nowhere in sight. That was okay,
he was yesterday's news.

Gianna knew she looked good. When she strutted into
Tucci's office, he rose, shock clearly clouding his features. She
was dressed as scantily as the dancers. Slowly, for effect, Gianna
slid the coat from her shoulders. Her short black knit sheath
dress hugged her curves like a second skin. The chunky belt ac-
centuated her narrow waist.

"Shut the door, Mario," Tucci commanded as he moved
closer to her. "From the outside."

"Hello, Mr. Tucci." Gianna extended her hand, and he took
it. His touch gave her goose bumps, but not the kind Gabe's
touch elicited.

"My God, Gianna, you look, fabulous. I . . . I'm speechless."

Gianna allowed his lips to linger on her hand as she set her
purse down, lens forward, on a waist-high book stand next to
her. She moved into Tucci so that he wouldn't see her adjust it
so that it had a straight shot at the cozy little sofa that had not
been in the office the first time she had been there. Looked like
Fabio expected to go cherry picking.

12

Gabe gritted his teeth as he watched and listened to Gianna turn it on with Tucci. He knew damn well how hot she looked in that skimpy little dress. He didn't need the minicam to show him. If she were his girl, he wouldn't let her out of the house in it.

Gabe leashed his escalating jealousy. Instead, he focused on the scene unfolding in front of him and decided right then and there that if it even looked like Tucci was going to do the dirty deed, he was out of the truck and in that office before he could alert his team.

Tucci slipped a possessive arm around Gianna's waist and walked with her to the sofa. Gianna sunk into the cushions and looked straight at the lens. A flirty smile twisted her lips. Gabe hissed in a breath. "Why, you little minx, you know I'm watching you."

When she pulled a Sharon Stone move and crossed her legs, giving a quick glimpse of her red-hot panties, Gabe's cock swelled. Tucci was as affected. He sidled up to Gianna, and like a little boy wanting to pet a pussycat, he held his trembling hand out toward her breasts. As if she were the queen of the world, Gianna turned a smile on Tucci. She leaned forward and almost allowed him to touch her. "Do you want to touch me, Fabio?" she softly asked.

He nodded, his head bobbing up and down. Gianna smiled that seductive all-knowing smile of hers and sank back into the cushions. "I have a few questions I'd like answered first."

Tucci slid closer. "Ask me anything."

Gianna cocked her head sideways and said, "I want the truth." She leaned toward him, her full breasts brushing the hands twitching in his lap. He palmed one. Gabe nearly climbed through the screen.

Gianna sat back and waved her finger under his nose. "Uh-uh, Fabio. No touching until I have my answers. I'll know if you're lying to me. And then"—she shrugged—"the only way you're going to get to my cherry is by forcing me." She smiled and leaned closer, her pouty lips an inch from the don's face. "And I don't think either one of us wants that, now, do we?"

Tucci shook his head.

Gianna smiled and sat back. Her gaze once again looked directly at the lens. "How did my father die?" she asked.

Tucci straightened. He took her hand and brought it to his lips. "*Bella mia*, I heard he fell down the steps and broke his neck."

Her eyes remained fastened to the lens. Gabe felt a swell in his chest. Even from where he sat, he could see the pain in her eyes. "I don't think he fell," she softly said.

"What are you saying?" Tucci asked, false concern lacing his tone.

Gianna moved her gaze to rest on Tucci's face. "I think someone pushed him, and I think you know who did it. I want you to tell me who it is; then I want to watch you kill him."

Gabe gasped. If he didn't know better, he'd think she was serious. Then he watched her eyes harden. Shit!

"*Bella*, if I—"

Gianna slapped him full across the face.

"Fuck!" Gabe said, standing up. That was going to land her on her back for sure. He hesitated when Tucci sat perfectly still. Gabe's eyes dropped to the mobster's crotch. He was wearing beige trousers, which suddenly inflated. Son of a bitch. He liked to be slapped around.

"Tell me who killed my father!"

Tucci took the hand she slapped him with and brought it to his lips. He kissed her fingertips, then sank his teeth into the tender flesh of her palm. Gianna cried out but did not try to move away. Instead, Gabe watched her figure Tucci out. She smiled and leaned into him. "You like to play rough, don't you?"

He nodded. She slapped him again, this time with her left hand. Tucci squirmed in his seat. "Tell me who pushed my father down the stairs and I'll slap you so silly you'll scream for me to stop."

"I went to talk to your father."

Gianna gasped. Tucci hurried with his words. "I wanted you, Gianna. I wanted the treasure between your legs. But Cappy wasn't selling."

Gabe watched her poker face and felt another hard tug at his heart for this brave woman.

"Go on," she softly said.

Tucci brought her hand to his chest. "I pleaded with your father. I told him I would forfeit all of his debt. I told him I'd spot him his next fifty Gs. He called me a *finnoch*!" Tucci pressed her hand to his crotch. "I'm not gay!"

Gabe spoke into his earpiece. "The fox is being hunted hard. Stand by for my word to move in."

Gianna grabbed her hand back from Tucci. Her eyes snapped with fury. She stood and looked down at him. "So, you go to my father and demand he hand his only child over to you for sex. He refuses. You push him down the stairs, then tell *me* that if I don't come up with the money or give up my cherry, you'll see to it I end up next to my father?"

"Gianna, please," Tucci begged.

"No! I'm going to the cops. I'm going to tell them everything."

He stood slowly, and his eyes morphed from begging to cold and calculated. Gabe held his breath. He had enough on Tucci right now, but a good attorney could get him off by saying Alberto's death was an accident.

"I would not do that," Tucci said so softly, Gabe wasn't sure he heard it.

"What are you going to do?" Gianna flung at him.

He grabbed her and yanked her hard against him. "Silly stupid girl. Your father was an ass. When he told me no, I told him how I was going to fuck you until I split you in half. Then I shoved him down those stairs. But he didn't die, Gianna. He was still alive. As I twisted his neck, I told him there was nothing he could do to keep you from me."

"Go!" Gabe yelled into his headset.

Gianna stood, terrified and furious. Her father was murdered for her cherry! She was going to kill Tucci herself.

He moved closer to her. But she held her ground, knowing it was just a matter of minutes before the calvary burst through the door.

"I'm going to fuck you right now," Tucci threatened. "Then let my boys have my sloppy seconds, then send you on a midnight cruise out into the deep blue Pacific."

Gianna laughed, the sound stopping him. She narrowed her eyes and dropped her cherry bomb. "I have a newsflash for you, Tucci. I'm not a virgin anymore!"

He slapped her. "Liar!"

Heat stung her, but she was locked and loaded for a fight. Gianna flung her hair over her shoulder and sneered. "You're not man enough to find out."

Tucci lunged at her, knocking her back onto the sofa. He grabbed at her panties, his nails digging into her thighs. Wildly, Gianna fought him off. She heard a loud thud against the door, followed by another. If she could just hold him off . . .

Gabe threw his shoulder into the door separating him from Gianna. The force of his muscles and his body hitting the thick wood as it opened sent him shooting into the room. He caught his balance and kept from tripping over Tucci, who was rolling on the floor and howling in pain, grabbing his balls. Gabe looked up to see Gianna standing over the howling don with her hands fisted at her sides.

"He's going to need some ice." She unbuckled the belt containing the wire and flung it at Gabe, then stepped over the mafioso and out the door.

As the rest of his team rushed into the room, Gabe went after Gianna.

"Gianna!" he called as the chilled October air hit him hard in the face. She'd exited the club, and in that skimpy dress and high heels, she stalked down the crowded sidewalks of the Tenderloin. If she didn't have that get-the-hell-out-of-my-way look on her face, Gabe was sure she would have been accosted more than once. As it was, anyone near her moved to get out of her way.

Gabe caught up to her and grabbed her elbow. She spun around and raised her fist to him. "Do you want a piece of this too?"

He grinned. He couldn't help it. All five foot four of her acted like she could take on the world and win. He sobered. Hell, after what he witnessed tonight, he bet she could.

"Gianna, you need to come back to the club."

"No, I don't. You have everything you need on film and on tape. I want you to leave me alone." She jerked her arm from his grasp and continued to stride down the sidewalk. Gabe watched her vanish around a corner. He should have been jubilant. They had Tucci right where they wanted him. He'd go away for the rest of his life. But instead of feeling good about the success of his operation, Gabe felt as if he had lost something so precious, he'd never be able to replace it.

13

"C'mon, Gianna," Tressie cajoled. "It's been three months, and you haven't wanted to go shopping once!"

Gianna smiled at her cousin. "I know I haven't been good company lately. But it isn't like you've been around a whole lot."

"I know! That's why it's important we have some cuzzy time."

Gianna smiled and continued to fold napkins at the bar. It was a quiet Monday afternoon, and the restaurant wasn't open for lunch on Mondays. She looked out the big front window to the gray afternoon. It had rained earlier and threatened to rain again. Shopping in the rain didn't excite her. In fact, not much did these days. She hated to admit it, but she missed Gabe. But he obviously didn't miss her. He hadn't made any effort to contact her. The last time she saw him was that night on the sidewalk in front of Roberto's.

Gianna let out a melancholy sigh. She missed the excitement he stirred in her. She'd tried to open up to the advances of several men. She'd even gone on a few dates, but she always said a polite thank you and shook her head when they asked if she'd like to go out again.

She decided that come spring, she was going to make arrangements to travel. Get out of her comfort zone and see the world.

"You still think of him?" Tressie asked.

Gianna smiled. She'd confided everything to Tressie. And while her cousin had been there for her, Tressie was of the opinion that Gianna should give the hunky Fed the opportunity to say what he had to say. Gianna refused. She was done putting herself out on a limb. Especially after Donna had filled Gianna in about Gabe. He was married to his job. He would never push it aside for a woman. At least not in her lifetime.

No, Gianna wanted a man she could trust. A man who came home most nights, a man she could build a life with. And while life with Gabe would be exciting and on the edge, it would always be on his terms and on his time. She deserved more.

A loud knock on the window startled both women. Gianna jumped in her seat and turned to see what caused the noise. Her stomach plummeted to her feet. Gabe!

Before Gianna could move, Tressie was up and at the door, unlocking it, inviting him in.

Gianna stood and put the bar stool between her and the man who had turned her inside out and left her hanging.

The months hadn't changed him. He was as big, as handsome, as sexy. He may have lost a little weight, but he still wore his fine threads like a runway model.

"I, um, have something to do in the kitchen," Tressie said, leaving them to stare at each other. Gianna scowled. She really needed to find a more loyal cousin.

"Gianna," Gabe softly said, "you look well."

"What do you want?"

"To talk."

"I'm sorry, but I have no time to spare you for conversation. Please leave."

He moved into the room. She sat at the bar, giving him her back, and proceeded to fold more napkins.

"I quit my job," he softly said.

Gianna's hand stopped for just a brief second before she continued to fold.

"I moved back up here."

She continued to fold the red cloth into little crowns.

Gabe moved to stand closer behind her. Gianna kept her breath as even as she could, not willing to read anything into his words.

"I've missed you, Gia," he softly said.

Her hand trembled. Her stomach slowly somersaulted.

"I wanted to apologize for, um, for taking advantage of you. I regret it. If I could take it back, I would."

Hot tears welled in her eyes. Anger simmered. Gianna spun around in the chair and faced him. "You regret it!" she shrieked. "You regret lying to me, then seducing me? Then taking what I should have given to a man who gave two shits about me?" She punched him in the chest. "Well, guess what, asshole? I *don't* regret it. I don't regret the biggest lesson I could learn. Men are pigs, and you're the foulest of them all!"

She moved off the chair and stood up to him. She only came to the top of his chest in her heels. But she felt like a tiger. Hot tears sprang from her eyes.

"I don't regret the fucking, Gabe. What I regret is the fact that it's going to take some serious research to find a guy who excites me the way you did, but one I can trust. One who won't go sniffing after the next piece of ass that wags under his nose."

She moved back to the bar stool and sat down. In a jerky motion, she began to fold the napkins again. "Thanks for stopping by and for your crappy apology. The door is unlocked. Please leave."

After several long minutes, when Gabe made no move to leave, she turned on him again. His soft smile stopped her cold. Against her better judgment, her heart began to thaw.

"Gianna, I have not stopped thinking of you since the day I watched you at your father's funeral from behind a bunch of oleander bushes with my asshole partner Gordo. I haven't touched another woman since that day." He moved closer. "I don't want anyone else but you, Gianna."

Her heart swelled, but it wasn't enough. "I can't trust you. Donna told me how you were unfaithful to your wife."

Gabe's jaw tightened. "I won't deny it." He let out a long breath. "I knew I didn't love Debbie the day I married her. It's why I didn't care if I came home or not. It was wrong, and I hurt her bad, but sometimes, Gianna, you can't see the forest through the trees."

He reached out and brushed a long strand of hair from her cheek. "I can tell you, I feel more for you than I have for any woman. It's why I didn't pursue you."

She looked up at him, confused.

"I knew I couldn't make a commitment to you, Gianna. Not when I was neck deep in a UC operation. It wouldn't have been fair to you. So I stepped back." He slid his fingers into her hair and pulled her to him. "But things are different now. I quit my Fed job. I'm done. I have almost a year's worth of vacation they owe me, plus all my years of hazard pay. I sold my house in L.A. and have a nice chunk of change. I've been rehired by SFPD. So long as I start within the next nine months, they'll guarantee my job."

Hope flared in her chest. "What are you saying, Gabe?"

"I'm saying I want to be here with you. Or wherever you want to go. I just don't want to spend another day without you in it."

Gianna stood for a long time and stared at him. His dark eyes held sincere promise. "I want to go to Italy and cook in all of the great kitchens."

Gabe grinned. "I want to eat everything you prepare and turn into a fat, happy Italian man."

"I'm afraid, Gabe."

He gathered her into his arms. "I'm afraid, too, Gianna. Afraid one day you'll wake up and not want me anymore. But it's a chance I'm willing to take if you are."

Gianna stood on her tiptoes and wrapped her arms around his neck, bringing his lips down to hers. "I'm game," and she knew she would not regret her decision.

Gabe kissed her hard and deep, like there was no tomorrow. Before she could protest, he swept her up into his arms and strode into the kitchen. Tressie jumped back from where she'd been eavesdropping next to the batwing doors. "I'm going upstairs to ravish your cousin. I don't think she'll make it down for dinner."

As Gabe continued his way through the kitchen, Tressie laughed and said, "I've got you covered, cuz!"

Gabe tossed Gianna on the bed, and instead of a slow seduction, he ripped her clothes off. "I'll buy you an entire new wardrobe, Gianna. Just help me get you naked."

As she shucked her stockings and shoes, Gabe stripped down to his birthday suit.

Gianna smiled and rose up on her knees. He stood naked and hard before her in all of his manly glory. Her blood quickened and she knew without hesitation this was the man she would spend the rest of her life with.

Touching a fingertip to the glistening bead of come on the tip of his cock, Gianna's smile widened. She rubbed her thumb across the full head of him, smearing the thick lubricant. Gabe hissed. "Are all men as big and beautiful as you are?" she softly asked as she lowered her head to him.

His body shook when she took him into her mouth, her tongue swirling around the wide head. She sucked him into her mouth and Gabe groaned, and if it were possible, his cock became thicker. Gianna wrapped her fingers around the base of his shaft, and slowly took more of him into her mouth. Her nether regions tingled, and heated. She wanted to devour him, then in turn be consumed by him.

Gabe dug his fingers into her hair and pressed hotly into her. "Jesus, Gianna, the first time I saw your lips I wanted them on me like this."

She smiled with him in her mouth, and in a slow rhythmic pump, between her hand, her lips, and her tongue, Gianna brought Gabe to his knees. When she cupped his balls with her free hand he groaned and shuddered and pulled away from her.

His dark eyes were hooded, the planes of his face sharp. On his hands and knees Gabe pushed her back into the pillows. "You're mine now, Gianna Cipriani. And that means I don't share."

She smiled and relaxed back into the pillows, parting her legs. She reached up and dug her fingers into his thick dark hair and pulled him down to her. "Neither do I."

Gabe smiled, breaking the tense moment, and in one long fluid motion he filled her. His warmth infiltrated her velvety muscles, loosing them more to accommodate the thick heat of him.

The sensation of him filling her combined with her full heart was so sublime Gianna felt as if she would burst into tears. She'd never felt so desired, so loved or so complete as she did at that moment.

In a slow unhurried motion, Gabe moved in and out of her, their bodies parting but coming back together as one. Each giving, each taking, and each knowing there was no place on earth they would rather be.

Gabe smoothed back her hair and looked deeply into her eyes, then whispered, "Gianna, I feel like I've come home." And she knew it was true for them both.

Will That Be All?

Jami Alden

To the real Vinnie,
a constant source of inspiration

1

"Screw you, Vince!"

Theresa Bellessi barely registered the words before the impact of another body slammed into her back. As she stumbled she made a desperate scramble for the glasses on her tray but it was a lost cause. The martini, the cosmo, and the glass of Sangiovese all went flying as the heel of her shoe twisted and she fell backward into a chair.

A chair already occupied by a Ciao Bella patron.

A very large, very muscular Ciao Bella patron.

The breath whooshed out of his chest, accompanied by a soft curse as Theresa slammed into him. "Excuse me, I'm so sorry," Theresa said as she tried to find her feet. But with her legs in an undignified sprawl and the tiled floor slick with alcohol, that was easier said than done.

Big hands closed around her hips as he tried to help her off his lap, and she was aware of thickly muscled legs moving under her own. She managed to shift her weight forward enough for her feet to reach the floor, only to have it skid through a puddle of God knows what as she tried to stand. She fell back in the same moment the customer tried to catch her, his big hand closing firmly over one of her breasts.

His fingers closed reflexively around it for a second. Then as he realized exactly where his hand was, he jerked it away and stood up. "Jesus Christ, I'm sorry," he said, his voice deep with a noticeable east coast accent. He grabbed her around the waist to keep her from falling.

She could feel the heat of his big hands through the cotton of her white button front blouse as he held her shoulders and turned her to face him. She groaned as she got an up-close look at the carnage she and her tray of drinks had wrought. Red wine plastered the fabric of what looked like a hellaciously expensive shirt to his mile-wide, muscular chest. Under different circumstances, she would have very much enjoyed the way the wet shirt clung.

But right now all she could see was a big, fat bill for a dry cleaner, or worse, a new shirt for the unfortunate customer. "I'm so sorry, sir," she said, heat searing her face as she sensed all the attention in the restaurant's crowded bar focusing on her. Great. Less than a week into her job as a cocktail waitress at Ciao Bella, her cousin Gia's restaurant, and Theresa was already making an impression. Unfortunately, not the kind she had hoped for.

"If you write down your name and address, I'll reimburse you for the dry cleaning, and of course your drinks and food are complimentary."

"It was an accident," he said, chuckling softly. "Besides, I think you got the worst of it."

Theresa glanced down at herself, and saw immediately what he was talking about. While the Sangiovese had hit him square in the chest, she'd received the brunt of both the cosmo and the martini. The front of her shirt was soaked and tinged pink. And since she was wearing white, she was giving the entire bar a nice peek at her lingerie.

She gave a small prayer of thanks that she'd decided to go with the bra with the fully lined cups.

"I'm so sorry," she said again. She grabbed the towel tucked into her apron and went to work trying to soak up some of the red stain. "I should have been watching—"

"What, you're gonna grow eyes in the back of your head? She knocked right into you." He grabbed her hand to still her frantic attempts to clean.

She looked up—way up—damn, the man had to be at least six-four—and finally got a good look at his face. He was gorgeous, but there was nothing pretty about him. The word that popped into her mind out of nowhere was chiseled. His chin was square and blunt, as if it had been carved from stone. His cheekbones were like sharp blades pushing through his tanned skin, and his long Roman nose spoke of his proud Mediterranean heritage. His hair waved off his forehead, thick and dark, maybe a shade lighter than her own. His espresso-colored eyes crinkled at the corners as he smiled, and were framed by outrageously long lashes, the only remotely feminine spot on an otherwise very masculine face.

He might have looked mean if his lips hadn't been quirked in an apologetic smile. "Really, don't worry about the drinks. Besides, it's my fault, if you want to know the truth. I'm Vince—the guy she was yelling at," he said.

Theresa finally unglued her tongue from the roof of her mouth. "Oh. Well, I should have worn different shoes," she said and gestured down to the black Mary Jane pumps on her feet. Unlike the ridiculous platform stilettos she'd been forced to wear at her previous job, these shoes were both cute and comfy, but obviously lacked the proper traction for working in a restaurant with tile floors.

"Yeah, well, the reason she stormed out in the first place is because she's pissed at me," he said. "That'll teach me to laugh in a woman's face when she tells me she wants to marry me."

He looked over her shoulder and sighed. "I better go and do damage control."

Theresa turned and looked out the window that faced the busy street. A tall, meticulously groomed blonde stood with arms folded across her chest glaring at them both.

The customer pulled his wallet out of his pocket and fished out a bill. When he went to toss it on the table, Theresa grabbed his wrist. "Absolutely not," she said, ignoring the shock of heat that went up her arm as her fingers brushed the warm skin of his arm.

"Come on," Vince said. "She knocked you over, I grabbed your—" His cheeks flushed dark as he gestured vaguely at her chest.

"I know you didn't do that on purpose," she said. And compared to what she'd had to put up with working at Slap Jack's, a minor boob graze was hardly worth mentioning. He tried to hand her the money again, but she shoved it away. As much as she couldn't afford to take care of his bill out of her own pocket, she couldn't accept his money, especially when he was being so nice about everything.

His mouth tightened as though her reply didn't sit well with him.

"Vince, I think Cameron—" Theresa's cousin Gia appeared at her side. "Whoa, what happened here?" Theresa's stomach knotted.

"I spilled my tray. All over him. It was totally my fault," Theresa said before Vince could get a word in edgewise. "Don't worry, I already comped him and offered to reimburse him for dry cleaning."

Gia nodded approvingly and some of the tension uncoiled in Theresa's midsection. Not that she expected Gia to go ballistic, but Gia had already gone out of her way to help her, and Theresa wanted to prove that she wasn't the irresponsible fuckup that the rest of the family thought her to be.

"Very sorry about that. As I was saying, Cameron asked me to come find you."

Vince shook his dark head and muttered something under his breath. "Guess I better get out there," he said, giving them both with a rueful smile.

"Why bother?" Gia said in a voice that only Theresa could hear. She looked at Theresa and did a double take. "Whoa. Now if this were Hooters, that look would work really well for you, but right now, I suggest you change before going back to work."

Theresa nodded and left. She grabbed an extra shirt from her locker and changed in the bathroom, wincing as she looked in the mirror. Though petite, she was, in a word, busty. Which meant that in order for a requisite white button front Ciao Bella blouse to fit, it had to be a size too big. Its boxy, unisex cut was already unflattering, and made Theresa's small but curvy figure disappear into a shapeless blob.

I should be grateful, she reminded herself, *that this place has a uniform that consists of more than pasties and a g-string.* Yes, she was grateful that she no longer had to dance in a cage or serve drinks in the near nude to generate enough income to pay the rent and cover a seemingly unending list of emergencies. Yet a vain, totally ridiculous part of her hated that her insanely gorgeous male customer had looked at her and seen a short, shapeless lump.

Although judging from his tall, sleek, model-perfect girlfriend, he wouldn't have looked twice at Theresa regardless of what she'd been wearing.

Theresa hurried back to the bar as quickly as the Friday night crowd would allow. Even with the bar this hopping, she had some work to do if she wanted to make up for having to cover Vince's tab and still make a nice cut. She was about to check on a big group to see if they wanted another round when Gia caught her by the arm.

"You must have made an impression," Gia said with a sly smile. "Vince left this for you."

Theresa gasped when she saw the hundred dollar bill in her cousin's hand. "I can't take that."

"He insisted," Gia said.

"But I wasn't even his server." Vince and his date had been seated in a section of the bar covered by Tanya, a short-haired brunette in her late twenties. "You need to give that to Tanya."

"He took care of her too, but he insisted I give you this."

"Why would he do that?"

"Because he's a really good guy. You'll see what I mean, he comes in several times a week."

Theresa reluctantly accepted the bill but couldn't suppress the uneasiness that had settled into her spine. In her experience, a man didn't throw around hundred dollar bills unless he wanted something in return.

She looked outside. Vince was still out there, having a heated discussion with the blonde. His face was pulled in tight lines and the way he raked his hands through his hair screamed of frustration. He reached out to take the woman's arm but she jerked away, and thumped her fist in the middle of his chest. It wasn't quite a blow, but it certainly wasn't a caress. Theresa's throat got tight as she waited for his reaction. Theresa remembered the last time she got physical with her ex that way. Her wrist still throbbed when it rained, a physical memento of his response.

She shook her head, reminding herself that not every man was like Mark. But that thought didn't make Vince any less intimidating. He was huge—not just tall but really muscular. Big enough to break the slim blonde in half if he wanted to. But all Vince did was calmly hold his hands up and say something to make the woman back off.

He reached for the woman's arm again, and this time she didn't resist. As he turned to guide her down the block, Vince glanced into the restaurant and caught Theresa watching. He gave her a quick, two-fingered wave and smiled.

Even as her entire body went warm, warning bells went off in her head and the hundred seemed to burn a hole in her front pocket. No way he could be that nice, that gorgeous, that perfect. When someone seemed too good to be true, it was because he was. She turned away without returning his smile.

Vince Mattera cracked open another beer and sank into the overstuffed cushions of his leather couch. Custom built to accommodate his size, the piece of furniture dominated the media room of his recently purchased house in San Francisco's posh Nob Hill neighborhood. *Nice fuckin' Friday night,* he thought as he aimlessly channel-surfed through the eight hundred satellite channels. Christ, after the week he'd had, all he'd wanted was a stiff drink, a good meal at his favorite restaurant, and an energetic fuck to take the edge off.

Instead he'd had his drink and his meal cut short by his freshly ex-girlfriend. At eleven o'clock, when he should have been recovering from his orgasm and gearing up for round two, his only companion was snoring and drooling next to him on the couch.

"Stupid Chester," he said and reached out to absently scratch the dog's ears. "Should have dumped her when she brought you home." That had been nearly two weeks ago, and Cameron had oh-so-casually mentioned that Chester, a nine-month-old purebred golden retriever who was as cute as he was obnoxious, would be the perfect "practice baby" for them.

Vince had oh-so-casually ignored that comment and asked her why Chester couldn't live at her apartment.

"Because you're the one with the yard, such a luxury in this part of the city." And in the time since Chester had moved in, he'd managed to dig up and crap on every square inch of his garden. Fifty thousand dollars worth of landscaping down the drain. Not to mention the two handwoven Persian carpets he'd crapped on and the huge sofa he'd disemboweled.

He needed to do something about the damn dog.

As though sensing his master's uncharitable thoughts, Chester opened one eye and raised a brow.

"I don't have time for this shit," Vince muttered. And he didn't have time for an overemotional, increasingly clingy girlfriend who bitched and moaned because he had to travel several times a month and was unable to squire her to whatever society gala she was supposed to attend.

He'd started dating Cameron when he was looking for a house. Somehow she'd managed to talk him out of a reasonably sized if still overpriced Victorian in favor of this six-thousand-square-foot brick home complete with a lavish garden and guest cottage. "So much better for entertaining," she'd said. "You could have dinner parties out on the terrace, casual get togethers in the kitchen."

From the beginning, she'd made no bones about her interest, never wasting an opportunity to flirt. At the time, dating her had seemed like a good idea. She was attractive in a sophisticated, well-maintained sort of way. As an added bonus, she had a lot of contacts in the business community, so he figured accompanying her to her many social engagements would be a good way to mix business with pleasure.

However, after only three months, it became clear that Cameron didn't view their relationship in such detached terms. When she'd talked about all that entertaining, she'd imagined herself as the permanent hostess. Lately she'd been making comments about his house being far too big for one person and how lonely he must be all by himself.

He hadn't taken the bait. And then Chester had shown up. Still, Vince hadn't said anything because he hadn't felt like having what he knew would be a difficult—and for her at least—painful discussion. Call him an asshole, but he had enough going on at work to stress him out. He didn't need his personal life in the mix.

He fended Cameron off as best he could because frankly, he liked the way things were. Liked having someone to go out with when he was in town. Liked that he didn't feel obligated to her when he had to work late or travel. And yeah, he was a guy, and he liked getting laid regularly.

Tonight at the restaurant, Cameron had run out of patience. "How's our baby?" she'd asked.

Vince had nearly choked on his carpaccio appetizer. "Baby?"

"Chester." Though she said it with a teasing eyeroll and a swipe at his arm, he could tell she was carefully gauging his reaction.

"The *dog*," he said, "is fine as far as I know." He took a fortifying sip of his vodka on the rocks.

"Did he miss his daddy while you were gone? Did you tell him mommy was sorry she couldn't come visit, but daddy won't give her a key to the house?"

He threw his fork down. "How about we cut the crap, Cameron," he said in the same sharp, no-bullshit tone that had earned him fear and respect in boardrooms across the world. "You got a problem with the way things are, spit it out."

Cameron sat up straighter, smoothed her glossy blond hair and took a sip of her pinot grigio. "I feel bad for the dog, is all," she said, her body stiff. "I mean, you're never home, and the poor dog is alone all day—"

"You knew that when you got the damned dog," he said, trying to keep a rein on his temper. He wasn't one to lose his cool, but he had no patience for people who chose not to say what they really meant.

"Well, I know," she snapped, "but all I can think is that if you can't even take care of a dog, how can you ever take care of a child?"

"Since I don't have any kids, and don't plan to anytime

soon, I don't think I need to worry about my parenting skills at this point."

He looked past Cameron's shoulder, his gaze locking on the little dark-haired cocktail waitress weaving her way through the crowd with a loaded tray. Gia must have hired her while he'd been out of town, because he didn't recognize her. And since he ate dinner at Ciao Bella almost every night, he was well acquainted with nearly all of the staff.

He couldn't see much of her—she was short and the crowd was thick—but he got the impression of dark, pretty hair, and a figure nearly swallowed up by the white button-down shirt with "Ciao Bella" embroidered over the pocket. He tracked her progress as she worked her way closer to their table, fully intending to flag her down and request another drink since his regular waitress was nowhere in sight. And since Cameron seemed inclined to talk all night about the state of their relationship, a few more drinks were definitely in order.

"Vince, are you even listening? Seriously, when we get married—"

That snapped him to attention like a drive-by bullet. "Married?" He couldn't help it. He burst out laughing. "I'm not marrying anyone," he said.

Then he felt bad when Cameron's face crumpled like paper and she gasped out, "Screw you, Vince!" She'd shoved back her chair and stood up just as the little cocktail waitress was trying to sidle by.

That was when all hell had broken loose.

Now he looked down at his wine-stained shirt and smiled bigger than he should for a man who wasn't getting laid anytime soon. But he couldn't help grinning at the remembered feel of the waitress's curvy little body squirming to get off his lap. Buried underneath the concealing waitress outfit had been a pair of lusciously plump breasts and a ridiculously tiny waist, nicely balanced by the lush, round, firm ass that ground against him as she'd struggled to her feet.

Then he'd seen her face and he'd felt like a dirty old man. At least she wasn't a teenager, he consoled himself. Hell, she had to be at least twenty-one to work in the bar of the restaurant, but he'd bet good money she'd been legal less than a year.

At thirty-five, he didn't exactly have one foot in the grave, but he was long past the days of chasing girls barely out of their teens.

Not to mention that the admiration wasn't mutual. The girl clearly felt horrible about spilling the drinks on him, but hadn't even given him a second glance. Call him arrogant, but he had a mirror and he knew he was good-looking. Combine that with an expensive, if understated wardrobe, and most women who looked his way saw something they liked.

But not her. She'd been focused on making amends, insisting she cover his drinks and appetizers, upset and afraid of his reaction. He would have much preferred to finish his dinner and reassure her that everything was fine, but Cameron hadn't stormed out and gotten a cab as he'd secretly hoped. Instead, she'd waited outside, obviously expecting him to come chasing after her.

Three hours later, he'd been summarily dumped. He supposed he should be more upset. Cameron was, after all, beautiful and successful, the kind of woman other women envied and other men coveted. But since he'd moved to San Francisco four years ago, his relationships always went the same way. He dated a woman for awhile, and though he never gave any hint of getting serious, eventually she wanted more than he was willing to give.

He couldn't blame Cameron for cutting her losses before she wasted any more of her time. She deserved to be with a man who could commit, a man who would marry her, give her what she wanted. Someday Vince would be that kind of man, but not now. At this point in his life, work was his priority, and everyone and everything had to be content with taking a back seat.

Vince jerked at the whiff of dog breath that hit his face right before Chester nailed him with a slobbery swipe of his tongue. "That means you too, buddy." Work was his life right now. He didn't have time to worry about anything else.

2

"What can I get for you?" The following Tuesday, Vince was back at Ciao Bella, smiling up at the cute dark-haired waitress who'd spilled wine on him. She waited to take his order. God, she was pretty. Young, he reminded himself sternly, but ridiculously beautiful, with big, dark eyes, smooth olive skin and bee-stung lips glossed to a high shine. The thought of kissing those lips, licking his way into the dark sweetness of her mouth, had his cock thickening against his zipper in a way that made him glad his crotch was concealed by the table.

She had no inkling of the direction his thoughts were going, and merely smiled a neutral, expectant smile until he finally managed to choke out a reply.

As the waitress went to retrieve his drink, Gia came over to say hello. He stood to kiss both of her cheeks, and Vince noticed something different about her, something he'd started to pick up on Friday but hadn't had time to think about after the commotion Cameron had caused.

In the time he'd known Gia, she'd always faded into the

background, but for the first time in four years, he realized Gia was damned attractive. No, scratch that, the woman was *hot.*

"Did you do something different? Buy a new outfit?"

Gia laughed and rolled her eyes. "Typical guy. Yes, I got a new outfit. I also chopped eight inches off my hair, had it styled, waxed my eyebrows and finally learned how to use makeup."

Vince smiled sheepishly and shrugged. "At least I noticed something."

"So . . . no Cameron?" Gia asked after a beat.

"No. Not anymore."

"Yeah, you look a little down."

He huffed a frustrated laugh and waved his hand dismissively. "Hell, Cameron's not the problem. It's that damn dog she bought me. Chester's gonna drive me insane."

Cameron might not have known it, but she got the last laugh when she'd saddled Vince with a dog.

Chester had been deemed too hyperactive for the atrociously expensive doggy day-care a colleague had recommended, and when Vince had tried taking him to the kennel he'd had a doggy mental breakdown. Chester needed personal, one-on-one attention, both during the days and when Vince traveled out of town. But his housekeeper had flat out refused to keep him in the house with her during the day. As a result, his neighbors had filed five noise complaints in the past week. Vince had had to pay a fine and animal control was threatening to seize the dog.

"I could take him to the animal shelter," he began, but stopped when Gia recoiled in horror. "Exactly my thought. Like I don't have enough to deal with, I have to worry about hiring a damn dog sitter."

The waitress reappeared with his drink and Gia gestured toward her. "I didn't have a chance to formally introduce you last week—Vince, this is my cousin Theresa Bellessi. She just moved back to town a couple weeks ago. Theresa, this is Vince Mattera, one of our best customers." She gave them both a play-nice smile. "Okay. If you'll excuse me, I have to go speak with the chef."

She left them alone.

Vince reached out to shake her hand. Theresa's hand was small, her long fingers tipped with short, buffed nails. But her grip was firm as she clasped his much bigger palm. "Great, now I feel even better about spilling drinks all over you and taking your ridiculous tip for it," she said with a rueful smile.

"Well I figured I better tip for the lap dance," he said, then immediately wished he could take back the obnoxious comment.

Color rose in her cheeks and her lips tipped up at the corners as she leaned a little bit forward and said in a low voice, "If I'd really given you a lap dance, you would have tipped me more than a hundred." A grin pulled at his lips as that image sank into his brain and took root as she straightened back up, once again all business. "Now, are you having dinner as well as cocktails tonight?"

Vince placed his food order and watched her walk away, his gaze pinned to the bounce of her ass under her slim black pants. That, combined with the knowing look that had accompanied her lap dancing comment was enough to send all the blood in his body surging for his groin. His neurons were firing images around his head, none of them suitable for dinner in the peaceful bar of a classy Italian restaurant.

He didn't go for strip clubs, didn't like the idea of having to pay a woman to undress and pretend that she liked him, but now he was gripped by a totally inappropriate fantasy of Theresa dragging him to a back room and slowly, suggestively stripping down to nothing but a g-string as she ground herself against his thighs. He watched her take an order from another customer, her friendly smile and neatly pulled-back hair so at odds with the lurid fantasy he was spinning.

He closed his eyes, banishing the images of a nearly naked Theresa from his brain, wondering what the hell was wrong with him. Theresa Bellessi was no doubt just like her cousin Gia. A nice, traditional, *sheltered* Italian girl, no matter what kind of snappy comments she came up with. And if he wanted to keep eating at his favorite restaurant, he needed to keep that firmly in mind.

Theresa snuck another glance at Vince, still seated in the bar. He'd already closed out his tab and was sipping his drink as his gaze aimlessly drifted over the other patrons. He exchanged greetings with several of the customers, all regulars like himself who she'd gotten to know in the brief time she'd worked here. He smiled at her and raised his drink and she jerked her gaze away, mortified to be caught staring.

"Gorgeous, isn't he?" Gia sighed.

"Who?"

Gia didn't buy her feigned ignorance for a second. "Give me a break. You've been eying him all night."

"Have not," Theresa said childishly as she punched a drink order into the restaurant computer. But she had, and was embarrassed that it hadn't gone unnoticed. She couldn't help it. There was something about him, a lethal combination of rugged good looks and earthy animal magnetism that drew her in like a tractor beam. She found herself wanting to run her fingers over all his hard edges and corded muscles, wondered how they would feel pressing up against her own soft curves.

The overtly sexual thought shocked her. It had been so long since she'd been even remotely interested in sex. For the last year, she'd been only going through the motions with her ex-boyfriend, feeling like that part of her had been lost somewhere in the wreckage that she'd let her life become.

Now, she felt the grip of arousal curl in her belly, completely unexpected.

Don't even go there, she told herself sternly. She'd come back to San Francisco to get away from the last guy who had turned her head. She needed to focus on getting her life back on track, and that meant not getting distracted by trivial things like hot, rich, successful men and the lustful urges they inspired. "He's good looking, I suppose, if you like really big, muscular guys."

Gia raised a skeptical, perfectly groomed brow. "And you don't?"

Theresa shrugged noncommittally. "I've got more important things to think about, as you well know."

Gia's face expression turned serious. "Did you find a place yet?"

Theresa swallowed back frustration and finished entering her drink order. "The only place I found that I could afford is a room on 14th Street."

She wrinkled her nose as she remembered her visit earlier that afternoon. Even in the middle of the day, Theresa hadn't felt safe walking around by herself. When her prospective roommate had opened the door, Theresa had been greeted by a female face rendered nearly unrecognizable from numerous piercings and tattoos. Which wouldn't have been that bad—Theresa knew lots of nice people with piercings and tattoos.

But the woman also had the gaunt, stringy frame and hollow-eyed gaze of an addict. And based on the track marks marching up and down the woman's scrawny arms, Theresa would bet that heroin was her drug of choice. She'd realized very quickly that unless she was willing to put up with lowlifes and the constant risk of having her stuff stolen, that wasn't the place for her.

"You can't live there," a deep voice laced with a heavy New York accent echoed her thoughts. "That neighborhood is full of junkies and criminals."

Theresa looked up to find Vince blatantly eavesdropping on

their conversation. She looked him up and down. With his five hundred dollar shoes and a Rolex that would have served as a nice down payment on a house, his look screamed Nob Hill. "Thanks for the tip, but we can't all afford to live in your neighborhood."

"How do you like dogs?"

Theresa frowned at the seemingly random question. Gia, in contrast, smiled as though in dawning comprehension. "Dogs?"

"Yeah. You like dogs?"

"I'm not sure I want to know where this conversation is going, but sure, I like dogs okay."

"Good. You can move in with me."

Theresa stepped back in surprise. "Isn't that a rather major step for this stage in our relationship?"

Vince laughed, his dark eyes crinkling at the corners. "Here's the deal. I have this dog. He needs attention, he needs training, and I don't have time to do it. Plus, I travel a lot and I need someone to stay with him when I'm out of town."

"You can't just hire a trainer?"

"Chester is," he pressed his lips together as though searching for the right word, "challenging." Gia laughed, unsuccessfully smothering it when Vince shot her a quelling look. "I need in-home care."

"Like a dog nanny," Theresa said.

He frowned as though not liking the way that sounded. "I suppose you could put it that way. Point is, I have a big place. I could let you live there in exchange for helping me take care of Chester."

Her gaze narrowed as she studied him, trying to see the truth behind that all too charming smile. Sure, he was beautiful to look at and seemed like a decent enough guy, but who knew what he was really like at home? And what if he was just luring her in with this whole dogsitting thing, then expected her to do more in exchange for a reduced rent?

Maybe that wouldn't be such a hardship, an evil little voice said.

"Sorry, I'm looking for female roommates only."

"You could take the guest cottage. It's a studio, no separate bedroom, but it's fully equipped with a kitchen and cable."

Theresa's brows shot to her hairline. "Guest cottage? Exactly how big of a place do you have?"

"Huge," Gia said before he could answer.

"You start work at what, five?" Vince fished a business card out of his pocket and scribbled an address on the back. "Come by tomorrow at twelve-fifteen and take a look."

He nodded good night to Gia and left without even waiting for Theresa to say yes, as though he was used to having people do exactly as he ordered.

"Take it," Gia said.

"I don't think so," Theresa said, shaking her head as she picked up her tray. "All I have to do is take care of a dog? There's got to be a catch."

"Not with Vince. He's been coming in here a long time. He's a straight-up guy. You have nothing to worry about."

Theresa wasn't convinced.

"You want to sleep on your mom's couch indefinitely?"

"Of course not," Theresa said. "But I don't think Vince's place is the answer."

Theresa began to rethink that the moment she stepped into her parents' house several hours later. She crept up the stairs of the old Victorian, feeling like a teenager sneaking in after curfew.

Not that she'd ever done that. She'd been a model daughter up until three years ago when she'd foolishly skipped town with Mark Silverton. Her father had yet to forgive her.

She winced as a stair squeaked under her foot. She didn't know what she was so worried about. Her parents were always in bed by ten, and it was nearly midnight. There was virtually no chance of running into her father.

She reached the top of the stairs and was headed down the narrow hallway to her room when she noticed that the kitchen light had been left on. She paused to turn it off and nearly jumped out of her skin when she saw her father sitting at the kitchen table reading the paper.

He looked up, and for a moment they locked eyes. It was the first time she'd seen him since her Uncle Alberto's funeral. Her father didn't look happy about it. Up until now it had been easy for him to avoid her, and Theresa was sure that was the only reason he'd given into Theresa's mother and let her stay with them until she found another place.

"Hi, Daddy," Theresa said tentatively.

His expression glazed over and he stared through her as though she wasn't there. *You're dead to me.* The last words he ever spoke to her echoed in her brain as a cold lump settled in the pit of her stomach. Judging from the way he'd turned his attention back to his paper without so much as acknowledging her presence, he hadn't changed his mind.

That's what happened when a twenty-first century girl finally rebelled against her father's nineteenth-century mindset. And that was just because she'd been "living in sin." Theresa didn't even want to think about her father's reaction if he ever found out more details about her last year in New York.

She walked slowly down the hall, her father's disapproval settling over her like a lead cloak. She snapped the light on in the room where she was staying. It used to be hers, but when she'd left with Mark her parents had removed any trace of her existence. Her posters, books, clothes were all gone. It had been reclaimed as a combination office and guest room. Where Theresa's double bed with its fluffy white comforter had stood, there was now a fold out couch that Theresa meticulously folded and put away each morning. Her white dresser and mirror had been replaced by a large desk topped by her parents' home computer.

She sank wearily onto the couch and kicked off her shoes. When Gia had called her and encouraged Theresa to come back home, Theresa had felt like she had a chance to get her life back on track, get it back to the way it was supposed to be.

Some life. She was twenty-four years old, broke, and had ditched her education and caused what appeared to be a permanent rift with her father to move across the country and shack up with her lowlife boyfriend. Now she had the honor of being an unwanted guest in her parents' house.

She pulled Vince's business card out of her pocket and studied the address he'd scribbled in his bold, messy handwriting. She recognized the neighborhood as one of San Francisco's ritziest. His offer dangled in front of her, tantalizing her. A place of her own in a beautiful, safe neighborhood. And all she had to do was play with a dog.

It sounded so perfect, but she didn't want to get her hopes up. She looked around her girlhood bedroom, now a sterile home office and thought of her father down the hall, barely tolerating her presence in his house.

Vince's offer sounded too good to be true—there had to be a catch.

Screw the catch. She needed to get out of here.

3

"How's the place?"

Theresa could hear the clang of silverware in the background as Gia spoke. "Good," Theresa grunted as she hefted another box of books and moved it over by the bookshelves. It was Saturday, and she was doing her best to get settled into the guest cottage before she had to go to work. "Thanks again for letting me borrow your car." Theresa hadn't had much stuff in storage, but she'd still managed to pack Gia's car to capacity.

"No problem. How's the dog? Is he giving you any trouble?"

Theresa checked out the blond, drooling lump in the corner. As though sensing her stare, Chester raised his head and gave his tail a thump. "I don't know what the big deal is. He seems like a good dog. Well, except for the humping thing, of course." When she'd first come to look at the place and meet Chester, the dog had responded to her scratch on the ears by immediately jumping up and going at her leg. Vince scrambled to yank the dog off, relieved that Theresa thought it was more funny than anything.

Vince came in with a box, his biceps stretching the sleeves of his T-shirt as his muscles strained at the weight. "Where do you want this?"

"Anywhere you can find space," Theresa said. Vince dropped the box and went out for another load.

"Was that Vince?" Gia asked.

"He's helping me bring my stuff in. And," she said in a lower tone, "providing excellent eye candy." That was the understatement of the year. In his threadbare T-shirt and well worn jeans, he should have looked like a slob. But somehow the shirt emphasized his wide, muscular shoulders and corded arms. And the way those jeans hugged his perfect ass should have been a crime. Theresa had considered herself dead below the waist for the past year or so, and it had been ages since she'd given a guy a second look.

But all day she'd found herself staring after Vince, tracking his moves with her tongue practically hanging out.

"If I didn't have Gabe, I'd be jealous," Gia sighed. "So maybe you and Vince—"

Theresa cut her off before Gia could even voice the thought. "Bite your tongue! The last thing I need is another man in my life to screw it all up. Besides, judging from the woman he was in with last week, I'm not even close to his type. And just between you and me," she said, her voice dropping to a stage whisper, "you should see how neat his house is. You wouldn't believe it, Gia, I mean, absolutely nothing is out of place. It's kind of creepy."

"What does that have to do with anything?"

"You have to wonder about a guy who takes cleanliness that seriously."

"You don't think Vince is gay?"

"No, not at all," Theresa said. "But I think he's kind of anal—you know, one of those guys who likes to put a towel down before sex so he doesn't mess up his designer sheets."

Gia laughed. "But I bet it would be a really nice towel."

"And he probably wouldn't want to mess that up either. Maybe he uses a tarp."

"I think this is the last of it."

Theresa felt her body go first cold, then hot with embarrassment at the sound of Vince's voice. Oh God, had he heard her speculating about his sexual habits? But Vince gave no sign of having heard as he stared at her expectantly and hefted the box in a way that made his forearm muscles shift and tighten under his darkly tanned skin.

Theresa hung up with her cousin and motioned for Vince to put the box on the bed.

"How about I show you the rest of the house before you have to get ready for work? I have to leave for New York tomorrow and I want you to know where everything is."

Theresa slipped on her flip flops, half anticipating, half dreading the tour of Vince's house. Mansion, really. When she'd come to look at the place earlier in the week, he'd just started showing her around when he got a call from the office and had to hurry back.

From that brief glimpse, Theresa had seen that Vince's house was perfectly, expensively decorated, and, as she mentioned to Gia, clean—as in eat off the floors or perform surgery clean. So clean Theresa almost took off her flip flops as she stepped inside the foyer, but then worried about the state of her feet.

It was nearly impossible not to gape as Vince led her through the entryway, the sound of her flip-flops slapping against her feet mingled with the clicking of Chester's nails against the floor.

"This is the sitting room," he said, opening a door to her left and gesturing inside. "I don't really ever go in there. That's the living room," he gestured across the hall. "I don't really go in there either.

"I'm sensing a theme."

His rough laugh tugged at someplace low in her belly. "I work a lot and travel several times a month, so I don't spend a whole lot of time here."

"Why do you need such a big place?"

"Believe me, I've asked myself that several times since I moved in." He led her down the hall to a gourmet kitchen, complete with a commercial-grade stove and double convection ovens. He opened one side of the stainless steel refrigerator and gestured inside. "Even though I eat most of my meals out, my housekeeper Magda keeps the fridge stocked with the basics. Feel free to help yourself to anything you want—"

"No really, I eat dinner at the restaurant every night, and I can make do with the kitchen in the apartment."

He held up a large, silencing hand. "I mean it, make yourself at home. I'm hardly here anyway, and trust me, you're not going to want to spend all day in your place with Chester."

Hearing his name, Chester came over and sat directly on Theresa's feet. "We can always go outside," she said, trying to get her feet out from under the dog's butt. But when she shifted, Chester scooted backward, keeping his furry ass firmly planted. "Or we can go to the park."

"Whatever," Vince said. "Just know that you have the run of the house."

He backtracked down the hall and Chester mercifully got up to follow him before the bones in her feet were pulverized. Vince trotted up the stairs, giving Theresa a mouthwatering view of his muscular butt flexing under his jeans. A hot flush seemed to cover her entire body. What the hell was wrong with her? Why, after so long, had her libido decided to return with such a vengeance? And why with Vince? Sure, he was thigh-meltingly hot, and rich to boot. What woman wouldn't want a taste of that?

But Theresa had known a lot of good looking men—hell, her ex-boyfriend could have been a model. So it wasn't just

Vince's rugged handsomeness she was responding to. Something else about him called to her, pulled at her, to the point where every room he showed her elicited fantasies of them in a naked, sweaty tangle. On the sitting room couch. On the grand piano in the living room. On the kitchen table.

Despite her comment to Gia, Theresa had the feeling sex with Vince would be earthy, lusty, and downright messy.

She was so absorbed in her thoughts that she didn't realize Vince had stopped. She bumped into his back, and her hands came up to grip his hips reflexively to steady herself. Her nose was buried in the deep, muscular groove that ran down the center of his back.

Without thinking, she took a long, deep inhale. He smelled delicious, dark and spicy and male. She took another long whiff. A wet doggy nose against her leg shocked her out of her lustful haze and she jerked away as though scalded.

Vince gave her a puzzled look. Thank God, he didn't seem to notice she was getting off from smelling him. She looked up and realized they were standing in the doorway of what had to be the master suite. An enormous, extra-long king size bed dominated one corner, and a leather upholstered bench sat at the foot. Decorated in shades of chocolate brown and furnished with heavy wood and leather, the room was a purely masculine retreat.

Theresa could too easily imagine herself on that bed, spread out like a feast while Vince flexed and strained over her. Appalled at the direction of her thoughts, she thrust the vision from her mind. She had to put a stop to this, make it clear to him and mostly to herself that nothing would ever happen between them. They were landlord and tenant. Employer and dogsitter. That was all.

"Why are you showing me your bedroom?" Theresa asked.

To be honest, Vince wasn't sure himself, and at this particular moment he wished he hadn't. Because right now he was having a really hard time coming up with a good argument against talking Theresa into spending the rest of the afternoon in his oversize bed with him.

Not for the first time, he questioned whether or not it was a good idea to have her move in, even if it was in a separate living space. He'd found her attractive from the start, but had stupidly convinced himself it was no big deal. He was a thirty-five-year-old man, not some horny teenager with no control over his emotions and sexual impulses.

Now he wasn't so sure. His attraction to her had only grown over the past week when he'd eaten at Ciao Bella every night as was his custom. His gaze had tracked her as she moved around the bar, his brain concocting more and more elaborate scenarios that all ended the same way—with him naked and her stripped of her oversize uniform shirt and tight black pants. Sometimes they were in the back seat of his Mercedes. Sometimes they were on the bar of the restaurant after hours.

But usually they were right here in his bedroom.

Her comment to Gia echoed in his head. Theresa thought he was anal, did she? He'd love nothing more than to show her that the only time any woman had ever called him anal in bed was when he was shoving his cock up her ass.

He knew exactly what it would be like, how good it would be to have her. Her dark hair would spill over the pillow. Her skin would be creamy and sweet as he ran his tongue up the inside of her thighs. Her small hands would grip the wooden slats of his headboard as he sank into her tight, lithe body. And she would be tight. He'd have to make her so wet first with his fingers and tongue—

"Vince? I asked you a question." He snapped his gaze up from where it had settled on Theresa's breasts to her face. Her eyebrows pulled down over her dark eyes and her full lips pulled down at the corners.

Whatever he'd been thinking, the feeling definitely wasn't mutual. Which was a good thing, he told himself. "It goes with the rest of the house," he said lamely. "Here's the bathroom." He walked through his walk-in closet into the attached bathroom with its slate tiled shower and oversize jacuzzi tub.

He backtracked through the bedroom and led her into the attached media room, where Chester had already made himself comfortable on the sofa. "And if you ever want to watch a movie, I've got the flat screen hooked up with surround sound, the whole nine yards—"

She held up a hand to put a stop to his tour guide shtick. "Look, let's get a few things straight," she said, pulling back her shoulders and raising to her full height. Which was still about a foot shorter than he was. "I appreciate you helping me out and letting me live here—"

"Believe me, you're helping me—"

"Let me finish. As I was saying, while I appreciate your help, I don't want there to be any misunderstandings about what's going on here. I'm taking care of Chester and that's it. I won't be taking care of you, if you know what I mean."

The last was accompanied by a crude hand gesture that left no room for misunderstanding.

Vince burst out laughing, despite the fact that he was offended she would actually think he'd expect sexual favors in exchange for letting her stay here. "I don't know what kind of people you've been hanging out with, but I can assure you I'll never expect you to pay rent on your back."

Theresa's face flooded with color and she cleared her throat uncomfortably. "Good. I'm glad we have that out of the way. And speaking of rent, I can't live here for free."

"Theresa, I don't need—"

"Yeah, it's pretty obvious you don't need money. But I'm not comfortable staying for free. I'm not a charity case."

She was so spunky and full of pride, but he didn't have to

look too hard to see life had thrown her a couple of major blows lately. It was ironic, all the women he had dated, successful career women who made very good livings on their own, and none of them had ever hesitated to let him pay for anything. In fact they seemed to accept expensive gifts and vacations as their due.

Then there was Theresa, scraping by on her waitress job, insisting on paying rent even when he clearly didn't need it.

Then again, Theresa wasn't his girlfriend. "I don't think you're a charity case," he sighed, rubbing at the bridge of his nose. "Pay me whatever you think is fair, but trust me. After you've spent more time with Chester, you'll realize you're doing plenty to earn your keep."

4

After nearly a week with Chester, Theresa was beginning to believe Vince when he said she would earn her keep.

"The dog is a menace," she groaned to Gia and tiredly surveyed the Friday night crowd.

"How many pairs of shoes have you lost now?" Gia asked.

"Counting my gold flats? That's four."

Suffice it to say, Chester had a chewing problem. She'd discovered it the last Sunday when she'd gone to work. Since Vince had already left on his business trip, she'd locked Chester in her apartment, thinking that since she had a smaller space there would be less for him to get into. Chester had entertained himself by reducing her beloved black Mary Jane pumps into a few scraps and a stray heel. Damn dog had to pick her favorites, and not the platform stilettos she kept meaning to donate to Goodwill.

The bartender, Nico, placed the last glass of wine on her tray. Theresa picked it up and winced as a sharp pain shot up her arm.

"Still bugging you?" Gia asked. "Maybe you should take the night off."

"I'm fine," Theresa said shrugging off her cousin's look of concern. No way was she going to leave her cousin short a server on a busy Friday night. Besides, Theresa couldn't afford to lose the tips. With steady income and the money she was saving on rent, she might be able to enroll in classes part time within a couple of weeks.

So she ignored the throbbing of her wrist and the twinge in her knee, both courtesy of Chester. Her injuries had happened at the first of Chester's obedience classes. They'd barely gotten inside the gate of the dog run at a local park before Chester, delighted to be in the presence of other dogs, had lunged forward, using all of his considerable weight to yank against the leash.

Theresa had been yanked off her feet and dragged several yards before she managed to untangle the leash from her wrist. As soon as he was free, Chester bounded across the dog run and had started exuberantly humping a hapless Rhodesian ridgeback. Theresa struggled to her feet and was met by the glares of the other students.

"You're going to have to keep better control of your dog if you want to keep attending class," the teacher said.

"I'm in class so I can get better control of him," Theresa snapped as she grabbed Chester by the middle and pulled him off the ridgeback, who seemed willing to take whatever Chester wanted to dish out.

The class had gone downhill from there, and at the conclusion the teacher observed that perhaps Chester would do better with a private trainer, and gave Theresa the card of someone she recommended.

By the time Gia dropped her off after midnight, Theresa felt like she'd been pummeled. Between her twice daily walks which were more like tug-of-war matches with Chester, and spending hours on her feet every night, she was beat. All she wanted was a hot bath, a glass of wine, and a long sleep. To that end, tonight she was putting Chester to bed in the main house instead of letting him sleep in her cottage. She knew Vince's housekeeper arrived at seven-thirty every morning and would let the dog out in time to prevent any accidents.

Or, she thought uncharitably, the housekeeper could clean up the accidents, since Vince no doubt paid her well. Right now, Theresa didn't care if Chester trashed the house—she just wanted to insure that she wouldn't be awakened at the crack of dawn by the feel of hot dog breath in her face.

She unlocked her door, relieved to see that Chester, for once, seemed to have left her shoes alone. "Come on, boy," she said, coaxing him out of the cottage and across the yard to the back door of the main house.

As she unlocked the door and punched in the key to the alarm, Chester pushed past her and hauled ass down the hall, the click of his nails against the wood floor echoing in the silent house. Damn. She took off after him, calling his name. If he was going to stay here, she had to shut him in the kitchen. She called again, and he didn't come. What next?

She heard the unmistakable thump-thump-thump of Chester trotting upstairs, and followed the jingling of his dog tags into Vince's bedroom. "Chester, come here!"

He barely spared her a glance as he climbed up onto the couch and settled into his favorite corner. She sighed, went over to the couch, grabbed him by the collar and tugged. Deadweight. Theresa collapsed on the couch and thought longingly of the bath and wine she'd been dreaming of all evening.

Make yourself at home. Vince's words echoed in her head. She shouldn't.

But now that the thought had entered her mind, she couldn't stop thinking about that gigantic spa-size tub just a few yards away. And she knew the "cheap" wine Vince kept in his kitchen for everyday consumption would be far superior to the bottle she'd bought on special at the grocery store.

Don't do it. Don't take advantage.

But he'd said to make herself at home when she moved in, hadn't he? He'd even said it again before he'd left last Sunday.

But he probably didn't mean take a bath in his bathroom.

Oh, but she wanted to soak in that tub, feel the pulsing jets massage her tired body. He wouldn't mind. He wouldn't even know, because he was out of town for another two days.

She pushed herself off the couch and went downstairs to get a glass of wine before she talked herself out of it. Feeling a delicious sense of naughtiness, like she was getting away with something, she filled the tub. Unfortunately, Vince didn't have any good bath oil or bubble bath, but she decided it was worth the sacrifice as she submerged her body in the tub and turned on the jets. Sipping at her wine, she let the heat of the water and the alcohol do their magic.

She leaned back and closed her eyes, luxuriating in the feel of the jets gently pummeling her body. Eyes still closed, she fumbled around for the soap and lazily ran it up and down her arm. She recognized its scent as the same soap Vince undoubtedly used, something that reminded her of evergreen and mint. It was pleasant, but nothing like when it was combined with the scent of Vince's skin.

She imagined she could smell him right now, that she had her face buried in the crook of his neck. She felt a pulse of arousal between her legs and started to push the inappropriate thoughts of Vince aside as she had every time they'd tried to invade her consciousness. *Just let go for once,* that naughty little voice encouraged her. *When was the last time you felt anything remotely sexual for anyone? Give yourself this little taste of pleasure. What harm could it possibly do?*

She kept her eyes firmly shut, knowing if she caught a glimpse of herself she'd chicken out. Tentatively, as though she was afraid of being caught, Theresa ran her palm over her stomach. Her own hand felt awkward against her skin, it had been so long since she'd touched herself like this. Not that she had a problem with it. But because she hadn't wanted to lately. Hell, not for a really long time.

But now, all she had to do was think of Vince. Oh, yeah, her body remembered what was what.

She skimmed her hand lower, over her thighs, imagining it was Vince's big, tanned hand pushing insistently between her legs. His palm cupping her sex and sliding his fingers in between flesh wet with more than water. She gasped in shock as her own fingers brushed her clitoris, having forgotten the sharp, almost painful pleasure arousal could bring. She slid her fingers up, down, around the hard knot of her clit, reacquainting herself with her body, reminding herself of how she liked to be touched. Her breath shortened and her hips rocked against her fingers as she stroked.

When the cab dropped Vince off, he noticed the lights on in Theresa's place. Even though it was late and he was exhausted from the long flight he momentarily considered knocking on her door to see if she wanted to come over for a drink.

But he quickly scrapped the idea because he knew damn well a drink wasn't all he wanted. He didn't know what it was about her, but she made him feel things he hadn't felt since, well, ever. Dark, primal, possessive things. He wanted to spend hours, days, exploring every bare inch of her creamy skin, wanted to suck and lick her luscious tits while he fucked her in every possible position. But at the same time, he had the strangest urge to take care of her, protect her, an odd feeling from a man who had learned to fend for himself and expected everyone else in his life to do the same.

He'd been relieved that he had a business trip planned for the week after she moved in. While he was gone, without the constant stimulation of seeing her, he'd managed to convince himself his attraction to her was a passing thing, easy enough to ignore once the initial novelty wore off. He'd dated some of San Francisco's most eligible single women, all of whom had left him, if not cold, at least unimpressed. He sure as hell wasn't going to be felled by a little Italian cocktail waitress easily ten years his junior.

Even if she was exactly the kind of little Italian girl his mother had always wanted him to bring home. But it was no secret that his family's idea of what kind of life he should live and his own were not even in the same ballpark.

Still, Theresa Bellessi seemed to have grabbed him by the balls and wasn't letting go any time soon. And any illusion that he'd gotten over his attraction during his time away was obliterated by the mouthwatering vision that greeted him now.

He stood in the doorway of his bathroom, afraid if he so much as took a breath she would disappear. He blinked hard, thinking she would vanish because there was no way this was real. He'd done nothing to deserve to have his fantasy come to such vivid life.

But Theresa was still there when he opened his eyes. Her dark hair spilled over the back of the tub, the jets making the water churn and surge around her small but voluptuous form. One arm was flung over the side of the tub, her fingers gripping the edge while her other hand . . .

He only had to look at her face to know what her other hand was doing. Her cheeks were flushed red, her lips even more swollen than usual. Her eyes were squeezed shut and her face was tense with pleasure.

Her lips parted and his cock surged against his fly as he anticipated her moan. But she didn't make a sound, just let out a harsh breath as her body shifted beneath the water.

It should have felt sordid, like the cheesiest of set-ups in low budget porn, but it was anything but. It was arousing, yes, almost unbearably so. And beautiful. So fucking beautiful it made his chest hurt as he fought the urge to snatch her from the tub and lay her across the upholstered chaise longue and finish what she'd started.

She shifted, arching her throat back. He wanted to run his tongue along the taut cords. His breath sped up to match hers. He was so hard he hurt, and he palmed himself through his pants, squeezing his dick as though he could will it down into submission. God, he should leave. This was so wrong, watching her during such a private, personal moment. But his feet were cemented to the floor, his gaze locked on her face as her face morphed into a mask of ecstasy.

She was about to come. He stroked his rigid cock, wishing with everything he had that he was the one giving it to her, that he was the one stroking and slipping his fingers against her juicy core. A man with any shred of decency would have left, but he couldn't. He needed to watch her, needed to experience her pleasure, even vicariously. Then, he vowed, he would go. Not before.

At that moment, her eyes flew open with a gasp. When she saw him, she gasped again, this time in shock. Vince's hand froze on his cock as he waited for her to start screaming.

Every cell froze in place as her brain registered the fact that this was no hallucination. That Vince was actually in the bathroom with her, watching her . . . touch herself. She'd been right on the edge of climax, so surprised she was still capable of one after so long, that her eyes had flown open at that first pulse emanating from her core.

And there he was. She should have felt embarrassed, humiliated to be caught doing this, while thinking of him, no less. But the sight of him, his dark eyes so hot and hungry as he stared at her like he wanted to consume her, only made that pulse of pleasure tighten into a near painful knot between her legs. Her gaze dropped lower, to where his big hand pressed against what looked like a mammoth erection. She licked her lips, imagining how it would look as it sprung free. So long, so thick, so perfectly designed to drive her insane.

As though it had a will of its own, the hand that had frozen between her legs when she'd seen him began to move again, fingers swirling, stroking, as she kept her gaze locked on Vince's burning stare. Some tiny part of her asked her what she thought she was doing. This was not like her. Despite her brief career of dancing nearly naked in front of men, she was modest, even reserved when it came to sex.

She did not do things like masturbate for an audience, especially in front of a man she barely knew.

But she couldn't stop. It was as though something had taken over, driving her to do this in front of him, do this for him. Because she knew he loved it, loved watching her, and knowing that made her want to do it more.

With a groan that almost sounded like a growl he kicked off his shoes and moved toward her. An unfamiliar, throaty purr emanated from her throat as she watched his progress. He tangled his fingers in her hair and her lips parted eagerly for his kiss. His tongue was hot and hungry as it slid between her lips, stroking and licking into her mouth. She brought both arms up to wrap around his neck, pulling him tighter as his spicy taste and scent flooded her senses.

She was soaking his shirt but he didn't seem to mind. He didn't even roll up his sleeve as he plunged his hand beneath the churning water to find her, nice and hot and slippery wet. One brush of his thick fingers and her orgasm, which had retreated in the shock of seeing him, was once again roaring to life. She moaned into his mouth and spread her thighs as he slid a finger down her slit and sank it inside her.

His thumb made lazy circles around her clit and she clutched his shoulders for balance as her hips rocked insistently against his hand. Pleasure was building again, and the fact that it was his hand, his fingers on her and in her, his lips on hers and his tongue in her mouth made it infinitely more intense than what she'd felt on her own.

His finger was joined by a second, pumping steadily inside her as his thumb worked the knot of nerves. Theresa was vaguely aware of someone making high-pitched, whimpering sounds, then realized, dazed, they were coming from her and Vince was eagerly swallowing them up as he stroked her higher and higher.

And then she was blowing apart, flying into a million little pieces as pleasure exploded against his fingers and surged in waves until every fiber of her being pulsed.

His kiss gentled and his hand cupped her sex almost protectively as the last little bursts of her orgasm sizzled through her body. She forced her eyes open, her lids feeling like lead. She met his gaze. He looked as shell-shocked as she felt.

And hungry. Like he was a lion and she was a juicy piece of red meat. Because he hadn't come yet, and he wanted to. More than that, he wanted *her* to make him come, and that thought alone was enough to make desire flare to life in her newly awakened body.

"I'm sorry," he said, his voice strained as he moved to take his hand away. "I shouldn't have done that—"

"Shut up," she said, more harshly than she'd meant to. But the last thing she wanted to hear right now was that he was sorry for being here, sorry for touching her. There would be time for her to regret this later—and she knew she would. She would be foolish to let another man get under her skin, have power over her, even if it was power born from pleasure.

Right now she wanted to revel in her newly awakened sexuality, wallow in the feel of a man's hands on her body. It had been so long since she'd craved the feel of a man's cock sliding thick and hard inside her. For so long sex had been about going through the motions, feigning interest and excitement long enough to get it over with. Now, out of nowhere, she was feeling again, craving again, wanting again.

She wasn't an idiot—she knew this sudden surge in her libido had everything to do with Vince. He made her want to strip him naked, run her hands and mouth over every ripple of muscle, taste him in her mouth, feel him inside her. And no matter how out of her league he was, no matter that she knew he would never view her as more than a casual fuck, tonight she wanted to experience everything he could make her feel, regardless of the consequences.

She rose from the tub, any self-consciousness over her generously curved form vanishing under the heat of Vince's dark, covetous gaze. She stepped out of the tub and pressed herself wet and naked against Vince's still clothed form. He cupped his hands around her ass and lifted her to meet his kiss, his touch almost frantic as he guided her legs around his waist.

He held her like she weighed nothing, his big hands firm and hot as they gripped her hips. She shifted her weight so his erection was nestled perfectly against her sex. Her legs gripped tighter as she ground against him, her body quivering in anticipation of accepting his thick length.

His groan rumbled through her and she felt the world tilt as he placed her on her back on the padded chaise, her legs still hooked around his hips as he came down over her. The damp cotton fabric of his shirt abraded her nipples, the wool gabardine of his pants chafed the skin of her inner thighs. She tugged his shirttail impatiently from his waistband and in a demanding tone she barely recognized as her own said, "I want you naked, Vince. Now."

Vince sucked the soft skin of her neck between his teeth, feeling like the tip of his dick was about to blow off as his clumsy fingers worked to undo the buttons of his soaking wet shirt. He couldn't believe this was happening, that instead of screaming and ordering him out when she'd caught him watching her, Theresa had stared at him, her eyes mirroring his pulse-pounding hunger. The primitive part of his brain took that as an invitation, even as his more civilized side warned him he was only seeing what he wanted to see.

But there was no mistaking the hungry way her lips parted under his, no mistaking the way she voraciously sucked his tongue into her mouth. And the way she'd eagerly spread her legs and clung to him when he'd fucked her with his fingers—there was no question she wanted it.

Feeling her come, watching her face as she exploded was one of the most perfect moments of his life. Still, he felt obligated to give her an out, to let her pull away and retreat to the safety of the cottage before he spent the night discovering how many ways and how many times he could make her come. Up until this point she'd shown no interest in him whatsoever, had made it clear she didn't want any kind of sexual relationship. He'd caught her at a weak moment, he reminded himself. At that moment, maybe any warm male body would do. As distasteful as that thought was, he had to acknowledge it.

But the way she said his name, so sure and strong as she demanded he get naked, and he knew, gut deep, that she wanted him too. If it was even half as much as he wanted her, he was in for a wild ride. His shirt landed with a plop on the tile floor and his pants followed. And then, holy-Mary-mother-of-God he was naked, his overheated body sliding against her wet silky skin. *Get a condom ready. Do the right thing.* He broke away long enough to grab a foil packet and got right back to her.

He threaded his fingers in her hair and brought his chest down to meet hers, groaning at the soft weight of her breasts pressed against him. She flattened her hands against his back, sliding her palms up and down the long muscles as she purred in approval.

His mouth ate at hers, sucking and nipping at her lips and

tongue. He liked kissing as much as the next guy, but he'd never wanted it like this, never felt like he couldn't get enough of a woman's mouth. He could kiss Theresa for hours, days, even as his cock surged insistently against the damp skin of her inner thigh.

Theresa squirmed under him, moving until she cradled his shaft between her legs. He squeezed his eyes shut and fought not to come as his cock slid between the plump lips of her pussy. He reached down and thumbed his cock into place, heard her breath catch as the broad head stretched her wide. One thrust of his hips and he would be buried deep.

He stopped, every muscle quivering with restraint as he struggled to hold himself back.

"What's wrong?" she said in a breathless voice that sounded almost apprehensive. "I want you—I want you to keep going." Was it him, or was there a slight note of surprise as she said that?

Even though it about killed him, he pulled free from the hot pressure of her body, kissing away her protests as his hands slid covetously up and down her sides. "I want you too," he said, "so much that if I get inside you right now I'm going to come too fast. I need to slow down," he said as much to himself at her. Pushing up on his arms, he spent several moments just looking at her. Her body was like a living wet dream. Her tits were lushly plump, with tight dark nipples puckered up into eager points. Her hips flared out from a waist so small he bet he could circle it with his hands.

His gaze roved farther south, to the sweet patch of curls that topped the hottest, tightest pussy he'd ever felt clenching and rippling around his fingers. He couldn't wait to feel her coming around his cock.

Which she wouldn't have the chance to do, not if he kept going at his current breakneck pace. And he didn't want it to end too soon, not with her. Even though he'd only known her a week, he had the weird sensation that he'd waited a lot longer for this moment, and he wasn't about to let it end with a couple of quick thrusts and lights out.

He enjoyed sex and had always been a considerate lover, but he'd never seen the point of drawing it out for long once his partner had gotten off. But tonight, he wanted it to be different. Different with her. Vince wanted to lick her and stroke her so that by the time he fucked her she was dripping wet, mindless with the need to have him.

She lifted her hand to cup his neck and threaded her fingers through his hair. He leaned into her touch like a pet seeking a scratch from his mistress. "It's okay," she whispered, running her other hand down his stomach until it hovered above the swollen head of his cock. "I've already . . . had mine, if you know what I mean."

His laugh was harsh as it exploded out of his chest. "Baby, you're not even close to done. And I've got all kinds of things I want to do to you before I get mine."

5

Theresa didn't think it was possible for her to get more turned on, but Vince's words, combined with the molten hot look in his dark eyes, sent a fresh surge of lust pounding through her body.

She'd never had a man look at her like he did, and that alone was enough to send her spinning out of control. Oh, men had looked at her with lust all right. Not too long ago, she'd made a living based on that fact.

But Vince's expression as he stared at her naked form was different. It was plenty lustful, but mixed in with the lust was need, even reverence. Like he was in awe to be naked in the same room with her.

She knew it was foolish to read too much into the simple fact that he was a guy who had found a naked, willing chick in his tub and was taking advantage of the situation.

But God, when he looked at her like that, when he said the things he said, she wanted to believe this was special. That *she* was special. That whatever it was about him that had awakened this wildly sexual side of her—he saw something similar in her.

She knew better than to let herself get swept away by her own romantic idealism. And tomorrow would be soon enough to deal with the harsh reality. Tonight she wanted to indulge in the illusion that all the intensity and emotion she sensed was real.

Theresa lay back and closed her eyes, tangling her fingers in the thick waves of his hair as he took her mouth again. Her hands swept up his back, loving the way his muscles rippled under his hot, silky skin. She shifted under him as his lips trailed down her neck and across her chest. His big, broad hands roamed up her stomach and sides, squeezing her hips appreciatively. His muscled chest brushed against her breasts, its light dusting of hair teasing her exquisitely sensitive nipples.

He was so big. The first night she'd seen him, she'd been struck by his size, conscious of how easy it would be for someone like him to overpower a woman if he wanted to. But now she wasn't intimidated at all, her body instinctively responding to his touch as though it knew he was solely focused on her pleasure.

Vince murmured a low sound of approval as his hand closed over the heavy weight of her breasts. Hot and wet, his tongue circled around one nipple before his lips closed over it with firm, sucking pressure. She arched eagerly against him, shifting her legs and hips until she could feel the firm pressure of his abs against her sex.

"God, you have gorgeous tits," he rumbled, sucking and nipping at her breasts until she was moaning and writhing underneath him, rubbing herself against him in an effort to ease the ache between her thighs.

"You want me, don't you?" he said in a rough whisper. "You want me to make you come again?" His hand slid down her belly, stopping just short of her mound.

The heat of embarrassment mingled with the heat of arousal at his words. She wasn't used to such frank language during sex, and she felt awkward and shy trying to put her desire into words.

"It's okay, baby, you don't have to tell me." His hand slid lower and she eagerly spread her legs as his fingers spread her open. "This tells me everything I need to know."

His fingers dipped inside her molten core. "You're so wet, you drive me crazy," he said. A shudder rippled through him and he buried his head in the deep valley of her cleavage. His lips moved hungrily down her stomach, sucking and nipping as his fingers circled around her clit in maddeningly soft strokes.

She rocked against his hands, craving the firm caress and thrust of his fingers he'd given her before. Suddenly his hand was gone, and before she could make a sound of protest she felt him hook her knees over his shoulders as his thumbs spread her open for his kiss.

"No," she said in a high, startled voice, and tried to squirm away from the startling heat of his mouth. Theresa had never managed to get comfortable having oral sex performed on her, even before her sex life with her ex-boyfriend went to hell. The few times she'd managed to get him to try it, he'd been so begrudging that she'd never gotten over her self-consciousness enough to enjoy it. And if it did start to feel good, her ex would inevitably ruin it by pausing and asking her in an exasperated voice if she was close yet.

"It's okay, you don't have to do that," she said, trying to squirm away, only to find herself pinned open by the wide sprawl of his shoulders.

He lifted his dark head from between her legs. "I know I don't have to," he said, pulling back to run his tongue up the smooth skin of her inner thigh. "But I *want* to." His next kiss landed on her stomach, right above the tidy patch of black curls, and she said a silent thanks that she'd kept up on her bikini waxes.

The way he said it, with such conviction, she almost believed him. "Hey, I know guys don't really enjoy this, so don't feel like you have to do . . . that."

He stared at her hard, his heavy brows knitting in a way that made her stomach sink. She'd ruined the mood. *Great job, Theresa. You're on the verge of having the best sex of your life after not even being interested for way too long, and you go and ruin it.*

"I don't know what idiot ever gave you that idea," Vince said, "and I don't want to do anything you don't want. But just so you know," he said, pushing himself up so he could kiss her, "I'm dying to go down on you." He swept his tongue inside her mouth, a bold demonstration of how he would lick between her thighs. "I want to suck on your clit and fuck you with my tongue and taste you coming into my mouth."

The dark, erotic words rippled through her and wetness flooded between her thighs. At this rate, he would be able to talk her into anything. Her fingers tangled in his hair as she met his kiss then slowly, tentatively, she pushed his head down.

He whispered something that sounded like "thank you" as he once again bent his head. He wasted no time, using his fingers to spread her wide as his tongue licked up, down and around, then dipped lower to spear inside her body. "You taste so good," he murmured, then sucked her clit between his lips in a way that made her womb clench and her toes curl.

All lingering self-consciousness fled as he buried his mouth against her, lapping, sucking, *savoring* her, like she was a ripe peach, bursting with juice, and he didn't want to miss a drop. She'd never felt anything like this, the hot pressure of his lips and the firm strokes of his tongue. Her moans echoed off the smooth surfaces of the room. Her heels dug into his back as she sought to get closer to his skillful lips and tongue.

Just when she didn't think it could feel any better, he shoved a thick finger inside her, making her arch and shake when his blunt fingertip pressed up against a bundle of nerves she'd never known existed. Her orgasm pounded through her, swift and intense, startling a harsh cry from her throat.

Theresa felt his big body shift and opened her eyes to find him braced above her, his weight balanced on his forearms as they rested on either side of her head. His full lips curled into a sexy smile. "Think you'll ever let me do that again?"

Her lips curved in an answering smile. "I could be persuaded." He kissed her and she could taste her own spice on his lips.

His cock pressed into her stomach, hot and insistent. She reached down and wrapped her fingers around the thick shaft. He was so big her fingers didn't meet, and she shivered as she remembered the feel of him pushing inside her before he'd pulled back.

It was going to be a tight fit, she thought as she stroked him from root to tip. To her shock she still wanted him, even thought she'd already come twice, harder than she ever had in her life. But as she felt his breath quicken, caught the spicy scent of arousal blooming on his skin, she knew she wouldn't be truly satisfied until she felt the whole of his thick length buried deep inside her.

"I want you, Vince," she whispered, testing the words, liking the way they tasted. She decided to go further. "I want to feel your cock inside me." She stroked her thumb across the plump head of his cock, spreading the thick bead of pre-come over his silky smooth flesh.

"Don't," he whispered harshly as every muscle in his body froze.

She felt a flash of self-consciousness, afraid she'd shocked him. Maybe he liked to be the only one talking dirty in bed. Maybe—

"If you keep saying things and touching me like that you're gonna make me lose it. And baby, I want it to be so good for you." He kissed her so hard her lips felt bruised, then abruptly jerked her into his arms and carried her into the bedroom and laid her down across the wide expanse of his king-size bed.

She watched him, her sex quivering in anticipation as he rolled on a condom.

She spread her legs wide as he knelt between them and took his cock in his hand. Keeping his eyes locked on hers, he slid the head up and down the slick folds, soaking himself in her arousal until she was ready to beg him to fuck her deep and hard.

And then he was squeezing inside her, his hips working in shallow thrusts as her body softened and stretched to accommodate him. His face was harsh, his mouth a tight line as he hooked her leg around his waist and slowly withdrew until just the head was inside.

"You're so tight," he said, sinking in a little deeper this time. "I don't want to hurt you."

Theresa rocked her hips to take him deeper, feeling anything but pain. "It feels so good, you feel so good—"

Her words disintegrated into a long moan as he sank in to the hilt, filling her, stroking so deep she could feel him all the way down to her toes. He was everywhere, on her and in her, so big he should have been overwhelming but she couldn't get enough. Her hands skated down his back to rest on his rock-hard glutes, her fingers clutching as his muscles flexed with every deep thrust.

She could feel another orgasm building, tightening low in her belly, and she rocked her hips harder and faster against him. As though sensing she was near the brink, Vince hooked her leg over his elbow and pushed it against her chest, adjusting his angle so his shaft slid against the pulsing bud of her clit with every stroke. His mouth swallowed her harsh cries as she clung to him, holding on for dear life as her climax roared through her with a force she wouldn't have believed possible. Red and gold sparks exploded behind her closed eyelids and rushed through her body until she tingled all over with the force of it.

Vince groaned in mingled relief and pleasure as Theresa's pussy clenched around him like a tight, wet fist. He sank into her, finally releasing the tight leash he'd kept on himself. She moaned and squirmed under him as he rode her through her orgasm, pounding into her with the full force of his need. He could feel the pressure of his orgasm building in his balls and the base of his spine.

He groaned and fucked her hard, shoving her across the bed with the force of his thrusts. She stayed right with him, her dark head tossing back and forth against the spread, her luscious tits bouncing in perfect time to the pumping of his hips. The sight was more than he could bear, and his orgasm shot through him with dizzying force. He came in hot, thick spurts, his cock twitching and jerking inside the molten grip of her body.

He collapsed on top of her, burying his head in the scented curve of her neck as he sucked air into his lungs. Her dark hair was damp from her bath, the wavy strands tickling his nose as he slowly came back to himself. "I don't think I've ever come that hard in my life," he murmured, unable to resist the temptation to suck on the silky skin of her neck. His orgasm was still running through him, sending crazy little aftershocks to all of his nerve endings.

"That makes two of us," she said, her voice muffled by the thick muscle of his shoulder.

"God, I'm totally crushing you," he said, feeling like it took all his strength just to roll off to the side. He had to lay there for a few more seconds before he was able to get up and dispose of the condom.

By the time he returned, Theresa had oriented herself the

right way in the bed and had the comforter pulled up to her chin. But for all her modesty, she didn't bother to hide her admiration as she watched him walk naked across the room. He slipped into the sheets beside her and pulled her close, sighing contentedly when she laid her head on his chest.

The sex was amazing, but this was pretty good too, he thought with some surprise. Post-coital cuddling wasn't usually part of his repertoire. More often than not, he had overseas phone calls to make or emails to catch up on and didn't tend to linger in bed once the sex was over. Or, if he didn't have work to do, he would rather roll over and go to sleep or watch Sportscenter than engage in pointless pillow talk.

But even though he was tired from the flight and jet-lagged from the three hour time difference, he didn't want to give into sleep just yet. He liked this, laying here with Theresa with her slender fingers running absently down his chest, liked the way his hand rode the lush curve of her hip. You couldn't have dragged him out of bed to do email if his job depended on it, he thought with a sleepy smile.

"Damn it, I forgot to put a towel down," he said with a grin.

Her fingers froze in the act of tracing concentric circles around his navel and she muffled a groan against his chest. "So you overheard that."

He laughed. "At least you didn't think I was gay."

"I'm sorry," she said. "I've just never known a guy whose place was so . . . tidy."

"I grew up with seven younger siblings who were always getting into my stuff. Now that I have my own place, I like knowing everything is where it's supposed to be," he said a little defensively.

"Seven kids? Your parents must be good Catholics."

"Yeah, my stepfather believed in doing his part to populate the world." He tried to keep the edge out of his voice as he remembered the sinking feeling he'd had as a kid when his mother announced every new pregnancy. As the family grew, Vince, a living reminder of her first marriage, had been pushed even more to the outskirts.

He ran his hand down Theresa's back, letting the sensation of her skin under his hand chase away thoughts of his childhood.

"You weren't supposed to come home until tomorrow," she said, her lips tickling his skin as she spoke.

"My meetings finished early and I decided I wanted to be home for the weekend." He crooked his head so he could grin down at her. "Disappointed?"

She gave him a sly smile. "No. Surprised, definitely, but not disappointed."

He pulled her up his chest so he could kiss her. The heavy weight of her breasts pressed against him, and to his amusement his dick made a valiant effort to revive. "Tell me," he said between slow, lazy kisses, "did you do that every night while I was away?"

"What?" She whispered, chasing his tongue into his mouth. "Take a bath?"

"Yeah, and masturbate while you did it," he said, catching her hand and guiding it to the base of his stomach where his cock was tenting up against the sheets. He groaned and arched up into her hand as she stroked along his length.

"Does the idea of that make you hot?" she whispered, kissing and nipping her way along his jaw to his ear. Her tongue flicked out to taste his earlobe, and he felt himself harden another inch.

His hands roamed restlessly over the silky skin of her back and sides. "It makes me fucking insane. The idea of you, naked and wet in my bathroom, touching yourself here." He reached between them and palmed her swollen heat.

"Tonight was the first time," she said, her voice a little shaky as he probed her folds with gentle fingers. She had to be sore, sensitive, but still she shifted her legs open to give him better access.

"What were you thinking about?"

She didn't answer, but he saw the truth in her dark eyes as they flicked up to meet his.

Renewed arousal shot straight to his cock, making him almost painfully hard. "You were thinking of me, weren't you? How it would feel to have me touch you, how it would feel to have me fuck you." Her face flushed red even as evidence of her need soaked his stroking fingers. He felt something unfamiliar tug at his chest.

She was such a contradiction. So sexy with her killer curves and take-no-crap attitude, yet surprisingly ill at ease when it came to sex. Before tonight he would have said it was a turn off—he liked his lovers self-assured and assertive, liked women who knew exactly what they wanted and weren't shy about telling him.

But tonight Theresa's unexpected blushes and flashes of uncertainty were driving him absolutely fucking wild. He wanted to indulge her in any and every fantasy she could think of. "Tell me what you imagined," he said, sliding his fingers deeper inside the slippery folds of her pussy. "What were you thinking of before you saw me there? How did you imagine me touching you?"

This was too much, Theresa thought, too intimate. The sliding strokes of his fingers between her legs, the thick invasion of his cock inside her—all that she could handle. But speaking her intimate, erotic fantasies out loud was well beyond her comfort zone.

Besides, her rusty sexual imagination hadn't been able to

come up with anything like what actually happened. "Trust me," she said in a shaky voice, "the reality of you is way better than anything I could have imagined."

His cock flexed in her hand, saving her from feeling like an inexperienced twit for admitting that out loud. She looked down and her mouth went dry at the sight of him in her hand. She'd never found penises particularly attractive, but his was gorgeous, the shaft thick and long, topped by a luscious plum-shaped head. She squeezed him firmly, loving the way his pulse pounded against her fingers, the way his breath caught and he seemed to get harder with every touch. Answering liquid heat gathered between her legs and he spread it around with thick, blunt-tipped fingers.

He pulled her more fully on top of him and she landed with her knees splayed on either side of his hips. His hands tangled in her wet hair and he held her still for his kiss. "I can't believe how much I want you," he said, almost as though to himself. "I just came so hard I almost passed out, and I already want you again."

His words filled her with the same uncharacteristic boldness that had urged her to return his kiss earlier, urged her to go with the flow of their explosive sexual chemistry and damn the consequences. Without breaking their kiss, she reached over to the bedside table drawer to find a second condom. Within seconds she had him sheathed and was sinking down on his thick, hard shaft.

He pulled her down so they were chest to breast, his mouth locked to hers as his hips rocked in an easy counter-rhythm. His big hands splayed across her back, roamed down to squeeze her hips and ass, slipped between their bodies to stroke and squeeze her breasts.

His hands gripped her hips, holding her still for his deep, probing thrusts. His tongue tangled with hers and his groans rumbled through her as his caresses became hungrier, his thrusts more frantic.

His pleasure sparked hers and she spread her knees wide to take him deeper. Her orgasm broke in a long wave, and as she rippled and clenched around him, she could feel him getting impossibly bigger, harder inside her. She knew he was close. Reaching behind her, she lightly cupped the heavy weight of his balls, drawn tight against his body as his climax loomed.

He came with a shout, his hands gripping her hips hard as he ground himself against her.

Afterwards, Theresa lay in the dark, listening to the soothing cadence of Vince's breath, completely overwhelmed by what had happened tonight. Not by the sex, amazing as it was. But boy how Vince made her feel. The way he touched her—it was as arousing as hell, but it also made her feel . . . cherished.

Theresa shoved the thought aside. She wasn't about to let herself get carried away by a few orgasms, no matter how good they were. Her three-year relationship with Mark Silverton had beaten had any romantic idealism she'd possessed out of her.

Literally.

She snuggled closer to him, unable to banish the depressing realization that he was the kind of man she should have waited for. If she'd only been smarter, more mature, less impetuous, less frantic to break free of her overprotective father, she might have become the kind of woman who stood a chance with a guy like Vince.

Well, she'd made her mistakes and now she had to live with them. The reality was she was a twenty-four-year-old cocktail waitress with only a year and a half of college under her belt, and a not so spotless past to boot.

Not exactly the kind of woman she'd seen on Vince's arm in the pictures taken at society galas featuring San Francisco's snobbiest. She'd googled him. So sue her.

But instead of getting out of bed and going back to her

apartment like common sense dictated, she snuggled closer to Vince, shivering in delight as he pulled her closer even in sleep. She would never be the kind of woman Vince wanted, but she was going stave off that harsh reality, if only for a few more hours.

6

Vince awoke to the familiar sensation of Chester's stinky dog breath huffing in his face. He cracked open one eyelid and that was all the encouragement the dog needed. Chester emitted a sharp whine and enthusiastically shoved his cold, wet nose against Vince's cheek. Vince barely managed to close his mouth before he was assaulted by a canine French kiss.

He felt a stirring next to him and smiled as he rolled over to see Theresa's dark head next to his on the pillow. She lay on her side facing away from him, one hand tucked up under the pillow. He slid his arm around her waist and drew her closer, sighing in satisfaction as his morning erection bumped up against the soft, warm curve of her ass. She sighed and snuggled closer, but just as Vince slipped one hand up to cup her breast, Chester padded over to her side of the bed. The dog put his paws up and lunged for Theresa's face, hitting her square on the chin with his big pink tongue.

Theresa groaned and buried her face in the pillow. "Five more minutes," she mumbled sleepily and rolled to face Vince. Her brow was knit into a frown, her eyes squeezed tight as though fiercely guarding her sleep. He looked at the clock. It was barely after six, but thanks to being on east coast time he was wide awake despite having spent most of the night doing anything but sleep.

Chester nudged Theresa again. She buried her face into the pillow with a frustrated sigh.

As much as he wanted to wake Theresa up with his tongue between her thighs, she needed her sleep. Especially, he thought rather smugly, after the way he'd tired her out last night. Unable to resist touching her one last time, he leaned over and pressed a soft kiss to her shoulder and whispered, "I'll take him out."

After a quick cup of coffee, he laced up his running shoes and took Chester for a long morning run. Maybe it was the lack of sleep, the eerie quiet of the San Francisco streets this early on a Saturday morning, but he felt like he was existing in some surreal, dreamlike state. It had started last night, when he'd come home to the totally unexpected sight of Theresa, naked in his bathtub.

His cock hardened at the memory, and he was glad no one was around to see since the baggy shorts offered nothing in the way of camouflage. The sex had been awesome, straight out of his wildest dreams. Hot housesitter. Naked and showing herself a good time the precise moment he walked in the door. Oh, yeah.

A dark thought entered his mind as he turned up the last steep hill before home. What if Theresa, in her dire financial straits, had decided to put herself out there to get a little extra beyond reduced rent?

The thought brought a bad taste to his mouth. But he didn't know why he cared. In the last several years since he'd really started making money, the women he'd dated had definitely appreciated his bank account as much as they'd appreciated him. He'd willingly spent the money to entertain them, understanding it was all part of the package.

But the idea of Theresa wanting him for the size of his wallet made him a little sick.

He shoved the thought aside. Of course she hadn't set it up. He'd gotten so used to everyone, including his own family, asking him for favors and hitting him up for money, that he was suspicious of everyone's motives. Theresa had had no idea he was coming home early, and besides, from what he knew of her from their previous interactions, she wasn't the type. Despite her gorgeous face and bombshell body, she had a certain reserve to her. An edge that warned people—especially men, he guessed— not to get too close.

But last night, he reflected as he opened the front gate to his house, that reserve had gone up in flames. He was so hard now he was aching just thinking about it. He hadn't been this attracted to a woman, ever. But he didn't know where it could go. A relationship was a complication he didn't need right now. Yes, he wanted her, with an intensity he'd never experienced before, but he was too old, not to mention too fuckin' busy, to be led around by his dick. No matter how much he liked and wanted Theresa, he didn't have time to go chasing around after a twenty-something waitress who happened to inspire massive hardons. Even if he wanted to actually have a relationship with her, he didn't have time to spend worrying about another person's wants and needs.

Christ, he thought as he unlocked the door and led Chester into the entryway, he couldn't even properly care for a dog, which was what had prompted him to ask Theresa to move here in the first place. He hoped she would understand where he was coming from. Underneath her tough girl exterior, he could sense she'd been hurt before. The last thing he wanted was to hurt her more.

Theresa jumped and dropped her spoon when she heard the front door close. She'd woken up to find herself alone in

Vince's bed, pleasurably sore in places she didn't know she had muscles and alternately horrified and aroused as memories of the previous night bombarded her. She pulled on her clothes and went back to her little place, relieved that Vince had apparently taken Chester out for his morning constitutional.

After a quick shower, she changed into sweats and forced herself to go back to the main house and wait for Vince. The urge to take off and spend all day avoiding him was almost overwhelming, but she had to get a few things straight, the sooner the better.

She didn't know what had come over her last night. She wanted to blame it on fatigue, on the wine, but she knew the truth. She had it bad for Vince Mattera, and had from the first moment she'd laid eyes on him. Reminding herself that she barely knew him didn't help. Neither did pointing out the fact that the last time she'd given into the notion of love at first sight, she'd wasted three years with a compulsive gambler and drug addict who'd knocked her around.

Not that Vince was anything like that. But nothing was likely to ever come of it, and since that was the case, she needed to nip this in the bud before anything else happened. Or, God forbid, he got any inkling of how she felt about him.

Now her stomach twisted into knots as she heard Chester's pounding paws coming down the hall, followed by Vince's heavier footsteps. She composed herself, determined to play it cool and casual, let him know that what happened, while no skin off her nose, could under no circumstances happen again.

Her mouth went dry as Vince walked into the kitchen. His dark eyes lit up and his mouth quirked into a sexy smile when he saw her sitting at the breakfast bar. "Good morning," he said, his voice melting over her like dark chocolate. His thick hair was damp and his T-shirt was dark at the neckline from exertion. She should have been grossed out, but all she wanted to do was rip his clothes off and use her tongue to catch every last drop of sweat.

She ignored the heat throbbing between her legs. "Thanks for taking Chester out," she said, striving for a casual tone. "I didn't mean to shirk my duties."

He poured himself a cup of coffee. "I figured you needed your sleep," he said with a knowing look.

Heat flooded her cheeks and she wished she didn't feel like an awkward, inexperienced teenager. She took her cue from Vince, who seemed to take having morning-after coffee with a woman in stride. He sat down next to her at the counter and opened the paper as though he hadn't spent most of last night exploring her naked body. Which was good, she told herself. It made what she had to say that much easier.

As it turned out, he beat her to the punch. "Theresa, about what happened last night," he began.

She might not have a lot of experience with guys, but she knew from his tone exactly what he was going to say.

"It was amazing."

She didn't reply. His compliment gave her an initial thrill, what he said next sent her promptly back to earth.

"But I don't have time for any kind of a relationship right now."

She pasted a smile on her face. "Oh my God, neither do I. I mean, honestly, I just got out of a relationship, and, no offense, but I think last night was, you know, rebound sex."

"Rebound sex?"

She barreled on as though she knew exactly what she was talking about, as though Vince wasn't only the second guy in the world she'd ever had sex with. "You know, rebound sex, to clear the slate until I'm, uh, emotionally open to a new relationship." She took another sip of her coffee, hoping he couldn't smell the bullshit. Because the truth was that if she thought she had even a remote chance of landing Vince, she would have opened herself way up, emotionally and otherwise.

He gazed at her with a faintly bemused look on his face. "Kinda like a sex aperitif?"

"Exactly," she said, finishing her coffee and hopping off her stool. "And as far as I'm concerned, a one-time thing."

"That's probably best," he said with a nod as though they'd just closed a business transaction. She felt inexplicably wounded, wishing he would protest, even a little. No, it was better this way, she told herself firmly. His swift agreement solidified her conviction that while last night had completely rocked her world, for him it had been nothing more than scratching an itch. For him it *had* been rebound sex. And while she felt this impossible, irrational, intense attraction to him, she was undoubtedly nothing more than a pretty woman who had conveniently shown up naked in his bathtub.

She couldn't have made it any easier for him if she wanted to.

Vince watched Theresa retreat from the kitchen, Chester trotting at her heels.

That had gone a lot smoother than he'd expected, especially given his recent breakup experiences. Not that he could really consider his discussion with Theresa a breakup, since you had to be in a relationship with a woman to dump her.

Or had she dumped him? She'd been so quick to jump in, had looked so horrified when the word relationship had popped out of his mouth. And called him a pussy, but her rebound sex comment kind of stung. He dumped the last of his coffee in the sink and went upstairs to take a shower.

He entered the bathroom and his gaze immediately locked on the bathtub. As visions of Theresa, slippery, wet, and naked flooded his brain, he was forced to admit that last night had been more than just a casual fuck, more than something as simple as rebound sex. At least on his part.

He ripped his gaze away, mentally going through his to-do list as he turned on the shower. He stripped down and stepped beneath the hot spray. What the fuck was wrong with him? Instead of being happy she was all too willing to dismiss what had happened as no big deal, he was pissed. Pissed she could so easily blow it off.

But mostly pissed that he wasn't going to have her again.

What was it about her that made him crave her like a drug? That had him hard as a spike and aching to hustle over to her apartment and throw her down on the bed? Maybe it was a taste of home—she reminded him of the girls he used to date in high school back in Queens. Good Italian Catholic girls who played hard to get until he got them into the sack.

Maybe after years of dating tall, lean WASP-y types, he was craving a taste of home.

Maybe so. For sure Theresa Bellessi drove him completely *pazzo* with her smooth skin, her lush ass, her beautiful big tits. He imagined her now, her dark, thick-lashed eyes looking at him like she'd looked at him last night. Like she wanted to cover him in whipped cream and lick him from head to toe.

And her mouth . . . God, her mouth was so full and pink. His cock ached, his balls tightened up at the thought of her lips and tongue on him. He soaped his palm and gripped his cock in his fist. Christ, he was pathetic, jacking off while the woman he wanted was less than a hundred feet away. But he couldn't stop the fantasy. In his mind Theresa appeared naked in front of him, her hair spilling, thick and dark over her shoulders. Her dark nipples would peek out from between the strands.

She would press herself against him, rubbing against him like a cat in heat before sliding to her knees. She'd soap up her tits and rub his cock all over them, circling her nipples with the head, stroking his shaft in her firm grip.

He pumped his fist faster, leaning back against the slate shower wall. Fantasy Theresa was just about to suck him between her lips when he came, muffling his shout as he spurted all over his fingers.

He squeezed his eyes shut, trying to hold onto the vision as harsh reality intruded. He was alone in his shower, his cock in his own hand. And, he thought ruefully, even in his dreams he hadn't managed to get a blow job.

Several hours later, Vince still couldn't get Theresa out of his head. He was supposed to be returning calls and returning emails, but he found himself staring out the window of his office, which happened to afford him an unobstructed view of the entrance to her apartment. She'd gone out late in the morning and had returned several hours later carrying a brown shopping bag.

He was working an excuse to go check on her when she left again, this time with Chester in tow. She was wearing stretchy yoga pants and a long sleeved T-shirt, but the way her breasts and hips filled them was somehow sexier than if she was wearing skimpy lingerie. While she was gone, Vince managed to power through his email backlog, only to be distracted again by Chester's happy bark upon their return.

Instead of going immediately back to the guest cottage, Theresa stayed in the yard with Chester. She unclipped his leash and took Chester through several obedience exercises, all of which the dog failed miserably. Vince's lips quirked in a smile and he couldn't help but admire her efforts. When he invited her to move in to take care of Chester, he'd expected her to simply keep the dog out of trouble. She'd surprised him by asking him if it was okay to sign Chester up for obedience classes, then presented him with a receipt for several dog training books.

He watched Theresa force Chester to sit by pushing on his butt, directing him to stay with a hand held up in front of the dog's face. It lasted for about all of two seconds before the dog walked over to her, tail wagging as he shoved his head into her hand for a pet. She patiently led him back to the other side of the yard and started the process over again.

She obviously took this seriously, and it was important for her to do a good job. Like at the restaurant—she could have easily skated on the fact that she was family, but she hustled around that bar more than anyone. She always remembered what the regulars drank and never forgot an order.

She took pride in her work and didn't want to take favors from anybody, he mused, remembering her insistence on paying him rent even though he didn't need the money. He admired her for wanting to pull her own weight, to make it on her own. He could relate. When Vince had announced his desire to go to college, his mother had shaken her head in puzzlement while his stepfather had laughed in his face.

"Where you think you're gonna get that kinda money, Vince? Whaddya need college for anyway? Your Uncle Lou already said he'd hire you."

Vince's stepfather hadn't understood that Vince wanted more from life than to work for his Uncle Lou's construction company, marry a girl from the neighborhood and have about a hundred kids.

He knew what was possible for a guy with his brains and his drive, and he wasn't about to waste it on a life that was "good enough." So he'd worked hard, gone to college on a football scholarship and worked as a trader straight out of school. When his firm had offered to send a select few junior traders to business school, Vince had made sure he was at the top of the list.

He, like Theresa, had worked his ass off at whatever job he happened to have at the time, whether it was doing construction work in the off season during college, or pulling ridiculous hours as a trader when he'd first started out.

Theresa repeated the sit/stay routine with Chester about a dozen times, until finally the dumb dog got the idea. Vince could hear her triumphant whoop through the double-paned glass and he grinned as she held out her arms to Chester, who bounded over and raised up on his hind legs, resting his paws on her shoulders.

He laughed at her exuberant response. She must have heard him, because her attention snapped up to the office window. Her eyes were bright, her face flushed, and she looked so pretty, it hit him like a kick in the gut. Heat curled low in his belly as he returned her sheepish wave.

He wondered what Theresa Bellessi wanted from life. Because right about now, Vince was ready to do give her anything she wanted for one more night in her bed.

"How's it going with Vince?"

Theresa jumped at Gia's question later that evening. Did Gia suspect? Was the fact that she'd spent most of the night rolling around naked with Vince tattooed on her forehead? From the way her body pulled and tingled with every slight movement, she felt like she might as well have been wearing a neon sign that read *I got lucky with a sexy zillionaire.*

But Gia's expression was one of casual curiosity, her brown eyes bright and friendly as usual.

"It's great," Theresa said as she waved to one of the regulars as he left the bar to be seated at his table. "He was gone all week, so I haven't seen much of him."

Okay, so that wasn't technically true. Because as of last night, Theresa had in fact seen *all* of him. Every big, muscled, scrumptious inch of him.

"Are you okay? You look a little flushed. You're not getting that flu that's going around, are you? I told you to get the shot."

"Thanks, Mom," Theresa said dryly. That was Gia, always trying to take care of everyone. "I'm fine. I've just been running around a lot today. Speaking of which, I finally have a new cell phone number."

She'd spent most of the day running errands, taking Chester for walks, anything and everything to avoid the house and Vince. Despite her determination that last night was a one-time deal, she was afraid that she would end up back in that vast bed of his with the slightest encouragement.

The upshot was that she'd finally taken care of miscella-neous life admin tasks, like getting a new cell phone number since she'd had to cut off service to avoid Mark's calls.

"There's no way for him to get this number, is there?" Gia asked as she jotted down the number.

Theresa shook her head. "It's unlisted."

"Are you sure you don't want to file a restraining order, just in case? Gabe can help you." Gia's eyes wide and worried.

"Don't worry about it," Theresa said, noticing a couple that had just sat down in her section. "He called because he wanted to annoy me, but he's not going to bother to come after me." Yes, Mark was pissed she'd left him, as evidenced by his multi-ple voicemails. They'd started out sweet and pleading, and swiftly turned angry and abusive. But she'd cleared the slate when she'd left, paid off his debts and his rent for the next month. There was no reason to come after her. "And even if she did," thinking out loud for Gia's benefit, "he wouldn't hurt me. Trust me, he's all bluster."

Now that was a blatant lie, and she had the healed fracture in her wrist and the memory of countless bruises to remind her. But even after all that, Theresa didn't believe for a second Mark had it in for her.

"As long as you're sure," Gia said.

"Mark's like a little kid, pissed that he didn't get his way. Now he's elevated drunk dialing to an art form. That's it. If he were really a threat, don't you think I'd have moved someplace a little less obvious instead of coming home?"

"If who were a threat?"

At the first deep-voiced syllable, all thoughts of her loser ex-boyfriend fled and every square inch of Theresa's skin bloomed with heat. She didn't need to turn around to know it was Vince. Even if his voice hadn't been a dead giveaway, she could pick up his fresh, spicy scent through the heavy smells of Ciao Bella's hearty Italian dishes. Like her body had a highly sensitive radar tuned exclusively to him.

She whipped around, drink tray clutched to her chest, to see him standing about six inches from her. "No one," she said quickly. He gazed at her steadily and quirked a thick, dark brow as though he didn't believe her. "What are you doing here?" she asked, wincing at how rude that sounded.

Gia shot her a puzzled look. "It's good to see you, Vince. We missed you this week." She looked pointedly at Theresa.

"Right, sorry," Theresa said, feeling the flush on her cheeks grow more intense. "I didn't mean it's not good to see you. Of course it is. I just didn't expect to see you tonight, since you didn't mention anything. But then, there's no reason to tell me your plans." Fine lines radiated out from Vince's eyes as he started to grin at her nervous chatter. And then his eyes got hooded as he looked at her, as though he was remembering her naked. Which made her remember him naked . . .

"Theresa, do you want to stop babbling and get Vince a drink?" Gia said sharply. Theresa could have kissed her cousin for giving Theresa an excuse to flee.

As she put in the order, she heard Gia offer to seat Vince in the main restaurant since they unexpectedly had a table free.

"No, it's late. I'll sit in the bar."

Theresa turned to see him sit down at a table in her section.

"Theresa can take care of me," he said with a knowing smile that fortunately seemed lost on Gia.

Theresa placed his usual drink, a vodka on the rocks with a twist of lemon, in front of Vince, then quickly scanned the bar, eager to make a quick getaway before she made a fool of herself all over again. So much for her plan of playing it cool and acting like sex with him was no big deal. She was handling this with all the finesse of a high school band geek with a crush on a football player.

Unfortunately, it was almost ten and though the restaurant was still nearly full of diners, the bar crowd had thinned out considerably. There were only four other tables occupied, and three of them were in the section covered by Tanya, the other cocktail waitress.

She turned her attention back to Vince and tried to keep her manner professional. "So what can I get you?"

He leaned back in his chair, one arm flung around the back as he kicked his legs out in a casual sprawl. "I don't know. I can't decide what I'm in the mood for."

He was dressed like almost every other guy in here, in dark wash jeans and button front shirt. It shouldn't have looked so sexy. But the way his broad chest and shoulders filled out his shirtfront, the subtle shift of muscle under the heavy denim of his pants made her mouth go dry as the area between her legs went embarrassingly wet. His shirt was open at the collar, displaying his strong, tanned throat to her hungry gaze.

She dragged her eyes up to his face, which was a mistake. He was staring at her, his full lips quirked into a half smile as though he knew exactly what she was thinking.

She cleared her throat and focused on taking his order so she could get the hell out of there. "Let's see. The chef has a special pasta tonight. Tagliatelle with prosciutto and peas. That's very nice if you want something light. Or if you want something heavier, we have our veal osso bucco." As she mindlessly recited the entire menu, Vince stared at her as though the only dish he was in the mood to consume was her.

She cut herself off in the middle of their wood-fired pizza options. "Will you stop that?" she whispered harshly.

"What?" Vince replied, eyes wide, big hands splayed as if to say, *who, me?* He blinked his big, coffee-colored eyes in false innocence. "I'm just trying to decide what I want to eat."

She glared at him, seizing onto annoyance like a lifeline. "Stop leering at me while you decide."

A laugh rumbled from his chest. "Can't a man look at a beautiful woman without getting his balls busted?"

"Vince, I thought I made it clear this morning—"

"Relax, Theresa. I don't know what you think is going on here." He took a sip of his drink. When he set it down, he caressed the rim with his fingers, circling the glass with a blunt fingertip. She was mesmerized by those fingers, remembering how they felt skimming along the sensitive skin of her inner thighs before sliding inside her. She moved her gaze to his face, only to find him watching her.

He knew exactly what he was doing, the prick. "I'll give you a few more minutes to decide." She turned in a huff and nearly ran into Gia.

"Is everything okay over here?" she asked, casting nervous glances between Theresa and Vince.

Theresa quickly moved to diffuse the tension, not wanting to put her cousin in the position of having to mediate between a family member and a favorite customer. She forced a laugh. "It's nothing. Vince was just busting my chops for Chester's slow progress in his obedience classes." She turned back to Vince.

Vince laughed. "Right. We were talking about the dog."

Theresa scooped up his drink, which still had a full inch or so of booze left. "Let me refresh this while you decide what you want to eat."

She didn't know what game he was playing. This morning he seemed eager—almost disappointingly so—to agree to her assertion that sex with him was only a one-time thing. Now he was deliberately toying with her, giving her looks that made her feel like she was being bathed in warm honey while he told her she was beautiful.

If he pushed any harder she was going to be in very big trouble.

But at least he didn't seem inclined to probe any further into the snippet of conversation he'd overheard earlier. The last thing she wanted was to have to share the particulars of her past with Vince. Besides what happened between them sexually, she genuinely liked and respected Vince, and wanted him to feel the same for her. And she didn't expect that he would if she shared the sordid truth about Mark and what she'd been willing to do, first in the name of love, later out of obligation—and fear.

After Vince finally settled on a plate of pasta pomodoro, Theresa served up his order in record time, hoping to hustle him out of there.

"You must be exhausted," Theresa said as she handed him his check. "It's already almost two a.m. Your time."

He smiled blandly, completely ignoring her hint. "I crashed for a few hours earlier, after you left. I'm wide awake. As long as I'm here, I'll walk you home."

Yeah, that was all her tenuous resolve needed, a walk home with Vince on a moonlit fall night. "Gia can give me a ride home."

"I insist," he said, and ordered a glass of vin santo.

So Theresa found herself walking home with Vince. She kept her mouth shut and her eyes fixed in front of her, but it wasn't nearly enough to block out his presence. At this hour on a Saturday night, North Beach was full of fashionably dressed San Franciscans hopping among the many hot spots. She couldn't help but notice that every single woman they passed raked Vince with a covetous gaze. Theresa forced down an irrational, territorial urge to clamp onto his hand and proclaim to everyone that Vince was hers.

But he wasn't. And he never would be.

She folded her arms more tightly around her chest and charged ahead, nearly falling on her ass when an obviously drunk guy stumbled into her. Vince steadied her with an arm around her shoulders. "Watch where you're fuckin' goin'," he said to the drunk's back.

The guy stiffened and turned around, chin tilted pugnaciously as his hands clenched at his sides. Then he got a good look at Vince, who topped him by a good six inches, and mumbled an apology to Theresa before hustling off to catch up with his friends.

"Idiot," Vince muttered. "You okay?" He gave her shoulders a little squeeze.

She nodded, but didn't immediately pull away. That big, muscular arm felt so good wrapped around her, it sent a shiver down her spine.

"You're cold," he said, and before she could protest the heavy weight of his leather jacket settled over her. His warmth and scent enveloped her, and she was so far from cold she was afraid she was about to spontaneously combust.

"I'm fine," she said, and tried to give the jacket back.

He refused, of course. "You wear it. I tend to be hot anyway."

God, did she know it, remembering the way heat had emanated from his bare skin as she lay curled up beside him.

They walked a few more blocks in silence. With every step that brought them closer to home, temptation grew. Every nerve ending was on high alert. Every so often her arm or shoulder would brush against him, and she felt the heat through the thick layer of his jacket. Her breath grew short, and she was glad she had the steep climb up Greenwich Street to blame. She prayed he remained ignorant of her arousal. God, if it got any worse she was in danger of becoming the first woman in recorded history to have an orgasm simply from walking next to a man.

By the time they reached Vince's front gate she was a wreck. As he keyed in the security code to unlock the gate, she planned her escape. She had to get away from him, as quickly as possible, before she did something unforgivably stupid.

But as she stepped inside the gate, poised to flee, she felt his hand wrap around her forearm. "Theresa," he said, his voice throaty with sexual intent. He bent towards her, his dark head illuminated by the outdoor lights.

"We're going to have more rebound sex, aren't we?" she blurted just before his mouth closed over hers.

"Yeah," he said, and she could hear the grin in his voice. "A lot more."

7

Vince slipped his hands under his heavy leather coat, circling his hands around Theresa's ribcage to bring her in to meet his kiss. She let out a small sigh as his mouth closed over hers, a little forlorn, almost like a sound of defeat. Her hand curled around his neck and her lips parted eagerly under his.

He took his time tasting her, savoring the feel of her hot tongue sliding against his. Heat exploded through his body at the first taste. His cock, which had been in a steady state of half hardness all day, rose to full attention, hard as a spike, as though it had been weeks instead of hours since he fucked her. It was absurd how much he wanted her. And more than that, how eager he'd been to see her. He'd fully intended to stay in tonight, give Theresa a little space while he figured out the best way to get himself back in her bed.

But when he'd woken up from a late afternoon nap, hard and aching, he decided to hell with that. The aggressive, straight-forward approach had always served him well both in business and the bedroom, so why not go with the tried and true?

She'd been so flustered by his appearance at the restaurant

he hadn't been able to keep from messing with her. Letting her know in no uncertain terms what was on his mind, making sure that thoughts of him, of *them* in a hot, naked tangle were front and center. His tongue thrust hungrily against hers as his hands came up to palm the full curves of her breasts. Her nipples were rock hard, pebbling against his hands. He pinched her through the heavy cotton fabric of her shirt, rolling the hard tips between his fingers until she made a soft, high-pitched sound in the back of her throat.

It went straight to his cock and he pulled her harder against him, rubbing his dick into the softness of her belly in an effort to ease the ache. Somehow he managed to steer them up the walkway and up the front steps until he had her backed up against the front door. He slid his hand down her back, dipping into the loose waistband of her pants where he found warm skin covered by wispy silk.

His fingers slid down further to cup one full ass cheek through the silk of her panties. He wondered what color they were. Sex-kitten black? Virginal white? Sinful red? His kiss got harder, hungrier as he imagined peeling her panties off as he sank to his knees, nipping and sucking at her firm curves before he bent her over and slid his cock into the wet, clenching heat of her pussy.

He fumbled with the lock, insane with the need to get her naked and under him. The door swung open and she stumbled inside. Vince lifted her up and hooked her legs around his hips and fumbled his way toward the stairs. He took two steps when he bumped his toe and went down, barely catching them both before he slammed Theresa into the wide wooden steps.

Not that she seemed to care. Without breaking their kiss she pulled him down on top of her, tugging at the buttons of his shirt until it was hanging open. His muscles clenched in delight as her hands ran up and down his abs, over his sides, around his back.

His fingers wrestled with her buttons, sending a few flying in his frenzy to get to the smooth, warm skin underneath. She was so soft, so warm. It was dark on the stairway, the only illumination from the moonlight spilling through the windows. He could make out the pale curves of her breasts above the even paler fabric of her bra. He tugged the cups aside so he could see her tight, dark nipples and feel them nudging his chest as he came down over her.

His cock fought the confines of his jeans as his hips nestled between hers, rocking against her. He could feel the heat of her sex even through the heavy fabric of their clothes, knew if he stripped her panties off he'd find her soaking wet and steaming hot.

He didn't know what had come over him. He was out of control, about to fuck her on the stairs, for Christ's sake. He didn't remember the last time he'd been so overcome that he couldn't make it to the bedroom.

Theresa deserved better than this, better than a quick hard fuck on the stairs that would leave bruises on the tender skin of her back.

Ignoring her protests, he scooped her up in his arms and carried her the rest of the way up the stairs. He flung open his bedroom door and switched on a low lamp so he could see her. He set her on her feet and they fumbled out of their clothes until he was naked and she was left in only her silky panties.

Pink. Wispy. And as he discovered when he palmed her through them, drenched with her sweet, hot juice.

She moaned and buried her face against his chest as he pressed his fingers against her silk-covered clit. He shuddered as her hand closed over his cock and her tongue flicked out to taste his chest. He backed toward the bed, sitting down heavily when his knees hit the back of the padded bench at its foot.

Theresa eagerly followed him down, lifting one knee onto the bench, cupping his face in her hands to tilt it up to meet her kiss. He cupped her breasts, loving the heavy weight of them in his palms, the way she gasped and moaned into his mouth when he ran his thumbs over the hard tips.

"I really wasn't going to do this again," she said as she sank into his lap and kissed her way down his neck. "I promised myself last night was only a one-time deal." Her mouth traced a scorching trail across his shoulders and down his chest.

"Why would you do a stupid thing like that?" He tangled his hands in her thick, dark hair, loving the way it spilled down her back and shoulders, falling forward to brush against his chest. He wanted to feel it tickling against his thighs as she bent her head to take his cock into her mouth.

"You know what they say about playing with fire," she said, sinking to her knees in front of the bench. "If I keep messing with you I'm going to be burned."

Something about her response nipped at his consciousness, bothering him. But he was so distracted by the feel of her lips working their way down his abdomen, he let it go. Because, oh Jesus, she was nearly naked in front of him, running her fingers up the insides of his thighs, leaning close enough for the tip of his cock to nudge against the heavy weight of her breasts.

He spread his knees wider and fought the urge to push her head down into his lap. He shuddered as she pumped him in her fist and cupped his balls in her other hand. He looked down and almost came when when he saw the look on her face. She stared at his cock, lips parted and wet as he swelled and surged under her attentions.

She flicked her gaze up to meet his, her eyes dark and knowing as a tiny half smile pulled at her plump, pink mouth. "Do you want me to suck your cock?"

The blunt, sexual words sounded even dirtier coming from Theresa, who, despite her ripe curves looked still had that good-Catholic-girl innocent air about her.

He couldn't have said no if he had a gun to his head. "God yes."

His head slammed back as the hot, sucking pressure of her lips slipped over the tip of his cock, her tongue licking the sensitive seam just under the head. His breath sawed in his chest and he fisted his hands against the bench so he wouldn't grab the back of her head and shove himself down her throat.

He fought not to come as he watched her with heavy-lidded eyes. Her lips stretched wide to take him, and his cock was shiny wet from her attentions. His balls grew tight and achy and each breath ended on a groan as she sucked him harder, her mouth moving up and down his shaft, taking him deeper into her throat. Hot little sounds emanated from her throat. She was getting even more aroused, just from sucking him off.

His eyes squeezed shut, his hands fisted in her hair. It was too much.

Theresa clenched her thighs together against the insistent throb between her legs. God, the taste of Vince, the feel of his cock so hard and insistent in her mouth was almost enough to send her over the edge. Gripping him in her fist, she slid her lips back up to the tip, running her tongue along the slit in the head to capture the pearl of pre-come that had formed there.

Her body's hungry response shocked her. She'd gone down on her ex, lots of times. Mostly as a way to get him off without having to actually have sex with him, which would require her pretending she was somewhat into it.

Vince was different, the salty, musky taste of him flooding her senses until she couldn't get enough. And the way he groaned her name and softly swore as she sucked him deep in her throat urged her on, heightening her own arousal to a fever pitch. She was so turned on she could feel a trickle of moisture running down her inner thigh. His hands fisted in her hair, and the

slight edge of pain made her moan around the thick staff filling
her mouth.

He was close, so close to coming in her mouth, and the very
idea made the creamy throbbing between her legs intensify to
the point of . . . *ohhh*. He pulsed against her tongue, his skin
stretching as he grew impossibly harder. Her fingers cupped
the tight weight of his balls as her fist pumped him.

She sucked him hard, anticipating the hot pulse of his orgasm. But before she could send him over the edge, he abruptly
pulled her from the floor and practically threw her on the bed.
Within seconds he had a condom on and was kneeing her legs
apart.

"Inside you," he muttered, barely coherent, as he positioned
himself against her. His fingers slipped between her legs, felt
how wet she was. "Yes," he hissed, fitting his cock against her
sex. "You're ready. So fucking ready."

Her body was shaking with need, the merest brush of his
cock against her sensitive folds sending bursts of pleasure
through her. And then he was inside her, so hot and thick she
started coming before he was even halfway in. He was relent-
less, pounding into her with hard, deep thrusts that made her
orgasm go on and on. She clutched at his hips, her head tossing
against the pillow as harsh cries ripped from her throat.

His hands hooked under her knees, spreading her wide as he
penetrated even deeper. His hips moved faster, harder, shoving
her up the bed with his urgency. His face was a harsh mask of
pleasure, the sharp planes and angles standing out in stark relief. "Theresa," he groaned and her name had never sounded so
beautiful to her own ears.

Then he was coming, pinning her hips to the bed as his cock
swelled and pulsed inside her.

Theresa pulled him down on top of her and threaded her
fingers through his thick, dark hair. He was a deliciously heavy
weight on top of her, his breath soft against her neck as the last

pulses of her orgasm fluttered around him. She couldn't seem to stop touching him, kissing the salty skin of his neck, skimming her fingers up his sleek back. She felt him soften and start to slip out of her, and her inner muscles clenched in protest.

She never wanted him to leave.

The thought sent a wave of panic through her. At the same moment, Chester bounded over to the bed and planted his paws squarely against Vince's shoulder and knocked him to the side. Theresa jumped out of bed and started gathering up her clothes.

"I better take him out," she said as she pulled her pants up her legs and threw on her shirt.

Vince rolled off the bed, and Theresa found herself mesmerized by the shift of hard muscle under all that tan, tight skin. He dealt with the condom and moved to pick up his boxers where he'd dropped them by the door.

Her gaze traveled down his broad, muscled chest, his rippling abs, between his legs where his penis hung heavy between his muscular thighs. He started to thicken and grow before her eyes, and her attention snapped to his face. He was watching her, lips quirked in that sexy, knowing smile.

"You keep looking at me like that and in about five seconds you're gonna find yourself on your back with your feet up on my shoulders."

That sounded like a pretty good idea to her, but before she could say so Chester let out an urgent bark and stomped his paws in a canine version of the pee-pee dance. Theresa snapped back to attention, grateful for the reminder that at this moment, it was probably best to put some distance between herself and Vince.

Not that he was inclined to let her get very far. He pulled on a pair of flannel pajama pants and a T-shirt to follow her outside and wrapped an arm around her waist when she would have followed Chester over to the rhododendrons.

"What got you so spooked all of a sudden?" he asked.

"Nothing," she insisted. Nothing except for the fact that after a couple rounds of fabulous sex, she was having inappropriate visions of living happily ever after with a man who was completely out of her league. "I don't want Chester to ruin thousands of dollars worth of landscaping." She tried to move away again, but he kept a firm grip on her forearm.

"I don't give a fuck about the landscaping," he said, pulling her hard against him. "I want to know why you're pulling away."

She ignored Chester and his enthusiastic digging for the moment and sighed against Vince's chest. "Sleeping with you complicates things."

"We're two consenting adults who had amazing sex. What's complicated about it?"

When he put it in that matter of fact way, she felt immature and unsophisticated.

"Me living here," she began.

"What could be more convenient? Listen, Theresa," he said, pressing a kiss to the top of her head. "I know you just got out of a relationship and you're not looking for anything serious. It's also become very clear to me recently that I'm in kinda the same place. But I really like sex," he said with a soft chuckle. Then, his voice going dark and deep, "And I especially like having sex with you. So why don't we stop worrying and just go with it?"

His mouth came down over hers, obliterating the protest on her lips. *Just go with it.* He made it sound so easy, so simple.

Maybe it was.

8

Just sex, Vince thought. Simple. Easy. Uncomplicated.

He only wished that were true as he watched Theresa move through the crowded tables at Ciao Bella. After almost a month of sleeping with her, his emotions toward Theresa were growing more fucking complicated by the day.

He'd figured the sex thing would cool down. He was, after all, thirty-five, and though he'd always had a healthy sex drive, his days of thinking about sex nonstop—not to mention doing it nonstop—had disappeared sometime in his twenties.

Man, had Theresa ever proven him wrong. He fucked her every single night, sometimes twice, and still he wanted her all the time. When he wasn't fucking her, he was thinking about fucking her. About peeling back her shirt and sucking her tits into his mouth, sinking to his knees so he could slip his tongue inside the delicious heat of her cunt.

He kept his thoughts deliberately crude, refusing to think of what they were doing as anything but fucking, pure and simple.

But as he watched her, nursing his drink until it was time to walk her home, he knew it was more than that. He didn't just

210 / Jami Alden

want her, he craved her. Ached for her. Until sometimes when he was at work he was unable to concentrate as thoughts of her invaded his brain. He never lost focus when he was in the middle of a deal, yet twice this week he had drifted off during conference calls, assaulted by fantasies of Theresa showing up at his office and spreading herself naked over his desk.

And the late nights weren't helping his focus either. Yet night after night, instead of turning in early so he could get some sleep, he lingered until the restaurant closed so he could take Theresa home.

Theresa looked over and caught him staring. She smiled, casual and friendly, giving no indication that in about forty-five minutes she was going to be naked and moaning as he did things to her that were still illegal in some states.

Unlike him, she seemed to have no problem whatsoever in keeping things casual. Not that she didn't feel the same intense chemistry he did—he was sure of that. But unlike every other woman he'd ever dated, Theresa wasn't inclined to share every single emotion she was feeling, didn't need to divulge every detail of her past and expect him to do the same. Even when he'd asked, she was remarkably closemouthed about what her life had been like up until the moment she ended up in his lap.

He knew her mother and Gia's were sisters, and knew that Theresa had left three years ago, and whatever happened caused a rift with the family. He'd deduced there was a guy involved but she refused to discuss it when asked. There had to be something going on. He'd known the Cipriani family for two years, and no one—including Theresa's mother or father—had ever so much as mentioned her name.

About all he knew about her was that she was smart, hardworking, funny, and sexy.

Sexy as hell.

His cock thickened as he wondered where they would do it tonight. In the past three weeks, they'd managed to christen every room in his house. He'd especially enjoyed having her in the kitchen. The breakfast bar was the perfect height for her to sit while he stood between her legs and fucked her.

"You don't have to wait for me," Theresa said as they walked home later. "Gia can always give me a ride home, or I can walk."

"I don't like you walking by yourself."

She snorted. "Believe me, I've made my way safely through neighborhoods a lot worse than this."

"Like where?" he pressed.

"You know, here and there," she said evasively.

His teeth clenched in frustration, but he didn't push. "I have to go out of town tomorrow for a few days. I want you to promise me you'll get a ride home with Gia."

"Where are you going?" He took small satisfaction in the stricken look that flitted across her face as he unlocked his gate.

"London," he said, taking her jacket and hanging it alongside his in the front closet. "I'll be gone until Thursday."

"Five days?" she asked.

"You gonna miss me?" he murmured, pulling her across the entryway to the sitting room. They hadn't done it in there for at least a week.

"Maybe," she laughed huskily as he pulled her down onto the silk-upholstered couch.

"Why don't you come with me?" he said. The question had been spontaneous, but now that he'd voiced it it sounded like a brilliant idea. Loath though he was to admit it, he dreaded leaving. In the past when business travel cropped up, he'd seen it as a welcome break in his routine, not to mention time away from the pressure of whomever he was dating.

Not this time. He was so covetous of every moment with Theresa he didn't want to spend one night away, much less five.

She laughed and seated herself in his lap. "Yeah, right, like I can afford to fly to London."

"I'll pay for your ticket."

"Even if I were willing to let you buy me a ticket to London," she said, the merest edge entering her voice, "I have to work."

"I'm sure Gia would give you the time off," he said, unbuttoning her blouse with practiced fingers. Baggy and unflattering though it was, Theresa's Ciao Bella blouse struck him as sexier and sexier every time he took it off her.

"I can't miss work. I need the money, especially since I'm starting classes next semester."

That was one small piece of personal information she had offered, her desire to finish school and get her nursing degree. He admired her work ethic, but selfishly he wanted her to blow it off so he could have her to himself. Not to mention that her schedule, the opposite of his, put a major damper on how much time they could spend together. Which had seemed like an advantage at first, but now just pissed him off.

"If you need money, Theresa, I can give it to you."

She went very still, her fingers frozen in the act of unbuttoning his fly. "What?"

He cleared his throat. In the past several weeks, he'd been hounded by the ever increasing need to protect her, take care of her. And the fact that she didn't seem to want it only made it that much worse. "I mean, if you don't want to work, so you can just focus on school, I'll give you the money. It's not like I can't afford it."

"You're offering to be my sugar daddy?" she asked, her voice dripping with scorn. Every line of her body was stiff. "Is that why you think I'm after? Is that what you think of me?" She shoved away and scrambled off his lap.

He jumped up after her. "I didn't mean it that way," he said. "I just want to help."

Her fingers fumbled with the buttons of her blouse, fastening them haphazardly in stiff, jerky motions. "I don't need your money, Vince. I can take care of myself."

"I know you can," he said, plowing his hands through his

hair in frustration. "Fuck it, forget I said anything about it." She moved for the door but he caught her, pulling her stiff and resisting body against his. "Don't be mad. It was a stupid idea, I know," he said, though he personally didn't think it was stupid in the least. "I just want to spend more time with you," he admitted, tracing his lips down her soft cheek, the sculpted line of her jaw.

"You spend every night with me," she pointed out, and he could feel her resistance waning as he licked and sucked the sensitive column of her throat.

He didn't argue the point, nor did he admit that much to his chagrin, the nights weren't enough. As he pulled her back down onto the sofa with him he realized that with Theresa, he would never get enough.

Theresa dragged through the next week, even though by rights she should have been happy about taking the first steps to get her life back in order. Not only had she managed to pay off her last credit card bill, she'd met with the head of the nursing program at San Francisco State. Despite her three-year break, Theresa would be able to jump back into the program where she'd left off. She had already registered for two classes starting in January.

And thanks to what she was saving on rent and the hefty tips she brought in from Ciao Bella, she would have no problem affording school.

None of that kept her from feeling downright crappy as she sat on Vince's couch, flipping through five hundred channels of nothing. She hated how they'd left things. Her brain kept stewing over their argument, beating her up for not having handled it better. She shouldn't have jumped all over him, but she disliked the idea of being taking care of. No, she wasn't a wildly successful city chick with a booming career, but she was damn well capable of cleaning up her own messes. She wasn't about

to let herself become dependent on Vince, financially or otherwise.

Still, it would have been nice spending the week with him in
London instead of here by herself. God, she missed him. More
than she'd ever expected, and more than she wanted to admit.

She'd tried so hard in the past few weeks not to let herself
get carried away, not to let herself get too attached. But she
missed everything about him, from his smile across the bar at
Ciao Bella, to his hot whisper in her ear when he was deep inside her.

She squeezed her thighs against the ache that bloomed between them. She *really* missed sex. And she missed the way he
pulled her against him afterwards, the way he would curl his
big body around hers so protectively. She hadn't been able to
sleep this week without him. She'd tried to convince herself it
was because she wasn't used to the smaller bed in the cottage.
So she'd sheepishly slipped into Vince's bed the second night,
only to toss and turn.

Which hadn't made Magda the housekeeper's suspicious,
censorious look any easier to bear.

As though sensing her depression, Chester picked up his
head off the cushion next to her and nestled his big golden head
in her lap. She couldn't help but smile. The crazy hairball was
actually making progress, if being able to maintain a sit-stay for
all of ten seconds was progress. He still regarded every piece of
furniture as his own personal doggie bed and had a tendency to
hump every new person he met, but at least he'd stopped chewing up her shoes when she left him to go to work.

She yawned and rubbed the grit from her eyes. Thank God
Vince was coming home tomorrow. The lack of sleep was starting to get to her, making her spacey at work and even a little
paranoid. The last few nights when she'd walked home after
work she'd had the strange sensation of someone following her,
only to look over her shoulder and see no one. She'd also re-

ceived a handful of hang-up calls on her cell phone. She'd chalked them up to a wrong number but they'd left her unsettled just the same.

She curled her fingers deeper into Chester's neck fur. "You'll protect me from the bad guys, right?" At the very least he'd lick them to death.

Right then her cell phone rang and she jumped about a foot, then rolled her eyes at her own skittishness. She didn't recognize the number, but picked it up anyway. If it was her hangup artist, she'd happily set him straight.

"Hey baby." Vince's rich, low baritone seemed to reach through the phone.

"Hey." Her voice was breathy with mingled pleasure and surprise. Vince hadn't called her at all this week. Not that she expected him to, because it wasn't like she was his girlfriend or anything. But deep down his neglect had hurt. "Is everything okay?"

"Everything is fine," he said, sounding weary. "I'm sorry I didn't call sooner, but the time difference makes it hard."

"It's okay," she said, doing her damnedest to ignore the little thrill she got at the idea he'd been thinking about her at all.

"I miss you, Theresa," he said his voice going low and husky. "Did you miss me?"

"Maybe a little," she said coyly.

"You don't sound convinced."

"Maybe you need to come home and remind me what I should be missing."

"Lucky for you I'm coming home tomorrow. I've been thinking about you all week," he chuckled. "I've been getting very creative."

Theresa felt her blood race in her veins and she settled back into the couch. "Really? Care to share?"

He paused and swallowed audibly over the phone line.

"Are you someplace you can really . . . talk?" she asked, running her fingers idly along her velour covered thigh. She'd never in her life had phone sex. In fact, it had always struck her as kind of weird. But right now she was running red hot at the thought of listening to Vince share his more creative moments with her. "I don't have to be at work for another four hours, so I have plenty of time to,"—she paused deliberately—"listen."

He was silent so long she was sure he was going to blow her off. Embarrassed heat crept its way up her chest and she braced herself for him to laugh at her and her hamhanded attempts at acting the femme fatale.

"Where are you right now?" he said, his east coast accent thickening like it always did when he was turned on.

"On the sofa in your TV room."

"What are you wearing?"

She looked down at her long sleeve T-shirt and stretchy yoga pants. "A black lace teddy, garters and stockings."

His laugh rippled over her like a caress. "Really?"

"I like to feel pretty when I'm watching TV."

"Honey, if you've been hanging out in lingerie in the middle of the afternoon, I'm going to have to start coming home for lunch."

"Yeah? What would you do?"

He paused and she could hear him clear his throat. "I'd call you first and let you know I was coming over. Give you time to think about it so by the time I got home you would already be primed."

Like she was right now.

"I'd tell you to get on the bed and wait for me. In fact, why don't you go over there right now."

"I'm walking," she said and went over to the bed in the next room. Chester stayed where he was.

"Now take off your T-shirt and pants," Vince said.

"Hey, you're ruining it." But even though she felt silly, she did exactly what he said.

"No, I'm not," he laughed. "I love thinking about you hanging out in your sweats. And I love thinking about what you have on underneath."

She looked down. "I'm wearing an ivory satin and lace bra—"

He made a low sound of approval. "The one where your tits almost spill over the cups?"

"Yes. And my underwear is the matching boy shorts with the stretch lace panel on the sides."

"Umm, the ones that do amazing things for your ass."

"I'm glad you think so."

"I wish I could be there now. Damn, the things I would do to you . . ."

"Tell me," she said, running her fingers idly along the lace trimmed edge of her bra, down the soft skin of her stomach. She closed her eyes, imagining how she felt to him.

"First I'd have to kiss you for awhile, because you know how much I love your mouth."

She licked her lips, his taste imprinted on them from hours of his deep, hungry kisses.

"Then I'd slide your bra straps down your smooth shoulders until your breasts were bare so I could lick your nipples like they were covered in cream."

A soft little whimper escaped her throat, and her hand trailed over her own breast to cover her nipple. It was as hard as though he'd sucked it, pressing insistently against her palm. The images he was evoking were so intense, so real, she could almost feel his hot skin sliding against hers as he came down over her. Which reminded her . . . "Are you naked yet?"

"For real? Or in this particular scenario?"

"Both," she laughed. "The way I see it, if I'm hanging out half naked by myself, you should be too."

"Fair enough." She heard the faint rustle of clothing being dropped before he got back on the line. "Now where was I," he said. "Right. I was sucking on your nipples, rubbing them with my tongue, sucking hard like I know you like."

She shifted restlessly against the sheets and pinched her nipples, trying to recreate the sensations with her own hands.

"By now you're so wet you've soaked your panties," he said, and she could hear his breath hitch over the phone line.

Proof that he was as aroused as she sent a pulse of heat between her thighs. "And you're hard, aren't you? Rock hard and dying to get inside me."

"Baby, you have no idea. But I'm going to wait a little while first, make sure you're really ready."

"I'm ready now," she said.

"Yeah? Do me a favor. Slip your hand inside your panties and tell me how you feel. Are you as wet as I think you are?"

Blushing to the roots of her hair, Theresa did as he asked. "Wetter." Her embarrassment melted into satisfaction at his deep groan.

"I want to go down on you so bad, lick up every drop of your sweet juice. Then I'd slide inside you, give it to you hard and deep."

She moaned and slid her fingers down and around her clit.

"If I close my eyes I can almost feel your sweet, tight pussy around me."

She slid her fingers inside herself, moaning at the penetration even though it was a pale imitation of what she really wanted. They slipped back up, dancing around the slippery bud of her clit. "I'm so close, Vince. Thinking about you inside me."

He let out a shaky groan. "Jesus, Theresa. I wish I was there right now. Tell me when you're coming, baby. I want to go with you."

She could hear his breath increase, and her own came in sharp pants. "I'm so close," her strokes grew firmer, faster as every sinew tensed. Her control snapped. "Now," she breathed, moaning, sighing, wanting him to feel her pleasure even from thousands of miles away.

He cursed softly and groaned her name as he found his own release.

She curled onto her side, into herself, feeling oddly empty. Even though the phone sex had been hot, and yes, satisfying, it wasn't the same when Vince wasn't here to pull her close. Right now she wanted to curl into his big, muscular body, breathe in his scent. Wanted it so much her eyes burned with tears. "I miss you so much," she whispered, unable to keep the emotion from her voice.

He sighed heavily. "I miss you too, Theresa, more than I ever thought possible."

Something bloomed in her chest, deep and intense. Something that felt an awful lot like love.

9

Vince's mind and body were spinning out of control. Phone sex. He was in the middle of one of the biggest deals of his career, and he'd nearly missed an important investor meeting because he was busy having phone sex with Theresa in his hotel room.

Even without Theresa actually there, it was still a sexually satisfying experience. Yet it left him unfulfilled and on edge, like giving a starving man a tiny taste of an appetizer when what he really needed was an all-you-can-eat buffet.

He was crazy about her. He'd realized his feelings were intensifying well past the point of merely sleeping together, but he hadn't realized how far gone he was until he was forced to be away from her for a week. Not even. Jesus, he was out of his mind after only five days away from her.

He thought about her nonstop, wondering what she was doing. Wondering if she missed him, embarrassed that he missed her as much as he did. He told her he hadn't had time to call, which was a lie. He'd forced himself not to call, trying to prove he could survive several days without talking to her, hearing her voice.

Because hey, their relationship was not about talk, not by a long shot. It was all sex, pure and simple. Out of sight, out of mind, right?

In a moment of weakness, he'd broken down and called her, and then she'd surprised the hell out of him by suggesting phone sex.

God, he couldn't wait to see her. His body was humming by the time his plane touched down on the runway. On the cab ride home he reminded himself that Theresa would be at work by the time he got home, so he'd have to wait several hours to see her. Touch her. Taste her. He needed to be patient.

Yeah, tell that to his cock.

He let himself in the front gate and did a double take when he saw the lights on in Theresa's cottage. Something that felt like butterflies erupted in his stomach at the prospect of seeing her. *Calm down*, he told himself sternly. *She probably just left a light on for the damn dog.* God, she had him as excited as a fifteen-year-old about to lose his virginity.

Then her door opened and she was calling his name. She stood in her doorway, smiling, wearing a short, satiny robe, her dark hair spilling thick and wavy over her shoulders. Vince swore he heard angels sing as he rushed across the yard.

He wasn't sure who moved first, but the next thing he knew his mouth was on hers and her arms wound around his neck as she stood up on tiptoe to press herself as close as possible. His suitcase and briefcase landed with a thump on her floor as he pushed her back inside. Somehow he shrugged out of his suit coat as he picked her up by the waist and maneuvered her to the closest flat surface he could find.

His hip bumped the small kitchen table. Good enough for what he was after, and that was getting inside her as fast as humanly possible. His mouth never left hers, sucking on her tongue, nipping at her lips as he yanked the silky lapels of her robe apart. He was vaguely aware of something pale and silky underneath, but he didn't take the time to appreciate it as her hands flicked open his belt buckle and unfastened his pants. She tugged his pants and boxers down over his hips and his cock sprang out like a beast, hard and aching and raring to go.

She produced a condom out of thin air and rolled it on. She knew exactly what he wanted, needed, because she shimmied out of her underwear and spread her legs wide, tilting her hips up as he plowed into her with a complete lack of restraint or finesse.

"Theresa," he said, but inside his brain he was screaming, *mine!* Then all he could manage was a strangled moan as her body tightened around him, surrounding him like a hot, wet fist as he pumped inside her.

Two strokes and he was already coming, unable to hold back his orgasm if his life depended on it. *Fuck.* He would make it up to her later . . .

But, sweet Christ, she was right there with him, moaning and squirming under him as her body convulsed around his, clenching and releasing in concert with his own release.

Afterward he felt like he'd been hit by a truck, unable to muster the energy to do anything but land the occasional kiss on her cheek.

She shifted underneath him, and he realized that this wasn't the most comfortable position for either of them: Theresa on her back on the hard table, her satin robe and ivory satin and lace bra twisted around her torso, and him still fully clothed and bent over her with his face resting on the table's faux wood finish.

Mustering the last of his energy, he scooped her up and staggered the few steps to the couch. Chester, who'd apparently been asleep curled in a corner, jumped up in surprise.

"Down boy," Vince muttered, settling on the couch with Theresa on his lap. "I thought you would be at work," he said, smoothing her sex-tangled hair.

"I told Gia I ate some bad fish and she found someone to cover for me," she said with a guilty smile. "I wanted to be here when you got home. I hope that's okay."

He laughed. "More than okay," he said, pulling her even closer. "I wasn't sure how I was going to make it until you got home from the restaurant, I was so excited to see you."

She lifted her head from his shoulder and cocked a dark, arched brow at him. "Yeah?"

He traced a finger down her cheek and grinned. "Are you kidding? I had to keep my briefcase on my lap the entire ride home so the cab driver wouldn't think I was some kind of pervert."

She laughed at that, and the soft sound rippled through him. He buried his nose in her hair, drinking in the soft, warm feel of her in his arms, the sweet, girly scent of her filling his head. In his life, in his work, he was rarely at rest, physically or mentally. He was always in motion, whether on a long run or running to his next big meeting. His mind was always thinking two, three steps ahead, chasing the next deal, cooking up a strategy for his next big move.

One of his ex-girlfriends had been really into meditation therapy and had tried to get him to try it. He'd refused, saying he had too much to do to waste any time sitting around with his eyes closed thinking about nothing. Needless to say, the relationship hadn't lasted long.

But one thing she'd talked about sprang to mind right now as he sat on the couch with Theresa curled in his arms. Being present in the moment. Right now he wasn't thinking about anything but Theresa, the way she felt, the way she sounded, the way she smelled.

The way she made him feel.

He'd been having a lot of these moments lately. Since he met her, in fact. She made the rest of the world fall away. It was kind of amazing.

And really fucking unnerving, especially for a guy like him, who had pretty much managed to convince himself that no-thing—especially not a woman—would ever distract him from his drive to succeed. Yet here he was, on the couch with his twenty-four-year-old maybe girlfriend, distracted.

Sometime later he carried her to the bedroom and made love to her again. This time nice and slow, paying special attention to all the parts he'd missed.

Afterward she lay back against the pillows, stretching and yawning with a look of complete satisfaction on her face. His gaze roamed over her body, over the lush curves of breasts and hips, the sweet little patch of dark curls between her legs.

Again that possessive urge swelled inside him. *Mine.*

Her hand reached for his face and she ran a thumb between his brows. He didn't even realize he was frowning until he felt his forehead relax.

"How can you possibly be in a bad mood after that?" she said, her words ending in a sleepy yawn.

"I'm not. I was just thinking about something." He held his breath, waiting for her, like every other woman in the world, to ask what. But Theresa, being Theresa, wasn't inclined to pry in-side his head. He caught her hand in his and kissed her finger-tips. "I got you something."

"Really?" she said, a hint of wariness in her voice. "You don't have to get me presents."

He shook his head and went to retrieve the box from his suitcase. He climbed back in bed and held out the flat velvet case as an uncharacteristic wave of nervousness washed over him. He hadn't bought a piece of jewelry for a woman in years, after realizing that they assigned way more meaning to gifts like that than he ever intended.

But when he'd seen the pendant in the Cartier window, he'd known he had to buy it for her. The rich red ruby would glow against her creamy skin. The stone was on the smaller side, in a setting that was faintly exotic, just like her. Luxurious, but not so flashy she couldn't wear it every day. That really got him off, the idea of her wearing it every day, the pendant nestled against the warmth of her breast.

Jesus, he was sounding like a lovesick chick even in his own head.

He knew what the gesture meant, even if he wasn't ready to admit it out loud, and the idea made his gut twist in apprehension. And the way Theresa was staring at the box, as though he were holding a snake in his hand, didn't help matters.

"Vince." she said warily. "I don't think—"

"Just open it," he snapped.

Eyes wide, she took the case from him and opened the lid, exhaling on a sharp gasp when she saw the pendant hanging on the delicate gold chain. "It's gorgeous," she breathed.

He started to grin.

She snapped the lid shut and shoved the case back in his hand. "It's too much. I can't accept it."

Patience, never his strong suit, fled in the face of fatigue, jet lag, and irritation. "Why the fuck not?" he said in a tone that had made many a CEO cower across a boardroom table.

She flinched almost imperceptibly. "It's too expensive. You buying me jewelry is not part of our deal—"

"C'mon, Theresa, I saw something and wanted you to have it, simple as that." Actually, it was more complicated than he wanted to explain, but he was too fucking tired to try logic to get through her resistance. "I don't see why you have to make such a big deal out of it."

"We already covered this before you left. I don't want you to give me money, or buy me jewelry like I'm your mistress—"

"Theresa, I offered to pay for school because I want to

spend more time with you. And I bought you the necklace because I wanted to buy my *girlfriend* something beautiful." He got up from the bed and yanked his pants on. The jewelry case lay on the bed. He picked it up and tossed it at her. "Take it or don't. Right now I'm too tired to give a shit."

Theresa's chest constricted as she watched Vince's retreating form. Through his anger and frustration, she could read his hurt. Big, tough, arrogant Vince's feelings were hurt. The realization cut her to the quick.

God, how had her foray into no-strings-attached sex become such a convoluted mess? She wasn't supposed to care so much.

And neither was he. But he did, and that realization sent such pure delight through her she thought she might burst through her skin.

She'd resigned herself to her own feelings, prepared herself to deal with the inevitable end of their affair. Not once had she allowed herself to consider he might return her feelings. She was a college dropout with skeletons in her closet she didn't expect him to get past. He was a high-powered, high-profile businessman who wore his wealth and success as easily as he wore his own skin.

But at this moment none of that seemed to matter, and for the first time since her life had spun completely out of control, Theresa allowed herself to hope for something so completely out of reach.

"Vince, wait," she said, shrugging into her short satin robe and grabbing the jewelry case as she hurried after him.

He turned to face her, his face a mask of impatience.

She held out the case to him. "Will you put it on me?"

He took the case warily and opened it. The thin gold chain and filigree of the pendant were even more delicate in his big, long-fingered hand. She lifted her hair and turned away from him so he could loop the chain around her neck and fasten it with deft fingers. He kissed her neck and turned her to face the mirror that hung over the couch.

The ruby's deep red was set off perfectly against her faintly olive skin and dark hair. "It's beautiful," she said.

"You're beautiful."

She turned to him and buried her face in his chest. "I'm sorry I was such an idiot," she said. "But this is moving really fast for me. I didn't expect—" She cut herself off before she admitted too much.

"This is way more than rebound sex, isn't it?" She could hear the hint of laughter in his question. She nodded and wrapped her arms around his waist.

After that, everything was different. Though they didn't spell it out in so many words, the energy between Vince and Theresa had changed, and they both knew it. Before, Theresa had tried to maintain a certain amount of distance. Sure, they'd slept together every night, but it had been more furtive, like she was sneaking over to his place after work only to have sex.

Now they spent every spare moment together, which admittedly wasn't much. Vince's work schedule was as jampacked as ever and Theresa's working nights didn't help any. But on weekends before she had to go to work, they spent long, lazy mornings in bed before taking Chester for meandering walks around the city.

When she had an evening off, he took her out to dinner, or even better, let her play around with all of his fancy kitchen equipment, often with mixed results.

"It's good," he insisted one night as he chewed doggedly at a piece of roast chicken so dry and tough it was like eating string.

She shot him a look and ate a bite of salad. "I didn't realize it would cook so much faster in a convection oven." She tried another bite of the chicken, just to be sure. Yep, it sucked. "This is worse than my mom's Thanksgiving turkey."

He blotted his lips and took a sip of wine. "Will you be spending the holiday with your folks?" he said, his voice carefully neutral.

She'd been trying not to think about the holiday coming up soon. "I have to work," she said. But that didn't leave her completely off the hook. Gia had reminded her several times about the Ciprianis' longstanding tradition of closing the restaurant on the Friday after the holiday to host a big dinner for the family and restaurant staff. Theresa would have tried to beg off, come up with some sort of excuse not to go, but she knew that this, the first major holiday after Uncle Alberto's death, would be especially hard on Gia. And after all her cousin had done for her, Theresa couldn't bail simply because she didn't want to face the family.

Including, of course, her parents. While she was thankful to be back in San Francisco, away from Mark and making a respectable living again, she wasn't too excited about the prospect of celebrating the holiday with her glowering, disapproving father. That is, if he wasn't still pretending she was dead.

"What are your plans?" They hadn't discussed the subject at all. On the one hand, Vince worked so hard he seemed like the kind of guy who would skip most holidays. On the other, she knew he came from a big Italian family like her own, the kind of family where things like holidays and traditions were important. "Are you going back east?"

"No," he said curtly with a smile that didn't quite reach his eyes. "I can really only handle one holiday a year with them, and this year it's Christmas. So I'll be around if you want to do something on your day off."

He turned his attention back to his plate. Theresa took a fortifying sip of wine, wondering if what she was about to propose would turn out to be a complete disaster. "I don't know if you'll be interested, but Gia's going to close the restaurant that Friday for a big family dinner. I don't suppose you'd, like, want to go with me?" Ooh, she was about as smooth as when she'd asked Tony Spinelli to the seventh grade dance. It was times like this when she wondered why Vince, who could have his pick of any single woman in San Francisco, seemed to be so enthralled with her. There was seriously no accounting for taste.

The smile that graced his face practically made her melt into a puddle on her chair. And if that wasn't enough to do it, the way he reached across the table and took her hand and said, "I'd love to," his dark eyes warm and intense, pretty much sent her over the edge.

It all felt too good to be true, she reflected several days later as she was walking to work. Somehow her life, which had seemed such a wreck only a month ago, was almost completely back on track. Okay, her father still refused to take her calls, but her mother hinted that maybe once she was back in school he'd be willing to give their relationship another shot. But on the plus side she had a good job she liked and she was set to start classes at San Francisco State in January.

And she had the most perfect boyfriend in the world. And though Theresa wasn't about to let a man define her life or be responsible for her happiness, she knew her renewed optimism was mostly due to him. The way he looked at her, the way he talked to her, made her feel like she was capable of doing anything. Almost like nothing bad could happen, as long as she could come home to him at the end of the day.

As she crossed Columbus Street and walked the last block to Ciao Bella, she couldn't quite banish the cynical little voice that warned her this was just too perfect. When life was going this well, something bad was bound to happen.

"Hey, Theresa."

Her blood ran cold at the sound of the familiar voice coming from behind her.

Damn, she really hated being right.

"What are you doing here?" she said, taking great pride that her voice betrayed none of her panic.

With his light brown hair, blue, blue eyes and sculpted, almost pretty features, Mark Silverton resembled a daytime soap star. It was only when you looked closely that you saw the signs of his true character. The slightly bloated belly on his lanky frame from too many nights of hard drinking. The red-rimmed eyes and pallor from too many hours in smoky back rooms over never-ending hands of poker. The almost undetectable redness around his nostrils from snorting controlled substances.

Theresa had seen none of this when she first met him. She'd been blinded by his good looks and the attention he paid her, and she'd thought his less than legal activities made him sexy after her years of only dating boys her parents approved of. Out with her friends, she'd met him at a bar and she'd been swept off her feet by that first charming smile. Too bad she hadn't been wise enough to recognize him for the snake he was.

For all the bravado Gia credited her with, Theresa wasn't that much more worldly than her cousin. Unlike Gia, she'd dated guys before she met Mark, but she'd still been a virgin when she met him. Growing up Catholic and under her ultra conservative father's rule meant she wasn't going to give it up to just anyone. She was saving it, if not for marriage, then at least true love.

And like an idiot, she'd thought Mark was it. She hadn't realized how wrong she was until it was too late. In a bold, impetuous, and, she now realized, childish, move, she'd jumped on Mark's invitation to move to New York City with him, seeing it as a chance for adventure and a way to get out from under her father's ever watchful eye. She was twenty-one, she'd thought, an adult, ready to make her own decisions. Even if they did prove disastrous.

It had taken her three years to get out of there, to finally cut herself loose. But here he was, turning up like a bad smell.

"Come on, babe, don't be like that," he said, his lips stretching into a smile that didn't warm up his blue eyes.

"Don't 'babe' me, Mark. What are you doing here?" He looked a little surprised at her firm tone. Not surprising, since she'd spent a lot of their relationship trying to keep him from flying off the handle. But she wasn't the same person who'd believed so blindly in love that she would do anything to keep him happy. And she was no longer susceptible to that empty smile and the sweet, cajoling tone. She knew too well what demons Mark hid, and knew how easy it was for him to take out that darkness on her.

His eyes narrowed. "Maybe I wanted to make sure you were okay. You left without a word, and I was worried."

A humorless laugh exploded from her. "Worry? That's what those hundred voicemails were about when you called me an faithless cunt?"

His attempt at charm fell away and his face settled into cruel, sulky lines. "You left me high and dry, Theresa. You spent all our money, and now Dante's goons are coming after me."

Disbelief stunned her like a physical blow. "Our money? Our money? That was my money. *I* earned it. I spent it all paying off Big Johnny to save your ass. And on rent so you wouldn't get evicted."

Even now it made her feel sick that, even at the end, even after all he'd done, she'd still worried about him. She'd known he was in bad shape and had paid off his dealer and advanced him rent so he wouldn't find himself out on the street.

"I should have let Big Johnny kill you." she said bitterly.

"I needed that money for Dante," he said. "You should have minded your business and let me handle it."

He took a menacing step towards her. She stepped back reflexively and cast a nervous look around, then stopped herself. He wasn't going to hit her, not out in the open, not with this many people around. It was 5 p.m. on a Wednesday night. North Beach sidewalks were crowded with people coming from their offices from the nearby financial district, meeting up for drinks or an early dinner.

Which meant Vince could be showing up any time. True, he usually stayed later at the office and showed up at the restaurant around seven-thirty, but it would be just her luck for him to show up right as Ciao Bella opened for dinner. "I don't have time for this, Mark." She turned to walk into the restaurant but he grabbed her by the upper arm. To a passerby it might look like a gentle hold, but Theresa could feel the painful press of his fingers into the muscle of her arm.

"Don't you walk away from me, Theresa. I told you I need money."

"And I don't see how that's my problem." She tried to jerk her arm out of his hold.

"It's your problem because you emptied out our bank account, and now I'm coming to collect."

"I don't have any money, Mark, and even if I did, why would I give you a single cent?"

WILL THAT BE ALL? / 233

"You talk to your father lately, Theresa?"

She frowned, taken off guard by the seemingly random line of questioning.

"He forgive you for moving out yet? For living in sin?"

She swallowed hard, not liking where this was going. "Why do you want to know?"

"Because I have some photos, Theresa, great photos from your stint at Slap Jack's. I think old Nello might appreciate some copies. Maybe a big poster-size print to hang over the mantel. Here, take a look at this one."

Theresa swallowed back her nausea and looked at the display screen on Mark's phone. Even knowing exactly what she would see didn't soften the blow. The resolution wasn't great, but she easily recognized herself. Yet it was such a different version of herself it was almost like looking at a stranger.

The actions were familiar. The image showed her leaning in to put a glass in front of a male customer. But while she was still a cocktail waitress, her attire was decidedly different from what she wore for her job at Ciao Bella.

Even on the tiny screen it was clear that her makeup had been applied with a heavy hand, intended to make her eyes more exotic and mysterious, lips painted a rich, deep red. Then there was her outfit, or lack thereof. Her full breasts were tipped with flesh-colored pasties, and her gold g-string barely hid the essentials. The rest of her body was decorated with artfully applied paint and sequins.

Those were the bad old days. Her job at Ciao Bella never required her to pause in her serving duties and dance around a pole.

"Think your dad will be proud to find out his little Theresa was a stripper?"

"I wasn't a stripper," she snapped, though she knew it was merely a technicality. Though she didn't actually take off her clothes and had never shown her nipples or given a lap dance, she'd danced nearly naked for tips. Most people wouldn't see the difference. Her father certainly wouldn't.

And she bet Vince wouldn't either.

"I don't have any money," she said. "The money I took out of our joint account to pay your bills was pretty much it."

"Cut the crap, Theresa. You think I don't know what you've been up to? I've seen where you live with your new boyfriend. Don't even start with this poor mouse shit."

So she hadn't been paranoid when those hang-up calls had given her pause and when she'd felt like someone was watching her.

She shook her head, refusing to let Vince get dragged into this. "He's not my boyfriend," she lied. "I take care of his dog."

"Then what's this?"

Theresa flinched as he reached out and hooked his finger through the chain of her necklace. She slapped his hand away. "It's nothing."

"Right. It sure as shit didn't come out of a Cracker Jack box. I bet it's worth two, maybe three grand."

Theresa felt the blood drain out of her face. She'd had no idea it had cost that much. And she trusted Mark's assessment, since he'd often taken his winnings in the form of jewels. "It's a fake," she said, tucking the pendant back into the neckline of her shirt. "I got it off a street vendor."

"It's Cartier," he said blandly. "And I have no doubt you're doing a hell of a lot more than walking his dog if he's buying you bling like that." He licked his lips and leered at her. "Your skills must have improved since I last saw you."

It made her physically ill to think he'd ever touched her. That she'd willingly, even enthusiastically, given her virginity to him, actually felt bereft when his sex drive had waned as his drug use went up.

She felt awful. Stupid and dirty for ever falling for him and his millimeter-thick veneer of charm. She yanked off the necklace and shoved it at him, feeling sicker as he closed his covetous hand around it. But she'd do anything to get him out of here, out of her life, to keep her father from finding out what her life in New York had really been like.

And most of all, to protect what she had with Vince.

"Take it," she snapped. "And take this." She yanked her wallet out of her bag and pulled out her checkbook as well. "I have a hundred or so here," she said, shoving a wad of bills at him, "and a little over a grand in my checking account." She wrote out a check, knowing she'd have to put off school for another semester, but she'd worry about that later. "Don't ever come near me again."

She wheeled around and slammed open the door of the restaurant, entering without a backward look at Mark. Her hands were shaky, iced with cold sweat, and her intestines knotted around each other like an unruly ball of yarn.

"Was that Mark?"

Gia's voice startled her, and Theresa took a calming breath before answering. "Yeah. But don't worry. It's no big deal."

Gia wasn't buying it, her big hazel eyes narrowing as her head tilted in a way that said she knew Theresa was bullshitting her. "He left dozens of threatening voice mails on your phone and now he shows up out of the blue. How can that be nothing?"

Theresa tied her short black apron around her waist. "He wanted to talk, that's all." The lie tasted bitter on her lips, especially since she was lying to Gia, the only member of her family so far to open up her arms, the only one who didn't treat Theresa like a huge fuckup.

"Let me talk to Gabe," Gia said, reaching for the phone. "He can help you with a restraining order—"

"I don't need a restraining order," Theresa replied, more sharply than she intended. "And that's nice of you to offer to call Gabe," she added, softening her tone, "but he's got much bigger problems to deal with than my stupid ex-boyfriend." Plus if Mark got wind that an FBI agent was sniffing around and that Theresa had filed a restraining order, a FedEx man would show up on her father's doorstep tomorrow, guaranteed. She pasted a smile on her face and gave her cousin what she hoped was a reassuring hug. "Thanks for worrying about me, but I can take care of myself."

Gia didn't look convinced, but put the receiver back on the hook.

"And Gia," Theresa said, deliberately casual as she wiped down a table, "don't say anything to Vince. I don't want him to worry."

Gia cocked an eyebrow and gave her a very pointed look. "You don't think Vince should know your ex-boyfriend is in town?"

Theresa's gaze skittered away from her cousin's hard stare and shame heated her cheeks. She hadn't spelled out her relationship with Vince, but Gia would have had to be blind not to notice that something was going on. She straightened her shoulders and met her cousin's look dead on. "There's no reason for Vince to know," she said, staring back at Gia in a way that told her if Gia spilled to Vince, Theresa would never forgive her.

"Everything okay?" Vince asked when Theresa hung up her phone. She'd practically jumped off the couch when it rang. Then she'd looked at the caller ID and breathed an almost imperceptible sigh of relief before greeting Gia on the other end. He wouldn't have even noticed if he hadn't been watching her so closely. But lately he'd been keeping a close eye on her every move, trying to figure out what the hell was going on.

Theresa was keeping something from him, Vince knew it. She was startled every time the phone rang, and when they were out, her eyes constantly roved over the crowd as though she was looking for someone. A few times in the past week he'd shown up at Ciao Bella to find Theresa and Gia in fiercely whispered conversation, only to have Theresa smile blandly at him when he asked what was going on.

"Gia just wanted to know what time we were going to show up on Friday. I told her around four, if that's okay with you."

"Fine," he said, taking in her wide, innocent-looking eyes and anxious smile. His years spent negotiating across boardroom tables had made him pretty good at reading people. He knew when companies were fudging numbers or overselling their "revolutionary" technologies. And he knew when someone wasn't telling him everything he needed to know.

It was frustrating as hell. He'd never met a more closemouthed woman. In the past, women had been all too eager to spill themselves over the table, telling him about their mommy issues, their daddy issues, their relationship issues, their issue issues, in an effort to get him to open up too. Theresa would talk about work, about school, and about him, but not much else. She'd once alluded to the fact that she and her father hadn't spoken much after she moved to New York with her boyfriend.

And forget any info about the boyfriend. Vince couldn't even get a name, not even from Gia, who finally told him point blank that if he had any questions about Theresa and her past, he needed to ask Theresa himself.

He was annoyed. At Theresa, for being so closed up when he thought they'd reached a turning point in their relationship. And at himself, for wanting to know every damn thing about a woman, and for using phrases like "turning point" about dating a woman.

Theresa, all five-foot-two and approximately one hundred ten pounds of her, was turning big, tough Vince Mattera into a goddamn chick.

"Are you going to tell me what the fuck's bugging you, or am I going to have to beat it out of you?" He'd meant to keep his tone light and joking, but he obviously didn't succeed if the way Theresa scooted herself into the far corner of the couch and folded her knees into her chest was any indication.

"N-nothing's bugging me. I'm a little nervous about seeing the family tomorrow, that's all."

"What do you have to be nervous about?"

He saw her throat work as she swallowed. "Big family gatherings get to me."

"Cut the bullshit," he said in the same no-nonsense tone he used for work. "I know something's bugging you that's got nothing to do with your family. Is it me? You don't want to show up with me tomorrow?"

Her mouth fell open in a genuine look of surprise. "Of course not. How could you even think that? In fact," she laughed humorlessly, "most likely they're going to wonder why you're with *me*."

"Why would you say something like that?" Okay, she'd said stuff like this before, casual comments he blew off as her insecurity about her age or income level in comparison to him. But lately he wondered if there was something more going on.

She shook her head. "Nothing. Forget I said anything."

"What is so bad about you that you think it's going to make me walk away from you?" he asked, hands flung out in exasperation.

Her lashes lay dark and thick against her cheekbones as she closed her eyes and her plump lips compressed into a tight line. Still she didn't say anything.

He'd never felt like this toward a woman, wanting to simultaneously shake her until she finally opened up to him, and wanting to hold her close and reassure her that nothing she revealed could ever make him turn his back on her.

Because he loved her.

His blood vessels constricted and his stomach bottomed out at the thought. But there it was.

He moved down his big leather couch until he was mere

inches from her. He reached out a hand that shook only a little and cupped her cheek. "Theresa," he searched for the right words, feeling like an incompetent ass. "I care about you." God, what a plain vanilla word that was to describe what he felt, but he wasn't quite ready to drop the L-bomb. "A lot. And I really want this to work out between us."

Her big brown eyes were getting watery. "I want it to work out too. But I don't know if it can."

"It can if you trust me enough to tell me what's going on with you."

"It's not that easy, Vince."

"Why not? I'm sitting here, telling you how much I want to be with you, telling you that nothing you say is going to change that."

She gave him a funny half smile and caught his hand in hers. "That's really sweet, Vince." She leaned forward, closing the distance between them and pressed her mouth against his. "But I don't want to talk anymore tonight." Her tongue teased open his lips, and a shaft of heat went straight to his groin. Her hand cupped him brazenly, stroking him through his fly.

She was using sex to distract him. And, he was ashamed to admit, he was an easy mark.

Sweet. She called him sweet. He sure as shit didn't feel sweet. There were a whole lot of intense, conflicting things churning around in his guts, and sweet definitely wasn't one of them. Anger, lust, need. Love, confusion, and fear.

All of it boiling up until it came out in a mad rush. He kissed her hard, his lips and tongue almost punishing as he yanked her shirt and pants off. His fist twisted in her silky panties until they ripped. The second she was naked his fingers probed between her legs, sinking inside her hot, wet core.

Satisfaction tugged low in his gut as his cock got superhard. She might be using sex to distract him, but she wanted him as bad as he wanted her. Her back arched as he dragged his fingers out, then thrust back in. He yanked the cup of her bra aside and closed his teeth over her nipple, biting down just hard enough to make her cry out before hitting it with the wet lash of his tongue.

He picked her up off the couch and carried her to the bed, tossing her down on the mattress as he paused to yank off his shirt. Socks, pants and boxers went flying, and he came down over her with all the subtlety and finesse of a Mack truck.

If this was the only way she would let him get close, then so be it. He wasn't going to waste his time trying to get in her head, to get her to tell him what she was thinking and feeling. But she was his, and it was about time she realized it.

He rolled her to her back and gripped her wrists in one hand, pinning them above her head as he kneed her legs apart.

She squirmed under him, trying to break free of his hold. "Let go of my wrists," she said, a hot flush of color blooming across her breasts and chest. "I don't like this."

He looked at her nipples, pointing vehemently at the ceiling, and he dipped his fingers into her slick folds. "Oh, I think you do, sweet thing." He drew his fingers out, spread her cream over her labia and clit for emphasis. Her hips rocked against his fingers, proving his point. He wanted to push her, see how much she could take, show her that her body knew exactly what she wanted.

She wanted him, no matter how she tried to push him away.

And he wanted her, with a soul-deep ache that made him half crazy every time he got in the same room with her. He bent to kiss her, sucking her tongue into his mouth, sliding his bare chest against the soft fullness of her tits. His cock rode the slick cleft of her pussy, slipping and sliding along her clit until they were both moaning from the delicious friction.

"Please," she whispered against his lips, "let me touch you."

"No," he said, "you want to fuck, fine, but tonight we're

doing this my way." Her dark eyes widened with confusion. He didn't blame her. He wasn't sure what had gotten into him either. But he'd be damned if he'd stop himself.

He bent his head to suck at the soft skin of her throat. A little mark appeared almost instantly, a tiny bruise marring the pale expanse. He liked that. Liked that he'd marked her. After tonight, she would have other marks in other tender places. Then tomorrow she'd sit across the table from him with the evidence of their sex on her. No matter how hard she tried to keep her distance out of bed, she wouldn't be able to escape those tiny, physical reminders.

He loved that.

He was fucking insane.

Theresa jumped under the almost painful pressure of his mouth as he rained firm, biting kisses down her neck, across her chest. He was different tonight, more forceful, more dominant than he'd ever been. As though he was calling her on her attempt to distract him with sex.

He hadn't let go of his anger and frustration, he was channeling it. Into his hard, forceful kisses, in the impatient touch of his hands. It freaked her out a little. Not just the way he was acting, but how much she liked it.

She moaned as his mouth closed hard over her nipple and his cock burrowed between her legs. She was pinned, helpless underneath him. Yet she knew with one thousand percent certainty that Vince would never, ever hurt her. Despite his much greater size and weight, he would stop the second she stopped liking it.

And, God, did she like it. Loved it. Loved the way he touched her with near frantic urgency. Loved the way his breath came hot and heavy over her skin. Loved the way his hard cock slid against her clit until she was dying for him to fuck her hard and deep. Her hands flexed against the pillow where he had them pinned, her biceps strained as she tried to free them. She wanted to feel the hard muscles flexing under his hot skin, trace the beads of sweat trickling down his abs with her fingertips.

He wouldn't give an inch. His mouth sucked at her nipples, his teeth adding an edge that rode a fine line of pain. Another surge of wetness soaked his erection, drenching him with the evidence of her need. "Vince, please," she whispered, shifting under him, trying to get the thick head aligned with her opening. "I want you inside me."

"Not yet." He lifted his head from her breasts. Her nipples were sharp, dark points, and the pale skin showed his love bites and the rasp of his whiskers. "You gotta be careful what you start with me."

The wealthy businessman had disappeared. He sounded like a menacing wiseguy, like one of those guys who'd tried to take the restaurant from Gia.

Somehow it turned Theresa on even more.

Vince leaned up and kissed her, and this time she gave as good as she got, sucking hard on his tongue, nipping his bottom lip when he tried to pull away. His eyes were wild and fierce; he licked his lip where she'd bit him and his mouth tilted up at the corner.

"Oh yeah? What are you going to do to me?" she taunted, arching her back and spreading her legs. His nostrils flared and he shifted his position so he was kneeling astride her hips.

His cock thrust aggressively from his hips, bobbing with every move. His balls were heavy and tight against his body.

He let go of her hands and palmed himself. Theresa unconsciously licked her lips as he pumped himself in his fist, once, twice.

Then he moved up her body, thrusting his hips until his cock rested in the deep valley of her cleavage.

"Push your tits together," he said in a gravely whisper,

shunting his hips against the soft skin until she could feel the head of his cock bump her throat.

She pressed her arms against her breasts, squeezing him so tight his shaft was buried in the giving flesh. Only the head of his penis was visible, huge and red and luscious as a plum.

Theresa bent her head, her tongue snaking out to dance around the tip. He groaned and thrust more firmly, the head of his cock pushing into her mouth as he fucked her tits. She sucked at him, licked at him, greedily swallowed the drops of pre-come that beaded at the tip.

He pulled away without warning, drawing his hips back when she would have closed her lips over him again. Before she could react he closed his hands over her hips and flipped her onto her stomach.

"On your knees." Even as a lick of uneasiness shivered down her spine, she didn't hesitate to obey. She propped herself on her forearms and tucked her knees under her, spreading them wide as she anticipated that first thrust.

Vince felt a rush of lust so hot, so thick, it almost made him light-headed. Theresa knelt before him, looking over her shoulder with a knowing, needy look. He'd meant to pull a power play on her, show her who was in charge. But for all that she was the one on her knees, he was the one who felt like he'd been slain.

Her body was perfection, her lush round ass tilted up, legs spread, giving him an unimpeded view of her juicy, succulent sex. It made him crazy to know how much she wanted him. Her smooth folds were shiny and slick, pulsing in deepening shades of pink. "So pretty," he whispered, dragging his fingers down her hot slit before donning a condom.

He wrapped one hand around her hip and used the other to guide his cock into her wet, willing body. As he sank deep, she let out a keening sound that went straight to his balls, grabbed on and didn't let go.

Thank God she was as aroused as he was, because he was beyond control, pumping and thrusting into her like a stallion over a mare. His chest heaved in and out like a bellows as he watched his cock sink inside her and emerge, shiny and wet. He gripped her hips and rode her hard, balls tightening as her cries grew more frantic with every penetration.

He hunched over her and slipped his hand between her thighs. His middle finger drew tight circles around the tight knot of nerves as he continued to pound into her. She heaved and bucked underneath him, her pussy clenching around his cock like she wanted to swallow him whole.

She yelled his name as she came, her cries muffled by the pillow. Vince could feel his own orgasm bearing down on him, gripping him by the balls, working its way up to the base of his spine. He dug his fingers into her hips, holding her still as he thrust as deep as he possibly could, his entire body jerking convulsively with the force of his climax.

He collapsed next to her, rolling her to the side so he could spoon her smaller body against his. She rolled to face him and burrowed her face into his chest. Her arms wrapped around him in a fierce, almost desperate grip.

He pulled her closer even as he mentally shook his head. One minute he could swear she was pulling away, and now she was clinging to him like he was a life preserver in the open sea.

A thousand questions about her, about them, swirled through his head, leaving him keyed up with a restless energy that even bone-deep sexual satisfaction couldn't diminish. He sighed heavily and ran his hand up her back, slipping it under her hair to rest on the back of her neck.

He played with the baby-soft curls at her nape, drifting, thinking about her words. *I want it to work, but I'm not sure it can.* What did she mean by that? Sure, they had their differences. Their age difference to start. Thirty-five and twenty-four wasn't exactly May-December, but they were definitely at different points in their lives. He was used to women who were straightforward about what they wanted, from him, from life. Women who didn't have a lot of time to fuck around.

Maybe that was the problem. He thought back to the relationships he'd had when he was in his twenties, what the women were like. There had been a lot of push-me-pull-you going on as he recalled.

Maybe Theresa was just young, playing games.

He sure as shit hoped not. He hadn't had the patience for it ten years ago, and he damn sure didn't now.

His fingers unconsciously tightened in Theresa's hair and she let out a little squeak of pain.

"Sorry," he murmured, disentangling his fingers from her hair and softly stroking the back of her neck. He ran his fingers up, down again, until it hit him. "Where is your necklace?"

She froze against him, only for an second, but this close he could feel her hold her breath, feel her heartbeat pick up speed. "I took it off when I took a shower this morning and forgot to put it back on."

A cold knot settled in his stomach. She was lying. He'd bet his life on it. But why?

"Why would you take it off to get in the shower?" he pressed.

"The clasp got tangled in my hair when I tried to wash it."

A perfectly plausible excuse, but pure bullshit. He knew it like he knew his own name. "Did you lose it?"

She pushed away, propped herself up on her elbows and glared at him. "No, I didn't lose it. What is with you tonight? Why are you so hellbent on picking a fight with me?"

He knew exactly why, but right now he didn't want to go there. He rolled off the bed and stalked to his walk-in closet.

"Where are you going?" she said.

"I need to catch up on some work," he said curtly.

"Vince, come back to bed," she said, and he felt a cold delight at the note of despair in her tone. Maybe she wasn't the only one playing games. "Don't be mad at me, please?"

"I'm not mad," he lied, coming over to the bed and placing a dry, perfunctory kiss on her forehead. "I really have work to do."

And for the first time, Vince left her to sleep alone in his bed.

11

The sound of thirty assorted Bellessis and Ciprianis hit Theresa as she and Vince walked into Ciao Bella the following afternoon. It should have been a comforting sound, a welcoming sound, but instead the loud, boisterous voices clashed in her head, rang in her ears, and made the nervous pit in her stomach take hold and grow roots.

Vince's silent presence beside her was small comfort. He'd been acting distant all day, and she knew why. Somehow he'd known she was lying about the necklace. She'd seen it in the way his eyes had narrowed, the way his mouth pulled tight.

She'd been in bad situations before, tasted the bitter edge of desperation. But she'd never spent a longer, colder night than last night, when he'd left her with a dismissive kiss. He'd taken her to the edge, taken her to the brink of falling apart. Taken her completely. Then left her, as though he had no more use for her.

That wasn't fair, she knew. He was angry and had every right to be. He wasn't a man who was often stonewalled. No, Vince Mattera generally got what he wanted.

She knew what he wanted. The truth. About her. And about

what had her jumping like a scared cat every time her phone rang. About the necklace.

But she didn't kid herself. She knew if he found out she'd given the necklace—along with the contents of her checking account—to her ex-boyfriend, and why, Vince wouldn't stick around.

And she still needed him to make it through today. She reached for his hand, breathing a sigh of relief as he wove his fingers through hers. As though sensing her anxiety, he pulled her to his side and bent his head for a brief kiss. "Relax. This will be fun."

"Says you," she muttered. This was the first time since her uncle's funeral that she'd seen the entire family. Then, everyone had been too distracted by grief and shock to do more than offer Theresa a brief hello.

Determined to be there for her cousin, Theresa had been able to block out the curious stares and whispers. She knew they wondered where she'd been, what she'd been up to, what she'd done to make her father refuse to speak of her for the past three years. She could only imagine the theories they'd come up with. Her large, loud, extended family was nothing if not imaginative.

"You look like you're about to face a firing squad," Vince said, running his big hand across her tight shoulders.

"I might as well be," she said, painting on a smile as her Zia Lola, her father's older sister, spotted Theresa and shrieked her name. With her big head of obviously dyed, teased black hair, red lipstick painted on with more enthusiasm than accuracy, and her big Italian ass stuffed into black pants a size too small, Aunt Lola was a living example of what Theresa would look like in thirty years if she wasn't careful.

"Tressie!" She enfolded Theresa in a hug so tight Theresa was afraid she was going to smother in her aunt's ample cleavage. Lola shoved her abruptly away and cupped her face so firmly Theresa's teeth cut into her cheeks. "You look so gorgeous. I meant to tell you at Alberto's funeral, God rest his soul,"—she crossed herself quickly—"but you were barely there." She lowered her eyebrows in an admonishing look. "Now I know you and your father aren't seeing eye to eye, but that's no reason to avoid the rest of us. Now you have to tell me—" Her gaze drifted past Theresa and locked on Vince. Her eyes widened with surprised delight. "Vince!" she said, and practically shoved Theresa to the floor to envelope Vince in an embrace so powerful Theresa heard the breath whoosh out of his chest.

"You two know each other?" Theresa said as Vince greeted her aunt with the affection of long acquaintance.

Her aunt released Vince just enough to look back at Theresa. "Of course we know Vince. He's been coming to the restaurant for years now and to Thanksgiving for the past, what, two years?" She looked to Vince for confirmation.

He grinned at Theresa's accusing look. "What can I say? Gia felt sorry for me."

"So if I hadn't invited you?" Theresa said.

He didn't get a chance to answer before Lola broke in. "You came with Theresa?" Her eyes flicked between them in rampant speculation. "Are you two—"

"I'm his dogsitter," Theresa said primly.

"Among other things," Vince said with a grin that made her want to smack him. "I'm going to go say hello to everyone." He kissed Theresa on the cheek and left her to meet her aunt's wide, slightly scandalized stare.

"You and Vince? Do you know what a catch he is?"

Theresa shrugged off her aunt's excitement. "Don't make a big deal out of it, Aunt Lola. It's nothing serious."

"You listen to me, Tressie, a man like Vince doesn't come around very often. Handsome, rich, good Catholic boy."

Like she needed someone to list all the reasons Vince was a great guy. And Lola hadn't even touched on the real reasons Theresa had fallen so stupidly in love with him.

"I always see him in these magazines with these socialites, these stick women who wouldn't know how to make a decent lasagna to save themselves. I told him he needed to find a nice Italian girl and settle down. Looks like he finally took my advice," she said, nudging Theresa with her elbow and winking conspiratorially.

"Even if Vince were looking to settle down, I'm not exactly a good little Italian girl. Just ask my father."

A shadow fell over Lola's eyes and her bright smile lost some of its vibrancy. "Nello was very upset when you left to live with that man, that is true. What you did, Theresa—" She shook her head and Theresa's heart swelled with old regret. "You broke his heart." She forced the brightness back in her smile and patted Theresa's shoulder. "But he'll come around. You'll see. Especially if you get a man like Vince to make an honorable woman of you," she said with another wink.

She let her aunt pull her to the table where everyone was mingling over glasses of chianti and trays of bruschetta. Gia bustled around, making sure everyone's glasses were full and the food kept coming. From the way everyone was casting speculative looks at her and Vince, Theresa knew they had drawn the same conclusions as Lola.

"How could you get engaged and not tell me?" Her mother's question made Theresa choke on her chianti. Vince, seeing her distress, ran over to pat her on the back.

"Who told you that?" Theresa choked out.

"Cousin Maria," her mother said indignantly. "I know we haven't spoken much, Theresa, but I shouldn't have to find out you're engaged from Cousin Maria."

"We're not engaged!"

"You don't need to sound so horrified by the idea," Vince

said, a note of laughter in his voice. "It's not a completely horrible idea."

"Vince," she said warningly.

"We haven't made it that far, Mrs. Bellessi," Vince said, leaning down to greet Theresa's mother with kisses on each cheek.
"Give us a little time."

Theresa had no idea if he was at all serious, but she wanted
to laugh and cry at the way he could even entertain the idea of
their engagement. Something that could never happen.

Her mother smiled girlishly and patted Vince on the cheek.
"Not that I would mind having you as a son-in-law, Vincent.
Someone needs to keep an eye on this girl, keep her out of trou-
ble."

Vince laid a proprietary hand on her shoulder. "I don't know
if any man is up to that challenge," he said, an almost imperceptible edge creeping into his voice, "but I'm certainly willing to try."

This conversation was taking Theresa's heart, her hopes, in a
direction they had no business going. "Where's Daddy?" Theresa
said, desperate to change the subject.

"He's over there, talking to Gabe," her mother answered.
Theresa looked over to the table where her father was waving
his hand enthusiastically while Gia's boyfriend listened patiently to her father's rant.

Theresa took a deep breath and started over to him. Better
to get it over with sooner rather than later. Her mother caught
her before she'd even taken a step.

"Come say hi to your cousin Frankie," she said, tugging her
in the opposite direction. "He was asking about you."

"But I haven't said hello to Daddy yet."

"It's Thanksgiving, Theresa. Don't get in his face today."

"Saying hello is hardly getting in his face." Blood rushed
into her face as she realized Vince was listening to all of this.

"Give it a rest, Theresa," her mother said tiredly. "I'm not in
the mood to deal with you both tonight."

A sick knot settled in her belly as she saw the tired slump in her mother's shoulders. Of course her mother was weary, tired of being caught in the middle of her husband and her daughter. "Maybe I should go," Theresa said. "I don't want to cause any trouble or make a scene just because Daddy and I aren't getting along."

"Oh please," her mother said, rolling her eyes. "Paola still isn't speaking to Uncle Angelo, and you know by the end of the night your cousin Frankie will be so drunk he'll try to pee in a potted plant. So don't worry about making a scene." The humor faded from the dark eyes, so like Theresa's own. "But don't press your father yet. He's just not ready."

Theresa swallowed back her bitterness. Railing against her father's medieval views of proper female etiquette wouldn't get her anywhere. She turned to the nearest relative, pasted a smile on her face and resolved to make the best of the evening.

As she helped Gia clear away the appetizers, she envied Vince's easy interaction with her family. She could hear his low rumble of a laugh as he listened to her family's stories, and she caught the bright flash of his grin as he winked flirtatiously at her aunt. He fit so well, like he was already part of the family.

Hell. She saw two of her older cousins avert their eyes when they caught Theresa's eye. Right now he was more a part of the family than she was.

In spite of the curiosity and speculation that pervaded every moment, Theresa enjoyed reconnecting with her family after so many years. She managed to dodge their pointed questions and glossed over the details of her time in New York. By the time they all sat down to dinner, she was comforted by the fact that Gia wasn't the only family member who was happy to have her back in the fold.

Everyone sat down to dinner, oohing and ahhing at the lavish spread Gia and the aunts had put out. Theresa's father sat across the table and four seats down from her, not even letting his gaze wander in her direction. *It's fine*, she told herself, ignoring the piercing ache in her heart. Maybe in a couple more months, if she stayed on track, if she kept Mark from spilling any secrets, maybe then her father would stop pretending she didn't exist.

Then as part of their family tradition, everyone around the table listed what they were thankful for this year, starting with Gia.

Her cousin tearfully raised her glass. "This has been a very hard Thanksgiving for me, the first without my father," she said, her lips trembling as she held back a sob. "But I am so very thankful to have all of you, my family," she said, gesturing with her glass over the group, "surrounding me with your love and your prayers."

"Alla famiglia!" Everyone enthusiastically raised their glasses and drank.

"I am also thankful," Gia said with a shy smile and a rosy blush, "to have my fiancé Gabe in my life. Not only did he help save this restaurant, my legacy, he's also brought me joy the likes of which I have never known."

There was a chorus of ahhs.

"Finally," Gia said, "I want to give thanks to another family member. I am thankful to have my cousin Theresa, the sister of my heart, back in my life. I am so glad you've come back to us," Gia said with a warm smile to Theresa.

Tears welled in Theresa's eyes at her cousin's gesture.

A fist slammed on the table, and thirty wine glasses quivered with the small earthquake. All eyes locked on Theresa's father, whose fists were clenched, his eyes stormy with barely contained rage. "I can't sit here. Not with her!"

"Zio Nello, she's your daughter," Gia said sharply.

"She stopped being my daughter the day she decided to become a whore!" He shoved back from the table and stormed from the room.

The room was dead silent. Theresa was caught in a spinning vortex of humiliation, every eye in the room spearing her with such force she was pinned to her chair, unable to move, to run, to hide.

"Theresa," Vince's voice broke through the haze. For the first time since they met it wasn't comforting, but only served to make her humiliation more acute.

She stood up on legs that felt about as steady as overcooked linguine. "I need to go." She swallowed back the burn in her throat. Her brain scrambled for an offhand remark, a snappy one-liner that would ease the tension in the room. All she could manage was, "Gia, thank you for a lovely dinner. It was nice to see all of you." Then she turned and walked as quickly as she could to the door.

She heard the scrape of a chair but didn't turn to see who was following her. "Theresa, please stay," Gia called. Theresa didn't spare her a backward glance, knowing if she tried to utter a single syllable she'd start bawling like a baby.

She stopped on the sidewalk outside the restaurant and struggled to compose herself. Hard, strong arms slipped around her. She buried her face into Vince's shirtfront, inhaling his warm, spicy scent, losing herself in the muscular security of his embrace.

"He didn't mean it, baby, he didn't mean it," he soothed.

"Yes he did," she said, squeezing her eyes against the onslaught of tears. "I thought he was getting over it, but he really thinks I'm a terrible person." And her father didn't even know the half of it.

She felt Vince's muscles flex and he held her even tighter as he pressed his cheek against the top of her head. "If he weren't your father, I'd go kick the shit out of him for hurting you."

"That won't be necessary, but I appreciate the thought." She slipped her arms around his waist and consoled herself that the day couldn't get any worse.

"Theresa, I thought I'd find you here."

Her blood turned to ice and she turned to look, praying as she did that Mark wasn't really standing behind her. That Vince wasn't staring hard at the wiry blond man who seemed to know Theresa very well. That her entire extended family wasn't inside. If Mark were so inclined, he could tell all and ruin her life in one fell swoop.

She pulled away from Vince and steeled herself against his hard, questioning stare. "Vince, can you excuse us for a moment?"

"Not until you tell me who he is," he said, not backing down an inch. Vince was bristling like a wolf at Mark's fake smile. She could practically smell the testosterone coming off Vince's big body, and kept herself carefully positioned between the two men.

"Mark is my ex-boyfriend," she said matter-of-factly. Vince already suspected she was keeping things from him, and she knew better than to try to to pass off Mark as no big deal.

"Tressie and I have a little unfinished business to discuss," Mark said, and Theresa winced at his use of her nickname.

Vince noticed too, if the way his big hands clenched into fists was any indication. "What kind of business?"

"Personal business," Theresa said pointedly, knowing she was on the verge of pile driving what she and Vince into the ground. "I need to talk to Mark alone for a moment."

"I don't like this," Vince said. "Whatever you have to discuss, you say in front of me."

"Just give me five minutes," Theresa pleaded, wondering how she could stand when her heart was squeezing so hard she could barely breathe. "Please, I need to talk to him. Alone." she finished pointedly.

He threw his hands up in frustrated defeat. "You know what? Take all the time you need." He turned and started walking up the block, his long strides eating up the pavement as his shoulders rippled under his shirt. Theresa wanted to call out, to beg for him to go, but Mark's voice stopped her.

"You're really afraid of what he'll think, aren't you?" How had she never noticed that oily undertone in Mark's voice? "That's good, because I'm going to need a little more to tide me over—"

She whirled around and shoved him in the chest, sending him stumbling back several steps. "Why are you doing this to me? I gave you everything. Everything! You have all my money, everything of value. I have nothing left to give you."

Mark grabbed her wrist in an iron grip, grinding the bones together. She gasped as white hot pain shot up her arm, but he kept the pressure on, right in the same place the bastard had broken the wrist a little over a year ago. He knew it, too. His cold blue eyes bored into hers as she stumbled helplessly after him. He dragged her down the block and around the corner, out of sight of the restaurant and her relatives.

"Don't fuck with me, Theresa," he said, shoving her up against a building's brick facade. "I need another two grand. You figure out how to get it to me in forty-eight hours, or else daddy dearest gets a lovely photo album to remember you by. And as a bonus, I'll make a copy for the big stud too."

"I can't—" she said, hating how weak her voice sounded.

"Forty-eight hours," Mark snarled. "I'm sure you'll find a way to make it," he said, giving her a head to toe scan that made her skin crawl.

Vince halted his angry pacing when he heard Theresa come through the front gate. She was only a few minutes behind him. That gave him some small measure of comfort. At least she hadn't disappeared with the little weasel and spent the afternoon fucking her ex-boyfriend as his fevered brain had envisioned. He'd left the Thanksgiving get-together shortly after he'd returned to Ciao Bella, gone home and tried to rip the sickening vision from his mind, simultaneously wanting to vomit or put his fist through a wall. He'd managed to quell both impulses, but just barely.

Chester, who had been pacing beside him and nudging his hand affectionately, trotted to the door to greet Theresa with an exuberant bark. Whoever said dogs were capable of reading human moods had obviously never met Chester, who was whipping his tail against Theresa's legs, spinning in happy doggy circles, completely oblivious to the tension emanating from them both.

"Down, Chester," she murmured, looking vaguely surprised when the dog actually obeyed. "Guess those classes are finally paying off," she said, a little too shrill.

"Are you fucking that guy?" he said bluntly, not about to let her brush him off.

"No!" she said with enough shock and conviction to convince him she wasn't lying. She hoped.

"Then what's going on?" He walked over to her, deliberately using his size to intimidate her as he backed her against the wall of the entryway.

"We had some things we needed to clear up."

"What kind of things?"

"He needed money, and I couldn't say no."

"Why not?"

"It's complicated," she said, her eyes sliding away from Vince's to focus on the buttons of his shirt.

"I'm smart," he said. "Explain it to me."

"I can't." Her voice was thick with tears. "I'm sorry."

"Are you still in love with him?" He held his breath for her answer. Hating her for putting him through this, hating himself for caring so much, for loving her when she was still hung up on her ex.

She sighed heavily. "No, I'm not in love with Mark any more."

He wanted to believe her, so much his heart was exploding with it. "Then promise me you won't see him or talk to him ever again."

She shook her head. "I can't promise that. You have to trust me—"

"Trust you?" he shouted, the words exploding out of him. "Give me one goddamn reason I should trust you! You barely tell me anything about yourself, you see your ex-boyfriend behind my back and you're apparently lending him money." His head snapped back as though from a blow as everything fell into place. "You gave him the necklace, didn't you? That's what happened to it?" Tears welled up in her eyes and her lips compressed and he knew he'd hit a bulls-eye. A rough laugh ripped its way up his throat.

It shouldn't matter. It was a stupid necklace. It had cost the equivalent of pocket change to him. But he'd bought it for her because he thought she was beautiful and wonderful and he wanted to see his gift hanging around her neck.

And she'd given it to that weasel like it meant nothing.

He laced his fingers behind his head and stared at the vaulted ceiling of his foyer as though it had the answer to how Vince Mattera, master of evading emotional entanglements, had managed to get his heart chewed up by a girl-woman he'd hired to babysit his dog.

"You should have told your boyfriend to keep a lower profile," he bit out. "Who knows how much you would have been able to siphon off to him."

"Vince, please—"

His heart cracked along with her voice, bleeding out inside his chest cavity. "Look, Theresa, I don't know what you have going on with Mark, but I'm too old and too busy to play fucked-up little games with a girl who doesn't know what she wants. So it's him or me. Decide what you want." He couldn't

WILL THAT BE ALL? / 259

let her go completely, not yet. Not without giving her one last chance.

"I wish it were that simple," Theresa said.

Vince felt the words like a blow. His heart wasn't breaking, it was imploding, collapsing on itself inside his ribcage. He wanted to fight, wanted to rage. But he wasn't about to sit around waiting for Theresa to figure out whether she wanted to be with him.

This had to end quick.

"You need to move out," he said, his voice so calm and cool it seemed like it was coming from a different person. "Take a couple of days to find some place to go, but I want you out by the end of the week."

She nodded but didn't say anything, just leaned against the wall with her arms wrapped around her waist like she was wounded.

He wanted her to argue, to beg him to give her another chance. The fact that she so easily accepted it pissed him off even more. "I'd offer you money to get set up," he said, unable to resist the cruel jab, "but I don't want you paying your pimp with any more of my cash."

Her body jerked as though she'd been shot and her face blanched. "I guess I deserve that," she said softly.

This was killing him. It was like all of the fight had gone out of her and she was bracing herself for another blow. But he steeled himself against the urge to take her in his arms, hold her close.

She pushed herself away from the wall, but instead of walking to the door she walked to where he was standing, stopping a few inches from him. Her dark eyes were weary, full of grief, anger, and helplessness. "I'm sorry, Vince. Sorrier than you'll ever know."

Theresa's heels echoed off the foyer floor as she walked out.

The click of the door shutting rang like a gunshot. Vince walked over to the stairs and sank down on the second step, feeling at least double his thirty-five years.

Chester managed to pull himself away from the delight of licking where his balls used to be long enough to finally notice his master's mood. His nails clicked on the floor as he ambled over. He pawed at Vince's leg twice, then laid his heavy furry head across Vince's knee. Vince absently stroked Chester's ears as the dog's eyebrows lifted in a look of canine concern.

"Looks like it's just you and me, dog," Vince said. "Alone again."

And for the first time in his adult life, being alone really sucked.

12

The next night, Theresa had barely gotten through the door of Ciao Bella before Gia enveloped her in a hug. "Tressie, why didn't you call me back? I was so worried after what happened." Theresa fought back tears at her cousin's concern. Frankly, her tears surprised her, since she was pretty sure she'd bawled out all the liquid in her body over the course of the last twenty-four hours.

"I'm okay, Gia," she said. "Nothing to worry about."

"One look at you and I know that's not true. You shouldn't let your father upset you so much. Now I know he's your father, and my uncle, but I swear sometimes that man makes me want to take a rolling pin to his head like Zia Catherine used to do with Zio Vito. Do you remember?"

Theresa managed a weak chuckle at the memory. "You don't have to bash any heads on my account. I'm just sorry I ruined your dinner."

"Please," Gia said, waving her off. "It's not a Cipriani-Bellessi holiday if we don't have a good brawl. But it makes me sad to see how much he hurt you. A father should never speak to his daughter like that."

Theresa nodded, not having the heart to tell her that her father's rage wasn't the worst of it. "I'm fine," she repeated. "But I have a favor to ask you. Two, actually."

Gia nodded absently and motioned for Theresa to follow her back into the kitchen. The rich, spicy smells of sauces simmering and meats roasting did little to settle Theresa's stomach. "Can I borrow your car this week?"

"Of course," Gia said, and asked the chef a question about one of the specials. She turned back to Theresa. "When do you need it?"

"Either tomorrow or Tuesday, depending on when I get packed."

She'd made very little progress today, spending most of her day the same way she had spent the long, sleepless night—in a semi-conscious fog on her couch in front of the TV.

Gia waved off a question from the sous-chef and focused all of her attention on Theresa. "What do you mean pack? Why are you packing?"

"That's the other favor," Theresa said. "I was wondering if I could stay with you for a little while, until I find a new place to live."

Gia's eyes widened with concern. She grabbed Theresa's hand and dragged her back to Gia's small office by the kitchen. She closed the door to insure privacy. "You and Vince are splitting up? What happened?"

"It didn't work out," she said. "It was never serious anyway, Gia. No big deal."

"No big deal. No big deal." Gia threw her hands up dramatically. "Your father disowning you, getting your heart broken. How can none of that be a big deal?"

"Please," Theresa said, feeling tired and weary and about a thousand years old. "I don't want to get into it right now. I just need a place to crash for a few days. I know you don't need me hanging around with you and Gabe, and I promise I'll be out by the end of the week."

Gia laid a small hand on Theresa's cheek and regarded her with dark, compassionate eyes. The big sister Theresa never had was coming through for her again. "Stay as long as you like. As for Gabe,"—she couldn't suppress a sly smile—"we can stay at his place. His bed is bigger anyway."

Theresa gave a nod, genuinely thrilled her cousin had found love at last, even if it did throw Theresa's bleak situation into stark contrast.

She worked that night in a sleep-deprived haze, always keeping one eye trained on the door, hoping against hope to see a tall, broad, familiar figure fill the doorway. But of course Vince wouldn't come here, not tonight. Probably not ever again. Great. As if she didn't have enough to feel bad about, she'd cost her cousin one of Ciao Bella's best customers.

She wondered what he was doing right now. He'd left early this morning. She'd roused herself from her vigil on the cottage couch to stagger to the window in time to see his retreating back. She wondered if he'd slept. She wondered if he felt bad about the pimp comment.

It still sliced at her like a straight razor. But as she'd said to him, she probably deserved that. Vince probably thought she was planning to milk him for what she could get and give it all to Mark.

Vince still wasn't home when she got back. There was a note on Theresa's door from the housekeeper asking Theresa to let the dog out. She collected Chester and let him do his thing. Instead of putting him back in Vince's house when he was done, she took the dog to her cottage, desperately needing the company. Even if said company shed tufts of blond fur all over her furniture and filled the small house with eau de dog breath.

"You need a Tic Tac," she said as Chester yawned, his breath wafting over to assault her nose. Chester climbed up on the couch and laid his head in her lap, settling in to join her for another sleepless night of mindless TV. "I'm going to miss you," she said, realizing it was true. She'd never been much of a dog person, or an any-pet person for that matter. But she would miss the dance of doggie delight Chester performed every time she reached for his leash. She'd miss how sometimes, when he was chasing a ball, he'd get his legs tangled up and tumble over in a full somersault. She'd miss the little grunts of pleasure he gave when she scratched his chest like she was doing now.

But most of all, she was going to miss taking Chester for walks with Vince at her side, holding her hand or with his arm slung over her shoulders.

Vince . . . She began to cry, then sucked it up. The only thing to do was to get on with it, keep pushing forward until the day came when she woke up and it didn't hurt quite so much any more.

Theresa hit the silence button on her cell phone as it rang for the tenth time that morning. She didn't even need to look at the display to know it was Mark, calling to say her forty-eight hours were up, and that he wanted the two thousand dollars she was supposed to magically pull out of nowhere.

She shoved her phone back into the pocket of her jeans, regretting her decision to give Mark her new number in the first place. But if she hadn't, he would have called the restaurant, or worse, shown up there to harass her in person. Theresa supposed she should be thankful that Mark hadn't cost her her job. Yet.

She hefted an over-stuffed duffel bag full of clothes into the trunk of Gia's car. On her way back to the cottage, she made sure the gate was propped open so she wouldn't have to keep opening and shutting it as she shuttled her belongings from the cottage to the car. She'd been up since six a.m, packing. Technically, she'd been up since three a.m., but it wasn't until six that she'd finally given up the battle for sleep and heaved her weary body out of bed. The temptation to pull the covers over her head and spend the day pretending the rest of the world didn't exist was almost irresistible. After all, today was her day off. She didn't actually have to be anywhere until work on Tuesday, so she had over twenty-four hours to mope around and feel sorry for herself.

And Vince had given her until the end of the week to move, so there was no rush.

She'd resisted the voices that wanted to throw her a pity party to end all pity parties and thrown herself into packing. Otherwise she knew she'd torture herself, gazing out the window, hoping to catch a glimpse of Vince. Like that would do anything to begin to fill up the massive crater where her heart used to be.

Strange that she could feel so much pain after such a short time. Was it really only a little over a month ago that she'd moved in here? She rubbed her eyes, scratchy from dried tears and lack of sleep. It felt like a lifetime ago. She'd found the man of her dreams and lost him in a big fat hurry.

Chester paced nervously around the boxes piled next to the door. He sniffed each one and whined softly, as though he knew something was up. Theresa paused in the act of picking up a box and knelt down next to the dog to give him a reassuring chest scratch. "It's all going to be okay, boy." Her nose burned with the effort to hold back yet another round of tears. "Pretty soon you won't even remember me." Her gaze involuntarily went out the window of the kitchenette, up to the window of Vince's office. Would he, she wondered, forget her just as easily?

She shook off the depressing thought and stood. As she reached for a box of books, Chester let out a sharp bark and whacked her in the leg with an enthusiastic wag of his tail. Her heart gave a lurch and her stomach flipped as she whirled around, unable to squash the irrational hope that Vince was here to beg her not to leave.

Her tentative smile vanished as she saw Mark in the doorway. Clammy sweat dampened the thin fabric of her T-shirt as she took in his cold, red-rimmed eyes and equally rosy nostrils. Great. As if he weren't already a dream to deal with, now he was coked out of his mind.

She cursed herself for leaving the front gate wide open, but stupidly, naively, she hadn't really expected Mark to show up here.

"You've been avoiding my calls, Theresa," he said with a sniff. "I hope that's because you have my money for me."

"Afraid not," she said, eying the door, trying to decide if she could run fast enough to get past Mark and up to the main house.

"You know that's not what I want to hear," he said, taking a step toward her, kicking boxes out of the way. "I told you two days."

She threw her hands up in exasperation. "I don't know what you expect me to do."

"I'm sure you can get a little cash from your boyfriend if you ask nicely."

She gestured at the boxes and suitcase crowding the small cottage. "Thanks to you, he's not my boyfriend anymore, so really, I'm out of resources." Not that she would give Mark so much as a penny from Vince's sofa cushions.

He rushed forward, grabbing her by the hair with such force she felt her knees start to buckle. "I don't think you understand the seriousness of the situation, Theresa. I need the money, and I need it now. Otherwise, the bad guys are going to do very bad things to me."

"Why should I care?" Theresa asked, blinking back tears of pain. She knew it was stupid to taunt him. She knew perfectly well what he was capable of in this state, but she refused to cower or give into his bullying again. She jerked her head to the side and felt a hank of hair at her nape get yanked.

"Don't push me, Theresa," he said, leaning so close she could feel the nasty heat of his ragged breath, "you know what will happen if you keep pushing me."

She kicked his shin, wincing as his hand fisted more firmly in her hair. "I don't give a shit. Show my father the pictures. Show Vince. Show the whole freakin' world for all I care."

It didn't matter anymore. Her father was never going to forgive her, and she'd already lost Vince. Terrified, she'd given into Mark's demands, and she'd lost everything anyway. What more did she have to lose?

Mark yanked her hard against him, never losing his grip on her hair as something cold and sharp kissed the tender skin of her throat. Her stomach bottomed out and her fingertips went numb as she froze, struggling to not swallow, to not so much as breathe against the icy cold pressure of the blade.

"Here's how it's going to go," he said, and Theresa could feel the faint tremors rippling through his body as the cocaine surged through his blood. "We're going to walk over to the main house. You're going to let me in. Then you're going to help me pack up your car with any items that I can hock or sell. Got it?"

"I'm not going to help you rob him," Theresa said, and immediately regretted it when she felt a keen slice and the warm trickle of blood down her neck. "Stop!" she said, trying to still her panic. "His house is protected with a really sophisticated security system. You'll never get past it without having me enter the security code." That might save her life, but it wouldn't buy her time. "We should wait until the housekeeper goes home." She looked at the clock, wondering frantically if Magda was still in the house. The last thing she wanted was to put anyone else in danger.

"I don't have time to wait. Let me handle her, you worry about getting me into the house."

* * *

Vince walked up the block to his house, brooding like a man possessed. He hadn't really intended to come home, hadn't intended to leave his office where he'd been hiding out pretty much twenty-four-seven for the last two days. But after the weekly partner meeting that had ended shortly before lunch, he'd called Magda, ostensibly to put in a request for her daily trip to the grocery store. Then, though he'd been trying to ignore her existence, he'd asked about Theresa.

Only to feel like he'd been punched when Magda informed him that Theresa had pulled a car into the driveway and was now loading it with suitcases and boxes.

She was really leaving. Even though he'd been the one to tell her to go, the actuality of it had him walking ten blocks home almost in a daze until he was standing in his own driveway, staring blankly at Theresa's cousin's car parked in his driveway, wondering why he had come.

To stop her?

To tell her not to let the door hit her on the ass on her way out?

He still wasn't sure as he walked through the gate she'd left propped open and started toward the door of the cottage, also left slightly ajar.

He froze when he heard a muffled male voice coming from inside.

Jesus, he thought as his blood pressure skyrocketed to a roiling boil, that took some fucking nerve on her part, to have Mark over here. He was about to walk away in disgust when he heard Theresa's muffled cry of pain, followed by Chester's frantic barking.

"Shut that fucking dog up!"

"Don't hurt him," Theresa cried. "Chester, shh! Be quiet!"

Vince was about to burst through the door but caught himself just in time. He had no idea what was going on in there. He flattened himself against the front of the small house and inched his way to the open door, carefully keeping himself out of sight as he peered inside the main room of the cottage.

Icy fear tripped up his spine at the sight that greeted him. He could see Theresa in profile, her face pale and strained as Mark held her tight, her back to his front. His left hand was fisted in her hair, forcing her head back as his right hand pressed a wicked-looking blade to her neck. A scarlet trail ran down her throat and stained the neckline of her thin cotton T-shirt.

Chester huddled in the corner by the kitchenette, looking as though he'd been kicked couple of times.

Vince's hands curled into fists as he struggled to control his rage. Every male instinct he had ordered him to go in there, rip Theresa out of Mark's hold and pound him into the floor. But a cautionary override reminded him that if he wasn't careful, he could end up getting Theresa hurt, even killed.

"Come on," Mark said, half dragging Theresa toward the door. "Let's get this over with."

They were coming toward the door. Vince pressed himself back against the house, waiting for an opening. Mark pushed Theresa out the door so hard she stumbled. As she fell, she pulled Mark partway down with her.

Vince seized the opportunity, clipping Mark with a hard punch to the temple. Stunned by the pain, Mark dropped his grip on Theresa and staggered back. He hadn't let go of the knife, and wheeled around clumsily to face his attacker, trying to shake off the pain that had to be ringing through his head.

"Vince, be careful," Theresa cried when Mark rushed at him, swinging his knife hand in a wild arc.

Vince was on the balls of his feet, hands loose, ready for him. It had been years since he'd been in a fight, but he'd spent enough time scrapping with the neighborhood toughs as a teen and now it all came back. And it helped that Mark still hadn't regained his equilibrium as he rushed at his target.

As Mark slashed viciously toward Vince's abdomen, Vince caught his wrist in an iron-hard grip. He squeezed, grinding the wrist bones together until Mark's hand opened spasmodically, sending the knife clattering to the stone pavers. Vince landed his other fist in Mark's face with a satisfying crunch, and Vince felt a savage satisfaction as blood spurted from the gory mess that used to be Mark's nose.

But Vince didn't stop there, landing blow after blow on the smaller man's body. He felt something tugging at his arm, but he didn't stop. He used Mark like a punching bag, exorcising the frustration and rage that had been dogging him.

"Vince, stop, you're going to kill him!" Theresa's voice, her grip on his arm, finally penetrated his consciousness.

He whipped around, fist raised. "Give me one fucking reason why I shouldn't!"

She jerked her hands away and flung her arm up in front of her face as though to ward off a blow. "Just don't!"

All the rage in his body drained out of him at her frantic plea. He let Mark slump to the ground as he turned to Theresa, feeling sick to his stomach at the way she flinched when he settled his hands over her shoulders. "Theresa, I'm not going to hurt you."

"I know," she said shakily, shaking her head as though to clear it. "I'm sorry. It's just reflex."

Anger kindled to life again. "Because of him." He slanted a scathing look at where Mark was moaning, semi-conscious.

She nodded, refusing to meet his eyes. "I'm sorry. Sorry about all of this."

She folded her arms around herself and started to turn away.

"Stop apologizing!" He grabbed her by the shoulders so she couldn't get away. "Just tell me what's going on here."

Her shoulders slumped. "He's trying to blackmail me."

"Blackmail you? How?"

* * *

In a hurried rush, she told Vince the story of her job dancing at the club, Mark's debts, and the slutty photos.

She didn't dare look at him until she was finished, not wanting to see his face, know what he thought of her until the last possible moment. When she finally met his eyes, she saw that they were dark and flinty with suppressed rage. His full, sensual mouth was drawn into a tight line. It was exactly as she feared.

"Why the hell didn't you tell me?"

The simple question threw her for such a loop, she couldn't find the words to answer.

He barreled through her stunned silence. "Why should I care if you danced naked—"

"I wasn't completely naked."

"Whatever. You could have just told me the minute this asshole started harassing you. You should have told me, Theresa," he said, his voice getting louder. "You should have trusted me enough to tell me."

"This was my mess," she said, her jaw tilting at a stubborn angle. "I didn't want to drag anyone else in."

"I could have helped you—"

"I didn't think you'd understand," she broke in impatiently. "I mean, I see how you live, the circles you run in. What was I supposed to say? Oh, by the way, my drugged-up, gambling addict ex-boyfriend is in town, threatening to send half-naked pictures of me to everyone I've ever known? How could I expect you to be okay with that?"

"Theresa, I didn't start out rich. If you'd bothered to ask, you'd know that me criticizing you for what you said you did would be beyond hypocritical."

She raised a skeptical eyebrow, taking in his tailored shirt and slacks, his five-hundred-dollar shoes, his twenty-thousand dollar watch. Okay, so his shirt and pants were bloodstained, and the hand attached to the watch was bruised from pounding on Mark's face, but still.

He met her look with a glare. "Let's just say my family's connected, Theresa."

"How connected?" she said.

"Connected enough that I've been audited by the IRS every year since I made my first million. And I guarantee that the FBI has a file on me. You hear that, asshole?" he said over Theresa's head to where Mark still lay in a pile. "You come near her again, I'll make sure you end up in a wood chipper somewhere, you got that?"

Mark made a feeble groan of acknowledgment.

He gave her a long, measured look. The same look her father used to give her when she had done poorly on a test. A look that said he wasn't merely angry, he was deeply, deeply disappointed. "You remember I told you once, there was nothing you could tell me that would make me turn away from you?"

She nodded, and a tiny seed of hope took root inside her. Maybe now that the truth was out, they could put this all behind them and start fresh.

"You should have believed me, Theresa."

That little seed of hope withered and died as he shook his head and turned away without another word. He pulled his cell phone out of his pocket and she heard him call the police.

By the time the cops had come and gone and taken Mark away in the back of a squad car, Theresa felt like she'd been hit by a truck. Her neck ached and her throat stung where Mark had cut her, but the full body ache came from the emotional blow she'd been dealt.

She'd lost Vince. She knew it. And along with that knowledge was the brutal realization that if only she'd told him the truth in the first place, she could have avoided this whole ugly mess.

He'd left her to follow the cops out and speak briefly with the detective. Now she stood alone amidst her packed boxes, wanting nothing more than to crawl into bed. Preferably with Vince.

But since that wasn't in the cards, the only option was to go along with her original plan for the day and get the hell out of here. By time the squad cars left and Vince walked up the driveway, she was loading up her last box.

He stood, thumbs hooked into the pockets of his pants. His wide shoulders were stiff and his jaw was tight with rage. His eyes were flat, grim, like he didn't want to look at her. "You got somewhere to go tonight?"

Please let me stay here. Please love me enough to give me another chance. But she stayed silent. Theresa Bellessi never begged. "Gia's." The name was all she could force past the softball sized knot in her throat.

He nodded, and she closed the trunk of the car and climbed into the driver's seat. She had nearly closed the door when he called out to her. "Yes?" she said, as embarrassingly hopeful as a death row inmate waiting for a pardon.

"I need your key back."

Her heart fell like an anvil, crashing through her insides to land somewhere around her feet. "Right." She dug through her purse, wondering when it had expanded to the size of the Grand Canyon as she raked through its contents. Having her vision blurred by tears did nothing to help. Finally she found the damn keyring and pried the key off with shaky fingers and passed it to Vince, praying she could get out of there before dissolving into tears again.

One fat droplet squeezed past her eyelashes and rolled down the side of her nose, landing with a plop on Vince's outstretched hand. She slammed the door shut and barely made it out of the driveway before she completely fell apart.

13

Vince stood outside of Ciao Bella, feeling more insecure than he could ever remember. It wasn't a sensation he was familiar with, and not one he enjoyed. And the fact that it was a woman who had him twisted in knots didn't make it any easier to take.

It had been a little over a week since he'd watched Theresa drive away. Coldly taken her key back and sent her away without so much as a "have a nice life." Nine days later, he was hovering outside Ciao Bella, having come to the realization that pushing her away was maybe the biggest mistake of his life.

Actually, it had only taken him about a day and a half to figure it out, but by then he'd been on a plane to Singapore and hadn't been able to do anything about it.

If he was completely honest with himself, he wasn't sure there was anything he could do about it now. Not after the way he'd treated her. He cringed every time he thought about the things he'd said, the way he'd acted. Every time he closed his eyes he saw her face, white and strained, mouth pulled tight as she struggled not to cry. His heart, which he hadn't ever given much thought to before, throbbed like a big bruise inside him.

Needless to say, he hadn't slept much in the past week and a half, and he knew better than to blame it on jet lag.

Now Vince lurked outside the restaurant, as he had for the past half hour, watching the last of the customers trickle out. He'd come directly from the airport, had the car service drop him off here and sent the driver home with his bag. He didn't want to waste any more time getting to Theresa.

So why was he standing out here like an idiot, watching her clear off and wipe down her tables and count her tips? For a guy who had a reputation for having brass balls and not taking no for an answer, he sure as hell was acting like a pussy.

"Loitering is illegal, you know."

Vince jumped. He hadn't see Gia come out the door, he'd been so focused on the sight of Theresa through the restaurant's window. "How is she doing?"

Gia looked at him like he was an idiot, which he supposed he was. "She's doing fine, considering in the past two weeks her father called her a whore, her ex-boyfriend blackmailed and attacked her, and you dumped her like last night's fish special." she said tartly.

His face burned despite the cold of the late fall night. "I fucked up," he said simply, voicing aloud the thought that had been playing on an endless loop since he'd last seen Theresa. "I never should have let her go."

Gia's expression softened by a degree. "Tell me something I don't know. The question is, what are you going to do about it?"

"Throw myself at her feet and beg for forgiveness?"

"Sounds like a good start." She grabbed his arm, pulled him over to the door and held it open. Before he stepped through she caught his arm, "I have to warn you, though. If you hurt her again—"

"I know, you'll send someone after me with a pair of cement boots."

Gia drew herself up to her full five-feet-two inches, looking mildly affronted. "To hell with that. I'll take care of you myself." She ushered him in before her, and as he stepped over the threshold, she called, "Theresa, there's someone here to see you," before she scooted past him to the back of the restaurant.

Theresa looked up expectantly, her hand freezing in the act of reaching for a cocktail glass. Her big eyes were sad and strained, her normally warm olive complexion looking sallow. But she was still so beautiful he felt like he'd been punched.

"Hey Vince," she said, wiping her hands on the short apron around her waist.

His tongue was thick, sticking to the roof of his mouth as he scrambled for something diplomatic, apologetic and highly romantic to say. His brain came up blank, save for one phrase flashing relentlessly like a neon sign.

"I love you," he blurted out.

Theresa met his blunt declaration with stunned silence. Every molecule in his body froze as he waited for her reply. She just stood there, staring at him like he was speaking Martian, her lips parted in confusion.

"I'm sorry," he tried again, rushing forward and stopping only inches from her. He grabbed her hand, laced her icy fingers through his. She didn't pull away, which he took as a sign of encouragement, even though she was still looking at him like she wasn't sure whether she wanted to kiss him or hit him. "I'm sorry," he repeated, "I shouldn't have said those things—I didn't mean them. I made a huge mistake—"

"Wait," she interrupted, halting his flood of inept apologies. "Can you go back? What you said before?" Her hand was gripping his, her fingers shakily clinging to his as wary hope poured through her big dark eyes.

"I love you," he said, bringing her hand to his lips, closing his eyes as the scent of her skin hit his bloodstream like a heavy narcotic.

Then, just like that she was in his arms, tilting her face up for his kiss.

"I love you too," she said, cupping his face in her hands.

Relief blew through him with such force it made his legs shake. "So you forgive me for being such an idiot?"

She laughed softly and kissed him hard. "Depends on what's in it for me."

"Everything," he said, lifting her by the waist to pull her closer. "Anything. Name it."

"Just you," she said, her face buried against his shoulder. "I just want you."

Theresa clutched at Vince's shoulders and buried her lips against his throat, absorbing his taste, his scent, not entirely convinced this wasn't an elaborate hallucination brought on by her recent lack of sleep. A distant part of her brain admonished her to resist, to play a little harder to get. He had dumped her. Without even trying to understand why she wasn't willing to blindly trust him with the truth about Mark and her past.

She let the thoughts percolate, tried to get angry. But then he said, "I love you" in the way that sent ripples of pleasure and need through her. And then, "I missed you so much." He pulled back and looked at her, his face marked with tired lines as he looked at her, passion in his beautiful dark eyes.

Okay. Some women might accuse her of being a weak-willed pushover, but she didn't see much point in fighting when he was giving her everything she'd ever wanted.

Her lips parted under his, opening for his tongue, eager for the wet slide, the hot taste of him. Her nipples puckered tightly against the satin of her bra and moist heat pulsed between her thighs. God, she had missed this, missed him. The feel of his big hands on her body, holding her flush against him, the thick rise of his cock pressing insistently against her.

A loud, deliberate throat-clearing broke through her lustful haze. She and Vince pulled apart and turned hazy eyes on Gia, who stood at the other end of the bar.

"Since everyone is gone," Gia said pointedly, "I'll leave you here to close up, Theresa. Try not to break any health department codes," she said and turned to leave through the back door of the restaurant.

Theresa broke away long enough to lock the front door and turn down the lights. Vince came up behind her, sliding his hands up her rib cage until his fingers teased the undersides of her breasts. "I just need to close out the cash register," she said a little breathlessly. "Then we can go."

"I don't think I can wait that long," he said, landing a hot, sucking kiss on the side of her neck.

Her gaze darted nervously out to the front window. It was late, and the foot traffic outside was scarce, but still.

"No one can see us," he said, as though reading her thoughts. His hands came up to cover her breasts, kneading her through the heavy cotton of her blouse. She could feel his cock rearing up against the small of her back. "And I can't walk home in this condition."

Frankly, she wasn't sure she'd make it either, what with the way all the blood in her body was pooling between her legs as the desire she'd suppressed for the past week and a half erupted in a rush of achy need. His hand slid down inside the front of her pants, over the silky fabric of her panties. She felt as well as heard his groan of pleasure when he found her wet.

"Turn around," he said, urgency lending an edge to his voice as his fingers fumbled with her buttons. He pulled the front open, the heat of his gaze rising another fifty degrees as he stared at her creamy flesh cupped in satin and lace. "So beautiful," he said, pulling his attention from her breasts to her face. "You are so beautiful to me, Theresa, and I love you so much."

Tears burned in her eyes at his words, at the way he looked at her, the way he touched her. He sat her on one of the tall bar stools and leaned her back against the bar as he kissed his way down her body. His lips pulled at her breasts, his tongue flicking her nipples into almost painful hardness. He slipped off her shoes and pulled her pants down her legs, turning his face to press a passionate, almost reverent kiss against the smooth skin of her inner thigh.

Any reservations she might have had about being seen from the street vanished at the first flick of his tongue. His palms pressed her legs apart, spreading her wide. His thumbs slid against her slick folds, parting her pussy lips to meet his kiss. He kissed her not with mere hunger, but with relish. Like she was the most delicious thing he'd ever tasted, like he wanted to lick her, kiss her, *pleasure* her, until she dissolved into a molten puddle. She braced herself against the bar with one hand and ran her fingers through his thick, dark hair with the other, reveling in the feel of his mouth against her, the slick texture of his hair sliding through her fingers, in the knowledge that he was *hers*. And she was his.

"Come inside me," she whispered, tugging his hair, urging him up. She shuddered as he gave her a last, lingering lick before coming off his knees to stand between her legs. She yanked his shirt from his waistband and they both struggled to pull it up over his head. She unzipped his pants and shoved his boxers down, and his heavy erection sprang into her waiting palm. "You have no idea how much I missed you," she breathed as she ran her hand up over his thick shaft.

"I can't believe I almost gave you up," he said. "I can't believe how lucky I am that you forgave me." His shaky voice echoed her own sense of happy incredulity.

"I can't believe we don't have a condom handy," she laughed.

He pulled one from his shirt pocket. "Always prepared."

"Get it on." She watched as he did.

"I love you," he said as his hips surged forward, parting her, stretching her for his thick invasion.

She came in a sudden rush, the combination of his words and the sensation of his cock surging inside her enough to shove her right over the edge. "I love you too," she moaned, wrapping her legs around him and pulling him deeper as her pussy rippled and contracted around him. Pleasure seared through her in a burst of heat and light as she pulled him close, her hands digging into the long muscles of his back as his hips pumped between her legs.

She'd never felt anything like this before, love and sex and pleasure, all the sweeter because she'd nearly lost it all.

He was right behind her, surging and thrusting between her thighs, pumping hard and fast. He came in thick, hot spurts, his hot skin blooming with sweat under her palms. "I'm never letting you go," he whispered against her neck, kissing his way up her throat. "Just so you know."

"Sounds good to me," she said, trying to keep herself from sliding off the bar stool and onto the floor.

They took care of getting it together, pulled their clothes back on, their progress impeded by frequent kissing and touching.

"At this rate we're never going to get home," he chuckled as her hand skimmed down the front of his pants. He caught it in his hand and drew it up to his lips. "No more of that. I've been dreaming of having you in my bed all week."

Home. In his bed. She loved the way that sounded.

She collected her tips and went behind the bar to grab her purse. When she came back around, Vince was surveying the restaurant with a calculating expression. "So you think Gia will let us have our reception here?"

That drew her up short. "As in wedding reception?"

"Yeah."

"Aren't you supposed to ask me first?" she said, feeling a goofy grin stretch across her face.

He grinned back. "I'll ask. But just so we're clear, we're definitely getting married."

Theresa didn't argue. And later that night, when he slipped a two-carat emerald-cut diamond on her finger, it took her less than a nanosecond to say yes.